**PRAISE FOR JOE HALDEMAN,
WINNER OF THE HUGO, NEBULA,
AND JOH**

"Haldeman has
comprehensive, an
a place deep wit
importantly, his
surviv

—Peter Straub

"Haldeman remains a nimble necessary figure
in sci-fi's pantheon."
—*Entertainment Weekly*

MARSBOUND

"As one of SF's most consistently inventive storytellers, Haldeman gets bountiful mileage out of this ingenious blend of Martian exploration and extraterrestrial anthropology."   —*Booklist*

"An intriguing story of first contact. The tale's inventiveness lies in the fact that the aliens are a mystery not only to the Earthlings who encounter them but also to themselves. They have only a limited sense of their own history, origins, and purpose—and only a vague, half-remembered notion of the forebears who left them on Mars millennia before. As the consequences of the encounter take on global, and then intergalactic, significance, Carmen must gather what allies she has in order to avert a catastrophe of horrific proportions. The stakes are high, but at its heart *Marsbound* is a thought-provoking meditation on time, history, and the potential for human evolution."   —*BookPage*

"Haldeman pens an entertaining and often humorous futuristic tale where tension and conflict abound, the mysteries of an alien race begin to unfold, and romance finds a way to thrive . . . The author has done a wonderful job in mixing in humor to keep things lighter, and as a whole it forms a very enjoyable read."   —*Darque Reviews*

continued . . . APR 18 2015

Fremont Library

THE ACCIDENTAL TIME MACHINE

"[A] smart, brisk, and even charming tale."
—*Entertainment Weekly*

"One of the most fun time-travel stories ever."
—*Rocky Mountain News*

"Joe Haldeman shows why he is a national treasure with this tremendous, thought-provoking thriller . . . This terrific science fiction time-travel tale feels like a throwback thriller starring a disingenuous antihero."
—*Alternative Worlds*

"Rather than being a riff on H. G. Wells's *The Time Machine*, this novel is closer in tone to Neil Gaiman's *Anansi Boys*, another charming yarn about a young man who's forced out of a boring rut. Producing prose that feels this effortless must be hard work, but Haldeman never breaks a sweat." —*Publishers Weekly* (starred review)

"The ever-inventive Haldeman offers a new twist . . . [His] ingenuity delivers cutting-edge technological speculation and irresistibly compelling reading." —*Booklist*

A SEPARATE WAR AND OTHER STORIES

"Unlike some other writers of hard science fiction who are too busy trying to wow readers with their knowledge of applied physics or molecular biology to be bothered with such trivialities as plot and character, Haldeman never forgets that even in science fiction it's all about us humans . . . Readers will be hard-pressed to find a subpar effort by science fiction master Joe Haldeman in *A Separate War and Other Stories*." —*The Baltimore Sun*

"A must-have collection." —*The Philadelphia Inquirer*

" 'For White Hill' is one of the most memorable tragic love stories ever written as SF . . . Haldeman's work is never less than clever and sometimes much more."
—*Publishers Weekly*

MARSBOUND

JOE HALDEMAN

ACE BOOKS, NEW YORK

THE BERKLEY PUBLISHING GROUP
Published by the Penguin Group
Penguin Group (USA) Inc.
375 Hudson Street, New York, New York 10014, USA
Penguin Group (Canada), 90 Eglinton Avenue East, Suite 700, Toronto, Ontario M4P 2Y3, Canada
(a division of Pearson Penguin Canada Inc.)
Penguin Books Ltd., 80 Strand, London WC2R 0RL, England
Penguin Group Ireland, 25 St. Stephen's Green, Dublin 2, Ireland (a division of Penguin Books Ltd.)
Penguin Group (Australia), 250 Camberwell Road, Camberwell, Victoria 3124, Australia
(a division of Pearson Australia Group Pty. Ltd.)
Penguin Books India Pvt. Ltd., 11 Community Centre, Panchsheel Park, New Delhi—110 017, India
Penguin Group (NZ), 67 Apollo Drive, Rosedale, North Shore 0632, New Zealand
(a division of Pearson New Zealand Ltd.)
Penguin Books (South Africa) (Pty.) Ltd., 24 Sturdee Avenue, Rosebank, Johannesburg 2196,
South Africa

Penguin Books Ltd., Registered Offices: 80 Strand, London WC2R 0RL, England

This is a work of fiction. Names, characters, places, and incidents either are the product of the
author's imagination or are used fictitiously, and any resemblance to actual persons, living or
dead, business establishments, events, or locales is entirely coincidental. The publisher does not
have any control over and does not assume any responsibility for author or third-party websites
or their content.

MARSBOUND

An Ace Book / published by arrangement with the author

PRINTING HISTORY
Ace hardcover edition / August 2008
Ace mass-market edition / August 2009

Copyright © 2008 by Joe Haldeman.
Portions of this book appeared in *Escape from Earth: New Adventures in Space* edited by Jack
Dann and Gardner Dozois (Science Fiction Book Club, 2006) and in *Analog* magazine, 2008.
Interior diagram by Joe Haldeman.
Cover art by Fred Gambino.
Cover design by Annette Fiore DeFex.

ISBN: 978-0-441-01739-3

ACE
Ace Books are published by The Berkley Publishing Group,
a division of Penguin Group (USA) Inc.,
375 Hudson Street, New York, New York 10014.
ACE and the "A" design are trademarks of Penguin Group (USA) Inc.

PRINTED IN THE UNITED STATES OF AMERICA

10 9 8 7 6 5 4

For Carmen and Catalin,
our alien invaders

Acknowledgments

Many thanks to Geoff Landis, my favorite Martian, for advice in science and math. Any inaccuracies, of course, were committed by the author alone.

The butterfly counts not months but moments,
and has time enough.
—Rabindranath Tagore

PART 1

LEAVETAKING

I

THE UNDEAD

It wasn't a lot of luggage for six years; for the longest journey anyone has ever taken. We each had an overnight bag and a small titanium suitcase.

We stepped out into the warm Florida night and carried our bags to the curb. I looked back at the house and didn't feel much. We'd only lived there two years and wouldn't be coming back. I'd be twenty-five then, and getting my own place anyhow.

Dad pointed out Jupiter and Mars, both near the horizon.

The cab hummed around the corner and stopped in front of us. "Are you the Dula party?" it said.

"No, we're just out for a walk," Dad said. Mother gave him a look. "Of course we are. It's three in the goddamned morning."

"Your voice does not match the caller's," the cab said. "After midnight I need positive identification."

"I called," my mother said. "Do you recognize this voice?"

"Please show me a debit card." A tray slid out and Dad flipped a card onto it. "Voice *and* card."

The doors opened silently. "Do you require help with your luggage?"

"Stay put," Dad said, instead of no. He's always testing them.

"No," Mother said. The luggage handler stayed where it was, and we put our small bags in the back, next to where it crouched. Its eyes followed us.

We got in, Mother and me facing Dad and Card, who was barely awake. "Verify destination," it said. "Where are you going, please?"

"Mars," Dad said.

"I don't understand that."

Mother sighed. "The airport. Terminal B."

"The undead," Card said in his zombie voice.

"What are you mumbling about?"

"This thing you humans call a cab." His eyes were closed and his lips barely moved. "It does not live, but it is not dead. It speaks."

"Go back to sleep, Card. I'll wake you up when we get to Mars."

Locked up in a spaceship with my little brother for six months. Plus parents and a couple of dozen strangers. We were lucky, though; six months was about the shortest possible flight. It can take more than a year when Mars is farther away.

When we come back, he'll be almost as old as I am now. That's only a little less strange than zombies.

2
GOOD-BYE, COOL WORLD

It's the only elevator in the world with barf bags. My brother pointed that out. He notices things like that; I noticed the bathroom. One bathroom, for thirty-six people. Locked in an elevator for two weeks. It's not as big as it looks in the advertisements.

You don't call it "the elevator" once you're in it; the thing you ride in is just the climber. The Space Elevator, always capitalized, is two of these climbers plus fifty thousand miles of cable that rises straight up into space. At the other end is the spaceship that will take my family to Mars. That one will have *two* bathrooms (for twenty-six people) but no barf bags, presumably. If you're not used to zero gee by then, maybe they'll leave you behind.

This whole thing started two years ago, when I was young and stupid, or at least sixteen and naive. My mother wanted to get into the lottery for the Mars Project, and Dad was okay with the idea. My brother, Card, thought it was wonderful, and I'll admit I thought it was spec, too, at the time. So Card and I got to spend a year of Saturday mornings training to take the test—just us; there was no test for parents. Adults make it or they don't, depending on education and social adaptability. Our parents have enough education for any four people but otherwise are crushingly normal.

These tests were basically to make *us*, Card and me, seem normal, or at least normal enough not to go detroit locked up in a sardine can with twenty-four other people for six months.

So here's the billion-dollar question: did any of the kids aboard pass the tests just because they actually were normal? Or did all of them also give up a year of Saturdays so they could learn how to hide their homicidal tendencies from the testers? "Remember, we don't say anything about having sex with little Fido."

We flew into Puerto Villamil, a little town on a little island in the Galápagos chain, off the coast of South America. They picked it because it's on the equator and doesn't get a lot of lightning, which could give you pause if you were sitting at the bottom of a lightning rod long enough to go around the Earth twice.

The town is kind of a tourist trap for the Space Elevator and the Galápagos in general. People take a ferry out to watch it take off and return, and then go to other islands for skin diving or to gawk at exotic animals. The islands have lots of bizarre birds and lizards. Dad said we could spend a week or two exploring when we came back.

If we came back, he didn't say. It wasn't like we were just moving across town.

Mother and Dad both speak Spanish, so they chatted with the taxi driver who took us from the airport to the hotel, where we would get a night's rest before ferrying out to the Elevator platform. The taxi was different, an electric jeep long enough to seat a dozen people, with no windshield and a canvas sun canopy rather than a roof. I asked what happens if it rains, and the driver summoned up enough English to say, "Get wet."

Card and I had a separate room, so Mom and Dad could have one last night of privacy. I hoped they were taking precautions. Six months of zero-gravity morning sickness? I wondered what they would name the baby who caused that. "Clean up your room, Barf." "No, you can't have the car, Spew."

(After all, they named Card Card and me Carmen, after an opera that I can't stand. "Tor-e-ador, don't spit on the floor. Use the cuspidor; that's what it is for.")

We dumped our bags and went for a walk, Card one way and me the other. He went into town, so I headed for the beach. (The parentiosas might have assumed we were going to stay together, but they didn't give us any specific orders except to be back at the hotel by seven, for dinner.)

My last day on Earth. I should do something special.

3

CAPTAIN MY CAPTAIN

The beach was less sand than rock, a jagged kind of black lava. The water swirled and splashed among the rocks and didn't look too great for wading, so I sat on a more or less smooth rock and enjoyed the sun and salt air. Real Earth air, breathe it while you can.

There was a big gray iguana on a rock, maybe ten yards away, who ignored me. He didn't look real.

With the noise of the surf on the rocks I didn't hear the man come up behind me. "Carmen Dula?"

I jerked around, startled. He was a strange-looking older guy, maybe thirty, his skin white as chalk. With a closer look I saw it wasn't his skin; it really was something chalky, some kind of absolute sunblock. He was dressed in white, too, long pants and long sleeves, and a broad-brimmed hat. Kind of good-looking aside from the clothes.

"Didn't mean to startle you." He offered his hand, dry

and strong under the chalk. "I'm Paul Collins, your pilot. Recognized you from the passenger roster."

"The climber has a pilot?"

"No, just an attendant. What's to pilot?" He smiled, metal teeth. "I'm the pilot of the *John Carter of Mars*, this time out."

"Wow. You've done it before?"

He nodded. "Twice as pilot, once as copilot, there and back." He looked out over the ocean. "This'll be the last one. I'm staying on Mars."

"The whole five years?"

He shook his head. "Staying."

"For . . . forever?"

"If I live forever." He squatted down and picked up a flat stone and spun it out over the water. It skipped once. The iguana blinked at it. "I have to stay on either Earth or Mars. I'm sort of maxed out on radiation."

"God, I'd stay on Earth." Was he crazy? "I mean, if I was worried about radiation."

"It's not so bad on Mars, underground," he said, and tried another stone. It just sank. "Go up to the surface once a week. And those limits are for people who want to have children. I don't."

"Me, neither," I said, and he was tactful enough not to press for details. "That's why you're so protected? I mean the white stuff?"

"No, more thinking about sunburn than hard radiation." He took off his hat and ran his fingers through his hair, what there was of it. It had obviously just been mowed, down to about a quarter inch except for a trim Mohawk. "I haven't had a tan since I was . . . just a little older than you?"

"Nineteen," I said, adding six weeks.

"Yeah, twenty-one. That's when I joined the Space Force. They don't encourage tans."

That was interesting. "I didn't know the military was in on the Mars Project." Officially, anyhow.

"They aren't." He eased himself down, stiffly, to sit on the rocks. "I quit after five years. It was all air flying. One suborbital, big deal. My tour was up, and this sounded more interesting."

"But you only get to do it three or four times?"

"There's that," he admitted, and threw a pebble at the iguana, missing by a mile. "They're way too conservative. I'm trying to change their minds."

"You couldn't do that better here on Earth?" I sat down next to him.

"Well, yes and no. Right now, if I stay there, I'll be the only pilot *on* Mars, in case something goes wrong and they need one." He threw another pebble at the lizard and missed by even more. "Can't throw worth a shit since I went to space."

I took aim and missed the creature only by inches. It glared at me for a long second and slid into the water.

"Not bad for a girl."

I decided he was joking, but you couldn't tell from his expression. "I've heard that spaceflight can be hard on the muscles."

"It is. Even though you exercise every day, you get weaker. I'm weak as a kitten in all this gravity."

Inanely, I said, "I left my cat behind. In Florida."

"How old was it? Is it."

"Nine." Half my age; I hadn't thought of that.

He nodded. "Not too old."

"Yeah, but she won't be my cat when we get back."

"Might be. They're funny creatures." He rubbed his fingers as if they hurt. "So you're out of school?"

I shook my head no. "Going to start university by VR in September. Maryland."

"That'll be interesting. Odd." He laughed. "I partied

through my first year; almost flunked out. Guess you won't have to worry about that."

"There aren't any parties on Mars? I'm disappointed."

"Oh, you have people, you have parties. Not too wild. You can't exactly send out for pizza and crack a keg of beer."

I had a sudden empty feeling, not hunger for pizza. I tried to push it away. "What *do* you do for fun? Go out exploring?"

"Yeah, I do that, go up and collect rocks. I'm a geologist by training, before I became a flyboy. Areologist now."

I knew about that; Ares is Greek for Mars. "Ever discover anything new?"

"Sure, almost every time. But it's like being a kid in a candy store, or it would be if you could find a store where they kept bringing in new candy. It's not hard to find stuff that's never been classified. You into geology?"

"No, more like English and history. I had to take Earth and planet science, but it wasn't my . . . favorite." My only C besides calculus, actually.

"You might learn to like it, once you have a new planet to explore." He wiggled a pebble out of the sand and looked at it: purple. Scratched it with his thumbnail. "Funny color for lava." He tossed it away. "I could show you around if you like. Mars."

Good grief, I thought, is the pilot hitting on me? Over thirty? "I don't want to be a bother. Just go out by myself and wander around."

"Nobody goes out alone," he said, suddenly serious. "Something goes wrong, you could be dead in a minute." He shrugged. "No 'could' about it, really. Mars is more dangerous than space, outer space. The air's so thin it might as well be a vacuum, for breathing."

"Yeah." It wasn't like I'd never seen a movie. "And then the sandstorms?"

"Well, they don't exactly sneak up on you. The main danger is getting careless. You've got ground and sky and gravity. It feels safer than space. But it's not." He looked at his watch and got up slowly. "Better get on with my exercise. See you tomorrow." He plodded off, obviously feeling the gravity.

I didn't ask whether he wanted company. Interesting guy, but we were going to be stuck in a room together for six months, and would see plenty of each other.

I didn't really feel like company at all. Maybe I could put up with the iguana. I picked my way out to the farthest place I could stand without getting my feet too wet, and watched the swirling, crashing water.

4

LAST MEAL

On the way back to the hotel, I ran into Paul again. He was sitting alone in the shade of a thatched-roof patio outside a shabby bar called the Yacht Club, drinking a draft beer that looked good. I sat down with him but asked for a Coke, out of a vague concern that Dad might come by. Drinking with a man, oh my. I didn't know the legal age, either; if I was carded, he'd find out I wasn't really quite nineteen.

It was a short date, anyhow. We'd just exchanged "where you from?" formalities when his cell pinged and he had to go off to the Elevator office. I did learn that he was from New Jersey but didn't have time to ask about Mafia connections or how to breathe carbon monoxide.

It was not a pleasant place to sit alone and wonder what the hell I was doing. My friends back home were about evenly divided between being jealous and wondering whether I'd lost my mind, and I was leaning toward the latter group. The Coke tasted weird, too. Maybe it was drugged, and when I slumped unconscious they would drag me into the hold of a yacht and smuggle me off to Singapore for a rewarding career in white slavery. Or maybe it was made with sugar instead of corn syrup. I left it, just to be on the safe side, and went on to the hotel.

Speaking of Coke, that was what we weren't having for dinner, no matter how much Card and I might have liked it. Or a pizza or hamburger or even a cold can of beans. Of course it was going to be fancy, the last real family meal for six years.

"Fancy" in the Galápagos was not exactly Park Avenue fancy. They don't serve up the iguanas, fortunately, but there wasn't much you'd find on a normal menu.

The hotel restaurant, La Casa Dolores, served mostly Ecuadorian food, which was not a surprise. I had picadillo, a Cuban dish that sounded like hamburger over rice, and pretty much was, although it tasted strange, like Mexican but with a lot of lemon juice and a touch of soap. Mother said that taste came from a parsleylike herb, cilantro. I trust they won't be growing it on Mars. Or maybe it's their only green vegetable.

Dad, being Dad, ordered the most outrageous thing on the menu: *tronquito*, bull penis soup, along with goat stew. I refused to look at any of it, and propped a menu up between us so I wouldn't be able to see his plate. Mother got ceviche, raw fish, which came with popcorn. It actually looked pretty good (I like sushi all right) but, excuse me for being practical, I had visions of thirty-six people waiting in line for that one bathroom. I didn't want too much adventure on the first day.

(Card ordered a sausage with beans, but only ate the beans. Maybe the sausage looked too much like Dad's soup. I didn't want to know.)

Mother asked what we'd done all afternoon. Card had a detailed analysis of the island's game rooms. Why go to

Mars when you can virtual yourself all over the universe, killing aliens and rescuing big-breasted babes? If we run into aliens on Mars, we probably won't have a single ray gun.

I told them I'd met the pilot. "You think he's only thirty?" Mother asked.

"Well, I haven't done the math," I said. "He was in the Space Force for five years? So he was at least twenty-six when he got out. He's been to Mars three times after that, and probably spent some time on Earth in between. Got a geology degree somewhere."

"Maybe in space," Dad said. "Passing the time. He looked thirtyish, though?"

Dad was still eating, so I didn't look at him. "He looked zombie-ish, actually. I guess he could have been older than thirty."

I explained about the sunblock, but didn't mention his offer to take me rock-hunting. Dad was being a little too protective of me, where males were concerned, and thirty-some probably didn't sound old to him.

"It's pretty impressive," Mother said evenly, "that he recognized you and remembered your name. I wonder if he knows all twenty-five of the passengers' faces. Or just the pretty girls."

"Please." I hate it when she makes me blush.

"Ooh, my pretty," Card said in his moron voice, and I kicked him under the table. He flinched but smiled.

"None of us are going to look all that great with no makeup," I said. Not allowed because of the air recycling. I wanted to get a lipstick tattoo when I heard about that, but neither parent would sign the permission form. It's not fair—Mother had a cheek tattoo done when she was not much older than me. It's way out of style now and she hates it, but that doesn't have anything to do with me. If you get tired of a lipstick tattoo, you can cover it with lipstick, brain.

"Levels the playing field," Dad said. "You'll be at an advantage with your beautiful skin."

"Daddy, don't." Mention the word "skin" and all of the acne molecules in my bloodstream get excited and rush to the surface. "I won't exactly be husband-hunting. Not with only five or six guys to choose from."

"It won't be quite that bad," Mother said.

"No, *worse*! Because most of them plan to stay on Mars, and I'm already looking forward to coming back!" I stood up and laid my napkin down, and walked out of the restaurant as fast as dignity would allow. Mother said, "Say *excuse me*," and I sort of did.

I managed not to start crying until I was up in the room. I was angry at myself as much as anything. If I didn't want to do this, why did I let myself be talked into it?

Part of it might have been the lack of boys where we were headed, but we'd talked that over. We'd also talked over the physical danger and the slight inconvenience of going to college a couple of hundred million miles off campus.

I put in my earplugs and asked for *Eroica*, the Tad Yang version. That always calmed me.

I stepped out onto the balcony to get some non-air-conditioned air, and was startled to see the Space Elevator, a ruler-straight line of red light that dwindled away to be swallowed by the darkness. Maybe the first two miles of fifty thousand. I hadn't seen it in the daylight.

The stars and the Milky Way were brighter than we ever saw them at home. I could see two planets but neither of them was Mars, which I knew didn't rise until morning. Dad had pointed it out to me on the way to the airport, which seemed like a long time ago. Mars was a lot dimmer than these two, and more yellow-orange than red. I guess "the Yellow Planet" didn't sound as dramatic as the red one.

I darkened the room and listened to the rest of the symphony, then went back down to the restaurant in time to get some ice cream along with a sticky sponge cake full of nuts and fruit. Nobody said anything about my absence. Card had probably been threatened.

Dad treated me his delicate girl-in-her-period way, which I definitely was not. I'd gotten a prescription for Delaze, and wouldn't ovulate until I wanted to, after we got to Mars. The download for the Space Elevator had described the use of recyclable tampons in way too much detail. I was just as happy I'd never have to use them in zero gee, on the *John Carter*. Vacuum sterilizes everything, I suppose, so it was silly to be squeamish about it. But you're allowed to be a little irrational about things that personal. I managed to push it out of my mind for long enough to finish dessert.

Card and I tried TV after dinner, but everything was in Spanish except for CNN and an Australian all-news program. There was a Japanese Game Boy module, but he couldn't make it work, which didn't bother me and my book at all.

The room had a little fridge with an interesting design. Every bottle and box was stuck in place with something like a magnet. If you plucked out a Coke or something, the price flashed in the upper right-hand corner of the TV screen, and a note said it had been added to your room bill.

The fridge knew we were underage, and wouldn't let go of the liquor bottles. But we were evidently old enough for beer—a sign said the age was eighteen, but the fridge wasn't smart enough to tell whether it was serving me or my brother. So I had two beers, which helped me get to sleep, but Card stayed awake long enough to build a pyramid of his six cans. I guess I could have been a responsible older sister and cut him off, but there wasn't going to be a lot of beer out on the Martian desert.

5

PIZZA HUNT

Our parents didn't say anything about the $52 added to our room bill for beer, but I suppose they took one look at Card and decided he had suffered enough. He'd told me he'd had beer "plenty of times" with his sag pals at school. Maybe it was the nonalcoholic variety. This was strong Dutch beer in big cans, and six had left a lasting effect. He was pale and quiet when we left the hotel and seemed to turn slightly green when we got aboard the boat, rocking in the choppy waves.

They didn't put the Earth end of the Space Elevator on dry land because it had to be moveable in any direction. Typhoons come through once or twice a century, and they need to get it out of the way. The platform it sits on can move more than two hundred miles in twenty-four hours, far enough to dodge the worst part of a storm. Or so they say; it's never been put to the test.

The ribbon cable that the carrier rides also has to move

around in order to avoid trouble at the other end—dodging human-made space debris and the larger meteors, the ones big enough to track. (Small meteor holes are patched automatically by a little robot climber.)

The platform was about forty miles offshore, and the long, thin ribbon the Elevator rides wasn't usually visible except for the bright strobe lights that warned fliers away. At just the right angle, the sun's reflection could blaze like a razor line drawn in fire; I saw that twice in the hour and a half it took us to cover the distance.

Paul Collins, the pilot, looked more handsome without the white war paint. He introduced himself to Card and my parents, proving that he could recognize passengers who weren't girls.

Before we got to the Space Elevator platform itself, we skirted around a much larger thing, the "light farm," a huge raft of solar-power cells. They didn't get power directly from the sun, but rather from an orbiting power station that turned sunlight into microwaves and beamed them down. Then it gets beamed right back up, in a way. The carrier's electric motors are powered by a big laser sitting on the platform; the laser's powered by the light farm. There's another light farm in the Ecuadorian mountains that beams power at the carrier when it's higher up.

The platform's like an old-fashioned floating oil rig, the size of an office building. The fragile-looking ribbon that the carrier rides spears straight up from the middle of it. The laser and the carrier take up most of the space, with a few huts and storage buildings here and there. It looked bigger from down on the water than in the aerial pictures we'd seen.

We took an elevator to the Elevator. There was a floating dock moored to the platform. It was all very nautical feeling, ropes creaking as the dock moved with the waves, seagulls squawking, salt tang in the air.

Our boat rose and fell with the dock, but of course the open-air elevator didn't. It was a big metal cage that seemed to move up and down and sideways in a sort of menacing way as we bobbed with the waves. If you were sure-footed, you could time it right and just step from the dock onto the elevator. Like most people, I played it safe and jumped aboard as the floor fell away.

We all had identical little suitcases made of light titanium, with our ten kilograms of personal items. Twenty-two pounds didn't sound like very much, but we didn't have any of the stuff that you would normally pack for a trip, since we couldn't take clothes or cosmetics. Three people had musical instruments too big to fit in the metal box.

The elevator clanked and growled all the way up. We clattered to a stop and got out onto a metal floor that felt like sandpaper, I guess some stuff to keep you from slipping. There was a guardrail, but I had a stomach flip-flop at the thought of falling back down the way we'd come. A hundred feet? Hitting the water would knock you out, at the very least.

Like we didn't have enough to worry about; let's worry about drowning.

To the salt air add a smell of oily grease and ozone tang, like a garage where they work on electric cars—and pizza? I'd have to check that out.

A guy in powder blue coveralls, the uniform of the Space Elevator corporation, checked to make sure we were all there and there weren't any stowaways. We each picked up a fluffy towel and a folded stack of clothes. There was a sign reminding us that the clothes we were wearing would be donated to a local charity. Local? The Society for Naked Fish, I supposed.

I'd just had a shower at the hotel, but no such thing as too clean if you're going without for a couple of weeks. Or five years, if you mean a *real* shower.

The women's shower room only took six at a time, and I didn't particularly want to shower with Mom, so I left my stuff stacked by the wall and went off to explore, along with Card, who was looking a little more human.

The climber wasn't open yet, which was okay; we'd be spending plenty of time in it. It was a big white cylinder, about twenty feet in diameter and twenty feet tall, rounded on the top. Not a vast amount of room for forty people. Above it was a robot tug, all ugly machine. It would pull us up a few hundred feet, before the laser took over. It also served as a repair robot, if there was something wrong with the ribbon we were riding on.

"Big foogly laser," Card marveled, and I suppose it was the biggest I'd ever seen, though truthfully I expected something more impressive, more futuristic. The beam it shot out was more than twenty feet in diameter, I knew, and of course it carried enough power to lift the heavy carrier up out of the Earth's gravity well. But it was only the size of a big army tank, and in fact it looked sort of military and menacing. I was more impressed by the big shimmering mirror that would bounce the laser beam up to us, to the photocells on the base of the carrier. Very foogly big mirror.

Three other young people joined us, Davina and Elspeth Feldman, sisters from Tel Aviv, and Barry Westling from Orlando, just south of us. Elspeth looked a little older than me; the others were between me and Card, I figured. Barry was a head taller than him, but a real string bean.

Elspeth was kind of large—not fat, but "large-boned," whatever that really means. You couldn't help but note that most of us future Martians were on the small side, for obvious reasons. Someone has to pay for every pound that goes to Mars. Mother spelled out the inescapable math—every day, you need twelve calories per pound to stay the same weight: someone who weighs fifty pounds more than you has to pig down everything you eat plus one Big Mac every day. Over the six-month flight, that's eighty-five extra pounds of food, on top of the extra fifty pounds of person. So small people have a better chance in the lottery.

(They call it a "lottery" to sound democratic, as if every family has an equal chance. If that were true, I wouldn't have lost a year of Saturdays to the cause.)

Thinking of food made me ask whether anyone had found out where the pizza smell was coming from. No one had, so we embarked on a quest.

The search led, unsurprisingly, to a shed with a machine that dispensed drinks and food, alongside a microwave in which someone had recently burned a slice of pizza. El-speth produced a credit card and everyone but my brother tried a slice. He didn't miss much, but we were more after the *idea* of pizza than the actuality. We didn't know for sure that there wouldn't be any pizza on Mars, but it seemed likely.

Barry and Card went off to play catch with a Frisbee while the rest of us sat in the shade. Neither Elspeth nor Davina was born in Israel; their family moved there after the war. Like ours, their parents are both scientists, their father a biologist and mother in nanotech, both of them in-volved in detoxifying the battlefield after Gehenna. Davina started to cry, describing what they'd had to do, had to see, and Elspeth and I held her until it passed.

Maybe there wouldn't be pizza on Mars, but there wouldn't be that, either. What hate can do.

6

FEARS

There was no privacy in the shower, and not much water—I
mean, all you could see in any direction was water, but I
guess the salt would froog up the plumbing. So you had
to push a button for thirty seconds of lukewarm unsalted
water, then soap up, push the button again, and try to get
the soap off in another thirty seconds. Then do it again for
your hair, without conditioner. I was glad mine was short.
Elspeth was going to have the frizzies for a long time.

She has quite a dramatic figure, narrow waist and big
in the hips and breasts. Mother describes me as "boyish,"
which I think is Motherspeak for "titless wonder." Women
built like Elspeth are always complaining about their boobs
bumping into things. Things like boys, I suppose.

I liked her, though. It could be a little awkward, the first
thing you do when you meet somebody is cry together, then
strip naked and jump in the shower, but Elspeth was funny
and natural about the latter. In the desert kibbutz where she

spent summers growing up, they didn't have individual showers, and the water was rationed almost as severely as here.

Light blue used to be one of my favorite colors, but it does lose some of its charm when everybody in sight is wearing it. We left our "civilian" clothes in the donation box and put on Space Elevator coveralls and slippers. Then we went to the media center for lunch and orientation.

Lunch was a white cardboard box containing a damp sandwich, a weird cookie, and an apple. A bottle of lukewarm water, or you could splurge a couple of bucks on a Coke or a beer out of the machine. I got a beer just to see Card's reaction. He pantomimed sticking a finger down his throat.

The media center was one room with a shallow cube screen taking up one end of it. There were about fifty folding chairs, most of them occupied by powder blue people. With everyone in uniform, it took me a minute to sort out Mother and Dad. Card and I joined them near the front.

The lights dimmed, and we saw a mercifully short history of spaceflight, with an unsurprising emphasis on how big and dangerous those early rockets had been. Lots of explosions, including the three space-shuttle disasters that all but shut down the American space program.

Then some diagrams showing how the Space Elevator works, pretty much a repeat of what we saw at the lottery-winner orientation in Denver a few months ago. Even without that, I wonder if anybody actually ever got this far without knowing that the Space Elevator was—surprise!— an elevator that goes into space.

It was interesting enough, especially the stuff about how they put it up. They worked from the middle out both ways, or up and down, depending on your point of view: starting at GEO, the spot that orbits the Earth in exactly one day, and so stays overhead in the same spot, they dropped stuff down to Earth and raised other stuff up into a higher orbit at the same time. That way the whole thing stayed in balance, like a seesaw stretching out both ways at the same time.

We were headed for that other end, where the *John Carter* and the other Mars ship had been built and would launch from.

They spent a little time talking about the dangers. Sort of like a regular elevator in that if the cable snaps, you lose. You just fall a lot farther before you go splat. (Well, it's not that simple—Earth elevators have fail-safes, for one thing, and the Space Elevator wouldn't actually go splat unless we fell from a really low altitude. We'd burn up in the atmosphere if we started falling at less than twenty-three thousand miles; above that, we'd go into orbit and could theoretically, eventually, be rescued. But if the cable snapped that high, on our way to where the *John Carter* is parked, we'd go flinging off into space. Then that theoretical rescue would really be just a theory. There weren't any spaceships yet that could take off and catch up with us in time.)

There's a lot of dangerous radiation in space, but the carrier has a force field, an electromagnetic shield, for most of that. There are huge solar flares that would get past the shielding, but they're rare and give a ninety-one-hour warning. That's long enough to get back to Earth or GEO. The Mars ships and GEO have hidey-holes where everybody can crowd in to wait out the storm.

I'd read about those dangers before we left home, as well as one they didn't mention: mechanical failure. If an elevator on Earth develops a problem, someone will come fix it. It's not likely to explode or fry you or expose you to vacuum. I guess they figured there was no reason to go over that at this late date.

When we left home, a lot of my friends asked me if I

was scared, and to most of them I said no, not really. They have most of the bugs worked out. It's carried hundreds of passengers to the Hilton space station, and dozens up to the far end, for Mars launch.

But to my best friend, Carol, I admitted what I haven't said even to my family: I wake up terrified in the middle of the night. Every night.

This feels like jumping off a cliff and hoping you'll learn how to fly.

7

CANNED MEAT

We walked up a ramp, took a long last look at sea and sky and friendly sun—it would not be our friend in space—and went inside.

The carrier had a "new car" smell, which you can buy in an aerosol can. In case you're trying to sell a used car or a slightly used Space Elevator.

There were two levels. The first level had twenty couches that were like old-fashioned La-Z-Boy chairs, plush black, with feet pointing out and heads toward the center. Each couch had a "window," a high-def shallow cube, all of which were tuned to look like actual windows for the time being. So there was still sun and sea and sky if you were willing to be fooled.

There was a little storage bin on the side of each couch, with a notebook and a couple of paper magazines. And that stack of barf bags.

Three exercise machines, for rowing, stair-stepping, and

biking, were grouped together where the ladder led up to the second level.

The woman who was our attendant, Dr. Porter, stood on the second rung of the ladder and talked softly into a lapel mic. "We have about sixty minutes till liftoff. Please find your area and be seated by then, strapped in, by one o'clock. That's 1300, for you scientists. I'll be upstairs if anyone has questions." She scampered lightly up the ladder.

I have a question, I didn't say. Could I just jump off and swim for it?

My information packet said I was 21A. I found the seat and sat down, half-reclining. Card was next to me in 20A; Mother and Dad were upstairs in the B section.

Card took a vial out of his packet and looked at the five pills in it. "You nervous?" he said.

"Yeah. Thought I'd save the pills for later, though." They were doses of a sedative. The orientation show admitted that some people have trouble falling asleep at first. Can you imagine?

"Prob'ly smart." He looked pretty much like I felt.

The control console for the window came up out of the armrest and clicked into place over your lap. On one side it had a keyboard and various command buttons, but you could rotate it around, and it was like an airplane tray table with a fuzzy gecko surface.

Card tapped away at the keyboard, which caused a ghostly message to cascade down the window in several languages: MONITOR LOCKED UNTIL AFTER LAUNCH. I touched one key on mine and got the same message, dim letters floating down in front of the fake seascape.

"They're just trying to make us feel comfortable," I said, but it was kind of disappointing. The window would normally be a clever illusion—you could play a game or read a book or whatever, but nobody could see what was on your monitor unless they were right in line with it. Sitting on your lap. From any other angle, it would look just like a window looking outside. It had something to do with polarization; the screen was actually showing two images, but you could only see one or the other.

With an hour to kill, I wasn't going to just sit and look through a fake window. I joined Barry and Elspeth in trying out the exercise machines, which were mainly for those of us going on to Mars. The others were just tourists going to the Hilton; they weren't going to be in space long enough for zero gee to turn their bones to dry sticks and their muscles to mush.

Then we went upstairs and took a look at the zero-gee toilet. We'd sort of trained on it in Denver, in the Vomit Comet, the big ancient plane that gave us fifty seconds of zero gee at a time—up and down, up and down, all day long. I was able to get my feet into the footholds and lower my butt into place, but that was it. I'd learn about the rest soon enough.

But not too soon. There was a regular toilet next to it, with a sign saying FOR USE UNTIL 0.25 G. So we had a few days.

The "personal hygiene" closet looked claustrophobic. Once a day you got a plastic bag with two washcloths wetted with something like rubbing alcohol. Get as clean as you can, then put the same clothes back on. It would be a little better on the *John Carter*, better but weirder—zip yourself up in a plastic bag?

The galley was on the opposite side of the room, just a microwave and a surprisingly small refrigerator, and a bunch of drawers of food and utensils. A fold-down worktable.

In the middle of both rooms, both levels, was a round table with eight seat-belted chairs, I guessed for socializing. Wouldn't it be smarter to have smaller, separate tables? Just in case there turned out to be somebody you couldn't stand the sight of?

After six months, that might be everybody, though, including the mirror.

Mustn't think negative thoughts, as Dad says. Only two weeks in this one, then a change of scenery for six months. Then a new planet.

"It's funny," I said quietly to Card, "on the boat over, I thought I could pretty well tell who were the rich people and who were the neo-Martians."

"Fancy clothes?"

"Or careful down-dressing. An ironed tee shirt—that's a dead giveaway. With clean old jean shorts?"

"But here—"

"Yeah, and it's not just clothes. No makeup or jewelry. That has to rag them. It's going to be interesting."

"Some of the Martians are rich, too," Card said. "Barry's dad's an inventor, and he has all kinds of patents. They came out in their own plane."

"Couldn't afford a ticket?"

"Sure, right. He's got two planes, two motorcycles, two cars, just in case one breaks down. They live on the lake in Disney."

Billionaires, but still. It seemed kind of wasteful to have two of everything, even if money's not an issue. But I didn't say anything. "Barry seems like a nice enough guy."

Card shrugged. "Sure. I think he's a little scared of his dad."

"I wonder if his dad eats bull-dick soup. *That's* scary." Card started giggling, and so did I. Mother gave us a warning look, and that made it worse. We climbed back downstairs, snorting, and managed not to break any bones.

8

STOP

I guess there's something to be said for launching the old way, riding three thousand tons of high explosive on a tower of fire. Dangerous but dramatic. When we took off, it was sort of like an elevator ride.

We were all strapped into our seats, probably just to keep us from wandering around. The tug above us made a whiny little noise, and there was a slight bump, and the platform below us slowly fell away. In a few seconds, you could see the big energy farm. I strained at the seat belt, but couldn't get close enough to the "window" to see the laser and the mirror—dumb of me. It wasn't really a window; if the camera wasn't pointed at the laser, I wouldn't see it.

The noise stopped, and there was another bump. "Switching over," Dr. Porter said over the intercom. A woman of few words.

The main motors were much smoother. There was a slight press of acceleration and a low hum, and in a couple of minutes we were up to our cruising speed, about 250 miles per hour.

After a couple minutes more of going straight up, we were higher than most airplanes, and you could easily see the curvature of the Earth as the Galápagos came into sight. My ears started to pop and crackle with the air pressure dropping. Upstairs, a couple of the younger kids were crying. Ears or fears?

It wasn't really anything new; we'd sat through a twelve-hour test of it at the Denver orientation, thin air with beefed-up oxygen, and everybody managed to live with it. We'll be breathing something like this for the next five years. (The high oxygen content was why we couldn't bring regular clothes—everything has to be absolutely nonflammable. And smokers have to quit.)

Little numbers in the corner of the window showed how high we were and what the gravity was. At seven or eight miles, the edge of South America was coming into view. The sky was getting darker and darker blue, and by twenty-five miles it was almost black. You could see a few stars, at least on this side. I craned my neck to see the windows behind me; the ones facing the afternoon sun were dimmed.

Soon the sky was inky black, and I shivered involuntarily. For all practical purposes, we were in outer space. Outside the Elevator, you wouldn't live a minute.

That would be true in an airplane, too. I told myself not to panic. I considered taking one of the pills, but instead just closed my eyes and took a few deep breaths.

When I opened my eyes, the gravity had fallen to 0.99. I'd lost a pound already, on the Space Elevator Diet. (Money-back guarantee—in one week, your weight problem will be gone!)

That was one advantage we had over the old astronauts. They went straight from one gee to nothing, and about half of them got sick. We had a week to get used to it gradually. But we did have barf bags, too.

That made me glance down to the pocket on the side of the chair. I did not count the number of bags in the stack, but rather pulled out the magazines.

We didn't get paper magazines at home, except for occasional catalogs. These felt funny, kind of heavy and slippery. I guess that was like the clothes, nonflammable paper.

One was the *Space Elevator News*, with a sticker on it that said, "Take this copy home with you." Not to Mars, I thought. The others were the weekend edition of the *International Herald Tribune*, which I'd read back at the hotel (for the comics), *Time*, *International Photography*, and *Seventeen*.

"God, you're reading a magazine?" Card said. "Look, South America!"

"I saw it miles ago," I said. But Earth really was starting to look like a planet, and we were only thirty miles up. I'd thought it would take a lot longer than that.

"You're free to unbelt now and walk around the carrier," Dr. Porter said. "Sometime before six, check off your dinner preference, and I'll call for you when it's ready." Doctor, chef, and waitress all in one, impressive. Though I suspected there wouldn't be much chef-ing involved, and I was right.

Once you got over the novelty of seeing the Earth out there, it was kind of like watching grass grow. I mean, it wasn't like Low Earth Orbit, where the real estate rolls along underneath you, constantly changing. I figured I could check it out once an hour, and tried the keyboard.

It worked pretty much like the console at home. Bigger picture and more detail. Out of curiosity I typed in a request for porn, and got an alphabetical menu that was a little daunting. I knew that Card would get ACCESS DE-NIED, which made me feel mature and privileged. (He'd probably devise a work-around in a couple of hours, but he could have it. I don't really get porn. After the first couple of times, it sort of looks like biology.)

There were a couple of thousand video and virtual channels, but unlike home, the console didn't know what I liked; there was no SUGGEST button. But I could goowiki anything.

The word "menu" started blinking in the corner of the screen, so I clicked on it. There were twelve standard choices for dinner, mostly American and Italian, with one Chinese and one Indian. Then there were ten "premium" meals, with wine, which had surcharges from $40 to $250. Some of them were French things I'd never heard of.

I clicked on beef stew, safe enough, and wondered whether Dad was going to rack up a huge bill ordering French stuff made of unspeakable parts of various animals. Mother would probably rein him in, but they both liked wine. There goes the family fortune.

You could toggle and zoom the window. I put the crosshairs on Puerto Villamil, and cranked it up to 250X, the maximum. The image wobbled and vibrated, but then cleared up. I could see our hotel, and people walking around, the size of ants. With careful toggling, I found the rocky beach where I'd spent my last time actually alone.

"Hey," said a voice behind me, "that's where we met?" It was the pilot, of course, Paul Collins, crouching down so he could see what was on my screen. Was that impolite?

"Yeah, where you nailed that iguana with a rock. Or am I imagining things?"

"No, your memory is perfect. I wondered if you wanted to play some cards. We're getting a game together before anyone else claims the table upstairs."

I was flattered and a little nervous that he had come down to find me. "Sure, if I know the game."

"Poker. Just for pennies."

"Okay. I could do that." The kids in high school had

stopped playing poker with me because I always won, and they couldn't figure out how I was cheating. I wouldn't tell them my secret, which was no secret: fold unless you have something good. Most of the other kids just stayed in the game, trusting their luck, hoping to improve their hands at the last minute. That's idiotic, my uncle Bert taught me; only one person is going to win. Make it be you, or be gone.

I got my purse out of the little suitcase and glanced at Card. He was wrapped up in a game or something, virtual headset on. Mental note: that way nobody can sneak up behind you and see what you're doing.

Upstairs, there were five people at the table, including Dad. "Uh-oh," he said. "Might as well just give her the money."

"Come on, Dad. I don't always win."

He laughed. "Just when I'm in the game." He actually was a pretty bad poker player, not too logical for an engineer. But he played for fun, not money.

We spent a pleasant couple of hours playing Texas Hold-'em and seven-card stud. I dealt five-card stud a couple of times, the purest game, but that wasn't enough action for most of them.

Dad was way ahead when I left, which was both satisfying and annoying. I learned that pilot Paul plays pretty much like me, close to the chest. If he stayed in, he had something—or he bluffed so well no one found out.

I went in with ten dollars and left with twenty. That's another thing Uncle Bert taught me: decide before you sit down how much you're going to win or lose, and stop playing at that point, no matter how long you've been in the game. You may not make any friends if you win the first two hands and leave. But poker's not about making friends, he said.

The gravity was down to 0.95 when I went back to my

chair, and I could almost tell the difference. It was a funny feeling, like "Where did I leave my purse?"

I could just see North America coming up over the edge of the world. Zoomed in on Mexico City, a huge sprawl of places you probably wouldn't like to visit without an armed guard.

Card was still in virtual, doing something with aliens or busty blondes. I put on the helmet myself and chinned through some of the menu. Nothing that really fascinated me. Curious, I spent a few minutes in "Roman Games: Caligula," but it was loud and gory beyond belief. Settled into "midnight warm ocean calm," and set the timer for six, then watched the southern sky, the beautiful Cross and Magellanic Clouds, roll left and right as the small boat bobbed in the current. I fell asleep for what seemed like about one second, and the chime went off.

I unlocked the helmet and instantly wished I was back on the calm sea. Someone had heard the dinner bell and puked. They couldn't wait for zero gee? There went my appetite.

After a few minutes there was a double chime from the monitor and a little food icon, a plate with wavy lines of steam, started blinking in the corner. I went upstairs to get it, hoping I could eat up there.

I was the second person up the ladder, and there was a short line forming behind me. They said they would call ten people at a time for dinner, I guess at random.

There were ten white plastic boxes on the galley table, with our seat numbers. I grabbed mine and snagged a place at the center table, across from the rich kid, Barry.

He had the same thing I did, a plate with depressions for beef stew with a hard biscuit, a stack of small cooked carrots, and a pile of peas, all under plastic. Everything was hot in the middle and cool on the outside.

"I guess we can say good-bye to normal food," he said,

and I wondered what dinner normally was to him. Linen and crystal, sumptuous gourmet food dished out by servants? "Water boils at 170 degrees, at this pressure," he continued. "It doesn't get hot enough to cook things properly."

"Yeah, I read about coffee and tea." All instant and tepid. The stew was kind of chewy and dry. The carrots glowed radioactively, and the peas were a lurid bright green and tasted half-raw.

Funny, the peas started to roll around on their own. A couple jumped off the plate. There was a low moan that seemed to come from everywhere.

"What the hell?" Barry said, and started to stand up.

"Please remain seated," Dr. Porter shouted over the sound. The floor and walls were vibrating. "If you're not in your assigned seat, don't return to it until the climber stops."

"Stops?" he said. "What are we stopping for?"

"Probably not to pick up new passengers," I said, but my voice cracked with fear.

Dr. Porter was standing with her feet in stirrup-like restraints, her head inside a VR helmet, her hands on controls.

"There isn't any danger," her muffled voice said. "The climber will stop for a short time while the ribbon-repair vehicle separates to repair a micrometeorite hole." That was the squat machine on top of the climber. It separated with a clang and a lurch; we swayed a little.

I swallowed hard. So we were stuck here until that thing stitched up the hole in the tape. If it broke, we'd shortly become a meteorite ourselves. Or a meteor, technically, if we burned up before we hit the ground.

"I heard it happens about every third or fourth flight," Barry said.

I'd read that, too, but it hadn't occurred to me that it would be scary. Stop, repair the track, move on. I swallowed again and shook my head hard. Two children were crying, and someone was retching.

"Are you all right?" Barry asked, a quaver in his voice.

"Will be," I said through clenched teeth.

"How about them Gators?"

"What? Are you insane?"

"You said you live in Gainesville," he said defensively.

"Don't follow football." An admission that could get me burned at the stake in some quarters.

"Me, neither." He paused. "You win at poker?"

"A thousand," I said. "I mean ten bucks. A thousand pennies."

"Might as well be dollars. Nothing to spend it on."

Interesting thing for him to say. "You could buy stuff when we stop at the Hilton."

"Yeah, but you couldn't carry it with you. Unless you have less than ten kilograms."

Maybe I should've saved a few ounces, brought back an Orbit Hilton tee shirt. Be the only one on the block.

The pilot Collins sat down next to Barry. "Thrills and chills," he said.

"Routine stuff, right?" Barry said.

He paused a moment, and said, "Sure."

"You've seen this happen before?" I said.

"In fact, no. But I haven't ridden the Elevator that many times." He looked past me, to where Dr. Porter was doing mysterious things with the controls.

"Paul . . . you're more scared than I am."

He settled back into the chair, as if trying to look relaxed. "I'm just not used to not being in control. This *is* routine," he said to Barry. "It's just not my routine. I'm sure Porter has everything under control."

His face said that he wasn't sure.

"You're free to walk around now," Dr. Porter said, her head still hidden. (I suppose pilots can walk around all they want.) "We'll be done here in less than an hour. You should be in your seats when we start up again."

Barry relaxed a little at that, and turned his attention back to dinner.

Paul didn't relax. He stood up slowly and took the vial of white pills from his pocket. He shook out two into his hand and headed for the galley, to pick up a squeeze bottle of water. He took the pills and went back to his seat.

Barry hadn't seen that, his back to the galley. "You're not eating," he said.

"Yeah." I took a small bite of the beef, but it was like chewing on cardboard. Hard to swallow. "You know, I'm not all that hungry. I'll save it for later." I pressed the plastic back down over the top and went over to the galley.

The refrigerator wouldn't open—not keyed to my thumbprint—so I took the plate and a bottle of water back down to my seat.

Card was reading a magazine. "That *food*?"

"Mine, el Morono. Wait your turn." I slid it under my seat but kept the water bottle. The pilot had taken two pills; I took three.

"What, you scared?"

"Good time to take a nap." I resisted telling him that if the Mars pilot was scared, I could be scared, too, thank you very much.

I pulled the light blanket over me. It fastened automatically on the other side, a kind of loose cocoon for zero gee.

I reached for the VR helmet, but it was locked, a little red light glowing. Making sure everyone could hear emergency announcements, I supposed. Like "The ribbon has broken; everybody take a deep breath and pray like hell."

After about a minute, the pills were starting to drag my eyelids down, even though the anxiety, adrenaline, was trying to keep me awake. Finally, the pills won.

❋

I had a nightmare, but it wasn't about the Elevator. I was with Elspeth, and we were working alongside her parents in the aftermath of Gehenna.

Whoever caused Gehenna had started it months before, by contaminating the water supplies of Tel Aviv and Hefa. People who had lived in those cities even for a few days became carriers of the azazel, an initially harmless nano-organism that migrated to the lungs, to wait. It wasn't even organic, just a submicroscopic machine.

Then the second part came. One minute after the beginning of Passover, thirteen car bombs and suicide bombs exploded simultaneously in Tel Aviv and Hefa and their suburbs. They were relatively small explosions, with a lot of smoke. It was a windy day, and the vapor from the bombs spread quickly.

They called it a "coadjuvent" reaction, which sounds cozy. Dust from the bombs activated the azazels. People's lungs stopped working. They could breathe in, but couldn't breathe out.

Respirators could delay death, for the ones who were already in hospitals. Two million others were dead in minutes.

So in my dream, Elspeth and I went from one rigid rotting corpse to another, collecting identification tags. Behind us was heavy machinery, digging a trench.

Mass burial was against Jewish law, or custom. But the smell was unbearable.

9

LOSING WEIGHT

I slept about ten hours, with no sense of rest. When I woke up it was right at midnight; the Elevator restarting hadn't awakened me. The window said we'd gone 2250 miles and we were at 0.41 gee. You could see the whole Earth as a big globe. I took the pen out of my pocket and dropped it experimentally. It seemed to hesitate before falling, and then drifted down in no hurry.

It's one thing to see that on the cube, but quite another to have it happening in your own world. We were in space, no doubt about it.

I unbuckled and pointed myself toward the john. Walking felt strange, as if I were full of helium or something. It was actually an odd combination of energy and light-headedness, not completely pleasant. Partly the gravity and partly the white pills, I supposed.

I went up the ladder with no effort, barely touching the

rungs. You could learn to like this—though we knew what toll it eventually would take.

Probably the last time I'd sit on a regular toilet. I should ask the machine when we were due to hit a quarter gee and switch to the gruesome one. Go join the line just before. Or not. I'd be living with the sucking thing for months; one day early or late wouldn't mean anything.

My parents were both zipped up, asleep. Several people were snoring; guess I'd have to get used to that.

There were four people I didn't know talking quietly at the table. Downstairs, two people were playing chess while two others watched. I took the copy of *Seventeen* from my chair and walked over to the bike machine. Might as well get started on saving my bones.

The machine was set on a hill-climbing program, but I really didn't want to be the first person aboard to work up a sweat. So I clicked it to EASY and pedaled along while reading the magazine.

So little of it was going to be useful or even meaningful for the next five years. Hot fashion tips! ("Get used to blue jumpsuits.") Lose that winter flab! ("Don't eat the space crap they put in front of you.") How to communicate with your boyfriend! ("E-mail him from 250 million miles away.")

I hadn't really had a boyfriend since Sean, more than a year ago. Knowing that I was going to be in outer space and on Mars for six years put a damper on that.

It wasn't that simple. The thing with Sean, the way he left, hurt me badly enough that the idea of leaving the planet was pretty attractive. No love life, none of that kind of pain.

Did that make me cold? I should have fallen helplessly in love with someone and pined away for him constantly, bursting into tears whenever I saw the Earth rise over the morning horizon. Or did I see that in a bad movie?

There weren't any obviously great prospects aboard the carrier. They might start to look better as the years stretched on.

And the Gehenna dream was still with me. I did start to cry a little, and the tears just stayed in my eyes. Not enough gravity for them to roll down your cheek. After pedaling blind for a minute, I wiped my eyes on a non-absorbent sleeve and cranked on. There was an article on Sal the Sal, a hot new cube star that everyone but me had heard of; I decided to read every word of that and then quit.

He was so sag beyond sag it was disgusting. Fascinating, too. Like if you can care little enough about everything, you automatically become famous. You ask him for an autograph, and he pulls out a rubber stamp, and everybody just comes because it's so sag. Forgive me for not joining in. I bet Card knows his birth date and favorite color.

Pedaling through all that responsible journalism did put me on the verge of sweating, so I quit and went back to my seat. Card had put aside the helmet and was doing a word puzzle.

"Card," I asked, "what's Sal the Sal's favorite color?"

He didn't even look up. "Everybody knows it's black. Makes him look 190 pounds instead of 200."

Fair enough. I handed him the magazine. "Article on him if you want to read it."

He grunted thanks. "Five-letter word meaning 'courage'? Second letter P, last letter K?"

I thought for a couple of seconds. "Spunk."

He frowned. "You sure?"

"It's old-fashioned." Made me think of the pilot, who seemed to have "spunk," Space Force and all, but was scared by an Elevator incident.

I sat down and buckled in and got scared all over again

myself. He had a point, after all. Accidents could happen on the way to Mars, but nothing that would send us hurtling to a flaming death in Earth's atmosphere.

Don't be a drama queen, Dad would say. But the idea of dying that way made my eyes feel hot and dry.

10

SOCIAL CLIMBING

The fear faded as we fell into routine, climbing up toward the Hilton midpoint. We grew imperceptibly lighter every hour, obviously so day by day. By the sixth day, we'd lost 90 percent of our gravity. You could go upstairs without touching the ladder, or cross the room with a single step. There were a lot of collisions, getting used to that.

It was getting close to what we'd live with on the way to Mars. We wore gecko slippers that lightly stuck to the floor surface, and there were gray spots on the wall where they would also adhere.

The zero-gee toilet wasn't bad once you got used to it. It uses flowing air instead of water, and you have to pee into a kind of funnel, which is different. The crapper is only four inches in diameter, and it uses a little camera to make sure you're centered. A little less attractive than my yearbook picture.

I hope Dr. Porter gets paid really well. Some of the little

ones didn't climb the learning curve too swiftly, and she had to clean up after them.

It didn't help the flavor of the food any to know where the water came from. Get used to the idea or starve, though. I found three meals on the menu I could eat without shuddering.

I mostly hung around with Elspeth and Barry and Kaimei, a Chinese girl a year younger than me. She was born in China but grew up, bilingual and sort of bicultural, in San Francisco. She was a dancer there, small and muscular, and you could tell by the way she moved in low gravity that she was going to love zero gee.

The smaller kids were going detroit with the light gravity. Dr. Porter set hours for playtime and tried to enforce them by restraining offenders in their seats. Then, of course, they'd have to go to the bathroom, and wouldn't go quietly. She looked like she was going to be glad to send them on to Mars or leave them at the Hilton.

I would, too, in her place. Instead, I got to go along with them, at least the ones who were ten and older. After we left the tourists at the Hilton, we wouldn't have anybody under ten aboard—if there were any small children in the Mars colony, they'd have to be born there.

Luckily, the two worst offenders were brother brats who were getting off at the Hilton. Eighty grand seemed like more than they were worth, and you'd think their parents would have had a better time without them. Maybe they couldn't find a babysitter for a few weeks. (Hell, I'd do it for less than eighty grand. But only if they let me use handcuffs and gags.)

We weren't supposed to play any throwing and catching games, for obvious reasons, but Card had a rubber ball, and out of boredom we patted it back and forth in the short space between us. Of course it went in almost ruler-straight lines, how exciting, even when he tried to put English on it—he needed speed and a floor or wall to bounce off, and a little bit of space for the thing to bounce around in. But even he was smart enough not to try anything that would provoke Dr. Frankenstein's wrath.

Elspeth and I signed up for the exercise machines at the same time, and chatted and panted together. I was in slightly better shape, from fencing team and swimming three times a week. No swimming pools on Mars, this century. Probably no swords to fence with, either. (The John Carter fictional character the ship was named after used a sword, I guess when his ray gun ran out of batteries. Maybe we could start the solar system's first low-gravity fencing team. Then if the Martians *did* show up, we could fight them with something sharper than our wits.)

Actually, Elspeth was better than me on the stair-step machine, since in our flat Florida city you almost never encounter stairs. Ten minutes on that machine gave me pains in muscles I didn't know I owned. But I could pedal or row all day.

Then we took turns in the "privacy module," which they ought to just call a closet, next to the toilet, for our daily dry shower. Moist, actually; you had two throwaway towelettes moistened with something like rubbing alcohol—one of them for the "pits and naughty bits," as Elspeth said, and the other for your face and the rest of your body. Then a small reusable towel for rubdown. Meanwhile, your jumpsuit is rolling around in a waterless washing machine, getting refreshed by hot air, ultrasound, and ultraviolet light. It comes out warm and soft and only smelling slightly of sweat. Not all of it your own, though that could be my imagination.

I fantasized about diving into the deep end of the city pool and holding my breath for as long as I could.

Six hours before we were due at the Hilton, we were asked to stick our heads into the helmets for "orientation,"

which was more of a sales job than anything else. Why?
They already had everybody's money.

The Hilton had a large central area that stayed zero
gee, the "Space Room," with padded walls and a kind of
oversized jungle gym. A pair of trampolines on opposite
walls, so you could bounce back and forth, spinning, which
looked like fun.

People didn't stay there, though; the actual rooms were
in two doughnut-shaped structures that spun, for artificial
gravity, around the zero-gee area. The two levels were 0.3g
and 0.7g.

The orientation didn't mention it, but I knew that about
half of the low-gee rooms housed permanent residents, rich
old people whose hearts couldn't take Earth gravity anymore. All of the people in the presentation were young and
energetic, and vaguely rich-looking in their tailored Hilton
jumpsuits, I guess no different from ours except for the tai-
loring and choice of colors.

We would stop there for four hours and could explore the
hotel for two of them. We were all looking forward to the
change of scenery.

"Don't use the Hilton bathrooms unless you absolutely
have to," Dr. Porter said. "We want to keep that water in our
system. Feel free to drink all of theirs you can hold."

The four hours went by pretty quickly. Basically seeing
how rich folks live without too much gravity. Most of them
looked pretty awful, cadaverous with bright smiles. We
looked at the prices at Conrad's Café, and could see why
they might not want to eat too much.

We did play around a bit in the weightless-gym area.
Elspeth and I played catch with her little sister Davina, who
obediently curled into a ball. Spinning her gave us all the
giggles, but we had to stop before she got totally dizzy. She
looked a little green as she unfolded, but I think was happy
for the small adventure and the attention.

I did a few bounces on the pair of trampolines, managing four before I got off target and hit the wall. Card was good at it, but quit after eight or so rather than hog it. I suppose two people could use it at once if they were really good. Only once if they weren't. Ouch.

The interesting thing about the jungle gym was gliding through it, rather than climbing on it. Launch yourself from the wall and try to wriggle your way through without touching the bars. The trick is starting slow and planning ahead—a demanding skill that will be oh-so-useful if I ever find myself having to thread through a jungle gym, running from Martians.

Dr. Porter had found a whistle somewhere. She called us to the corridor opening and counted noses, then told us to stay put while she went off in search of a missing couple. They were probably in Conrad's Café guzzling hundred-dollar martinis.

I mentioned that to Card and said there wouldn't be any vodka or gin on Mars—and he bet me a hundred bucks there would be. I decided not to take the bet. Seventy-five engineers would find a way.

The missing duo appeared in the Elevator, and we crawled back home to wait in line for the john. The carrier seemed cramped.

The *John Carter* would be about three times as big, but nothing like the Hilton. After that, though, a whole planet to ourselves.

II

UP AND OUT

The trip from the Hilton out to the end of the tether was more subdued than the first leg. Only twenty-seven of us and all headed for Mars, except Dr. Porter. We did the gravity thing in reverse, slowly weighing more until we would (temporarily) have full Earth weight at the end of the tether.

We couldn't go back to using the gravity-operated toilet. Didn't want us to get used to it again, I suppose. When they fling us off to Mars, it will be zero gee again.

We spent a lot of time sitting around in small groups talking, some about Mars but mostly about who we were and where we came from.

Most of us were from the States, Canada, and Great Britain, because the lottery demographic was based on the amount of funding each country had put into the Mars Project. There were families from Russia and France. The flight following ours would have German, Australian, and

Japanese families. A regular United Nations, except that everybody spoke English.

My mother talked to the French family in French, to stay in practice; I think some disapproved, as if it was a conspiracy. But they were fast friends by the time we got to the ship. The mother, Jac, was backup pilot as well as a chemical engineer. I didn't have much to do with their boy, Auguste, a little younger than Card. His dad, Greg, was amusing, though. He'd brought a small guitar along, which he played softly, expertly.

The Russians kept to themselves but were easy enough to get along with. The boy, Yuri, was also a musician. He had a folding keyboard but evidently was shy about playing for others. He would put on earplugs and play for hours, from memory or improvising, or reading off the screen. Only a little younger than me, but not too social.

He did let me listen in on a bit of Rachmaninoff he was practicing, Rach 3   Piano Concerto no. 3   and he was incredibly nimble. (I studied piano for five years and quit as soon as Mother would let me. I'm an avid consumer of music but will never be a producer of it.)

Our doctor on the way to Mars would be Alphonzo Jefferson, who was also a scientist specializing in the immune system; his wife, Mary, was also a life scientist. Their daughter, Belle, was about ten; son, Oscar, maybe two years older.

The Manchester family were from Toronto, the parents both areologists. The kids, Michael and Susan, were ten-year-old twins I hadn't gotten to know. I didn't know Murray and Roberta Parienza well, either, Californians about our age (Murray the younger) whose parents came from Mexico, an astronomer and a chemist.

So our little UN among the younger generation was two Latins, a Russian, two African-Americans, two Israelis, and a Chinese-American, slightly outnumbering us plain white-bread North Americans.

We'd all be going to school via VR and e-mail during the six-month flight, though we started going on different days and, of course, would have class at different times, spread out over eleven time zones. If Yuri had a class at nine in the morning, that would be ten for Davina and Elspeth, eleven for Auguste, five in the afternoon for us Floridians, and eight at night for the Californians. It was going to make the social calendar a little complicated. As if there was anything to do.

Meanwhile, we could enjoy the extra elbow room we got from dumping off the nine tourists. I moved upstairs to sit next to Elspeth, which put Roberta on my right. Dr. Porter rolled her eyes at three young females in a row, and told us to keep the noise down, or she'd split us up. That wasn't exactly fair, since the little kids were the real noisemakers, and besides, most of our parents were on the second level, too.

But you had to have some sympathy for her. The littlest ones were always testing her to see how far they could go before she applied the ultimate punishment: locked in the seat next to your parents with the VR turned off for X hours. She couldn't hit them—some parents wouldn't mind, but others would have a fit—and she couldn't exactly make them go outside to play, though if she did that once, the others might calm down.

(It was no small trick to get a recalcitrant child back to its place while we were still in zero gee. They'd push off and fly away giggling while she stalked after them with her gecko slippers. Hard to corner somebody in a round room. The parents or other adults usually had to help.)

What finally worked was escalating punishment. Each time she had to strap a kid in, she added fifteen minutes' VR deprivation to *everyone's* next punishment, no exceptions. At ten, they were old enough to do the math, and started policing themselves—and behaving themselves, a small miracle.

We went a little faster on the second half, and it would've taken only four and a half days, except we had to stop again while the robot repaired a tear in the tape ahead.

I had a vague memory of watching the news when they started building the two Mars ships eleven years ago. They'd taken the fuel tanks from the old pre–Space Elevator cargo shuttles, cut them up, and rearranged the parts. The first one, the *Carl Sagan*, was assembled in Low Earth Orbit; the second up at GEO, where the Hilton is now. I guess the Elevator wasn't available for the first. Anyhow, they both took a long crawl up here, spiraling slowly up with some sort of solar-power engine. The first one took off while they were still working on ours.

The *Sagan* had made two round-trips, and was on its third, in orbit around Mars now. Ours had only been once, but at least we knew that it worked.

Of course a spaceship doesn't have to be streamlined to work in outer space, with no air to resist, but the fuel tanks these were built from had gone through the atmosphere, and so they looked kind of like a hokey rocket ship from an old twentieth movie, though with funny-looking arms sticking out on the left and right, with the knobs we'd be living in.

We could see the *John Carter* a couple of hours before we got there, at least as a highly magnified blob. Slowly it took shape, the stubby rocket ship with those two pods. Once we were on the way, it would start rotating, once each ten seconds.

The carrier slowed down for the last couple of minutes. Strapped in, we watched the spaceship draw closer and closer.

It wasn't too impressive, only ninety feet long, unpainted

except for the white front quarter, the streamlined lander. We were going in through the side of that, a crawl tunnel like we'd used for the Hilton, but with gravity.

The carrier came to a stop, and Dr. Porter and Paul put on space suits to go check things out. They came back in a few minutes and said things were fine, but a little cold. The air that came through the open air-lock door was wintry— colder than it ever gets at home. Paul said not to worry; we'd warm it up.

They opened the storage area under the exercise machines, and we all pitched in, carrying things over. There were some pretty heavy boxes, a lot of it food and water for the trip. "Starter" water, that would be recycled. I'd almost gotten resigned to the fact that a little bit of every drink I took had gone through my brother at least once.

You could see your breath. I had goose bumps, and my teeth started chattering. Barry and his parents were the same way, fellow Floridians. My parents and Card seemed to have some Eskimo blood.

A lot of the stuff we stored in the Mars lander, under Paul's supervision. Some of it went into A or B, the pods where we'd be living.

That was sort of like the Hilton in miniature. There was a relatively large zero-gee room, a cylinder twenty-two feet long by twenty-seven feet wide. On opposite sides there were two four-foot holes, A and B, with ladders going down. No elevators.

It was all kind of topsy-turvy, with the temporary gravity we got from the Elevator cable's spin. Up and down were normal in the little spaceship, the lander. Pretty much like an airplane, with seats and an aisle. But carrying stuff back into the zero-gee room, we walked along the wall. We carried stuff down a ladder into B and strapped it into place. Then we waited back in the Elevator while they turned the thing around 180 degrees. Then we could go down A's ladder.

I couldn't get warm. Fortunately, one of the things I delivered was a bundle of blankets for "Sleeping A." I was A-8, so after we finished, I liberated one of the blankets and wrapped it around myself.

Saying good-bye to Dr. Porter was more emotional than I would have thought. Tears that acted reasonably, rolling down your cheeks. She hugged me, and whispered, "Take care of Card. You'll love him soon enough."

She went back to the carrier, and the air lock closed. Paul warned us we all had thirty minutes to use the toilet, then we'd be strapped in for almost two hours. I didn't really need to go, but might as well be prudent, and I was mildly curious about what I'd be putting up with for the next six months. I got at the end of the line and asked my reader for a random story. It was an amusing thing from France a million years ago, about a necklace.

The zero-gee toilet was the same as the carrier's, without the little camera. I didn't miss it; nor did I miss the target.

We strapped into our seats in the lander and waited for twenty minutes or so. Then there was a little "clank" sound, the cable letting go of us, and we were in zero gee, flung away.

Most of the speed we needed for getting to Mars was "free"—when we left the high orbit at the end of the Space Elevator, we were like a stone thrown from an old-fashioned sling, or a bit of mud flung from a bicycle tire. Two weeks of relatively slow crawling to the top built up into one big boost, from the orbit of Earth to the orbit of Mars.

We had to stay strapped in because there would be course corrections, all automatic. The ship studied our progress, then pointed in different directions and made small bursts of thrust.

It was only a little more than an hour later when Paul gave us the all-clear to go explore the ship and get a bite to eat.

Compared to the Space Elevator carrier, it was huge. From the lander, you went into the zero-gee room, which was about three times the size of our living room at home. The circular wall was all storage lockers that opened with the touch of a recessed button, no handles sticking out to snag you.

You climbed backward down the ladder, in a four-foot-wide tunnel, to get to the living areas, A or B. Both pods were laid out the same. The first level, for sleeping, had the least gravity, close to what we'd have on Mars. Then there was the work/study area, basically one continuous desk around the wall, with moveable partitions and maybe twenty viewscreens. They were set up as fake windows, like the carrier's "default mode"—thankfully not spinning around six times a minute.

The bottom level was the galley and recreation area. I felt heavy there, after all the zero gee, but it was only about half Earth's gravity, or 1.7 times what we'd have on Mars, the next five years.

It had a stationary bicycle and a rowing machine with sign-up rosters. You were supposed to do an hour a day on them. I took 7 A.M., since 8 and 9 were already spoken for.

Elspeth and Davina found me down there, and we had the first of a couple of hundred lunches aboard the good ship *John Carter*. A tolerable chicken-salad sandwich with hot peas and carrots. Card showed up and had the same. He made a face at the vegetables but ate them. We'd been warned to eat everything in front of us. The ship wasn't carrying snacks. If you got hungry between meals, you'd just have to be hungry. (I suspected we'd find ways around that.)

It was a lot more roomy than you'd expect a spaceship

to be, which was a provision for disaster. If something went wrong, and one of the pods became uninhabitable, all twenty-six of us could move into the other pod. Then if something happened to *it*, I guess we could all move into the zero-gee room and the lander. I don't know what we'd eat, though. Each other. ("It's your turn now, Card. Be a good boy and take your pill.")

I sat down at one of the study stations and typed in my name and gave it a thumbprint. I had a few letters from friends and a big one from the University of Maryland. That was my "orientation package," though actual classes wouldn't start for another week.

It was very handy—advice about where to get a parking sticker, dormitory hours, location of emergency phones and all. More useful was a list of my class hours and their virtual-reality program numbers, so I could be in class after a fashion.

It was a little more complicated for me than for the kids actually on campus. Up in the right-hand corner of the screen were UT, Universal Time, and TL, time lag. The time lag now, the time it took for a signal to get from me to the classroom, was only 0.27 of a second. By the time we got to Mars, it could be as much as twenty-five minutes (or as little as seven, depending on the distance between the planets). So if I asked the professor a question at what was to me the beginning of the fifty-minute class, he'd already be halfway through, Earth time. He'd get my question while everybody else was packing up their books, and his answer would get to me twenty-five minutes after class was over.

Actually, it would be even more complicated once we were on Mars Time, since the day is forty minutes longer. But I didn't have to worry about that until we got halfway there, and switched.

Ship time was Universal Time, until we hit the halfway

point, which put us on the same schedule as people living just downriver from London, which I guess had made
sense when they were planning things on Earth. Why not
go straight to Mars Time? Whatever, I got a few pages into
the college catalog, and my body said sleep, even if it was
only two, 1400, to the folks in Merrie Olde Englande. I
dragged my blanket up to the light-gee sleeping floor and
wrapped myself up in it, and slept till the dinner bell.

12

TROUBLE

The first week or two we were under way, I was asleep as much as awake, or more, which got Mother worried. She had me go talk to Dr. Jefferson, who asked me whether I felt depressed, and I'm afraid my response was a little loud and emotional. I mean, no, I wasn't depressed; I was just imprisoned and hurtling off to some uncertain future, probably to die before I was legally an adult, and I asked him aren't *you* depressed?

He smiled and nodded (maybe not "yes"), and gave me a light hug, the big black bear, which might have made me slightly telepathic. It wasn't so much the abstract danger. I was really upset at not being able to concentrate, falling asleep over my college homework . . . but what was that, compared to being the only doctor aboard, waiting for someone to need an appendix out, or even a brain tumor? Or just pulling a tooth or looking up someone's ass with an ass-o-scope. He only had to take care of twenty-six of us, but anything could happen, and he was responsible for our lives or deaths.

He probably had a suitcase full of pills for depression, and said he'd give me some if I needed them, but first he wanted me to keep a personal record for a week—how many hours asleep and awake; when I lost my temper or felt like crying. After a week, we would talk about it.

He said he was no psychologist, but that seemed to work, maybe because I wanted to impress him, or reassure him. After a week, I was sleeping eight hours—counting the hours lying with my eyes closed listening to music—and pretty much awake the rest of the time. And I was undramatically less sure that space wanted to kill us all, especially me.

All of us between ten and twenty had "jobs," which is to say chores. Mine was easy, cleaning the galley after meals, a lot less mess than the kitchen at home, with nothing actually cooked. Card had to clean the shower, which I suppose enriched his fantasy life.

Everybody spent thirty minutes a day learning about Mars. That was mostly boring reinforcement of stuff we already knew, or should have known. I tolerated the half hour until regular classes started, and really just sort of thought about other things while it droned on. Nobody was testing me on Mars facts, but I had exams in history and math and philosophy.

Of course, Mars would test me on Mars. I knew that and didn't think about it.

School was absorbing but tiring. Part of it was that every professor was kind of a star—I suppose every subject, every department, picked its most dramatic teacher for the VR classes, but the net result was almost like being yelled at—"This led to the Hundred Years War—how long do you think that war LASTED?" "Look where potassium and sodium are on the Periodic Table—what does THAT suggest to you?" Socrates and Plato getting it on, more than I wanted to know about student-teacher relationships. And could I have just one subject that's not supposed to be the most important thing in the world? I should've taken plumbing.

Actually, the stories and plays in the literature course all promised to be interesting, no surprise, since that has always been the most enjoyable part of school. It didn't have any exams, either, just essays, which suits me.

I didn't want to major in lit, though. I couldn't see myself as a teacher, and I don't think anybody else gets paid to read the stuff for a living. I didn't have to choose a major for a couple of years. Maybe I could become the first Martian veterinarian. Wait for some animals to show up.

Something I would never have predicted was that the virtual-reality classrooms smelled more real than our real spaceship. If someone was chewing gum or eating peanuts near where you were "sitting," it was really intense. Our air aboard the *John Carter* was thin, and it circulated well. When you peeled the plastic off a meal, you could smell it for a few seconds, but then it was pretty much gone, and a lot of the flavor as well.

Roberta and Yuri were also starting college, though in Yuri's case it was more like a practical conservatory. Most of his courses were music. (I wondered how the time lag was going to affect that. When I suffered through my first piano lessons in grade school and middle school, I cringed in anticipation of the *whack-whack-whack* Ms. Varleman would make with her stick on the side of the piano whenever I lagged behind. I might have liked learning piano if the teacher was twenty-five minutes away!)

My life settled into a fairly busy routine. Classes and homework and chores and exercise periods. A blood test said I was losing calcium, and so my forty-five-minute exercise requirement went up to ninety minutes; two hours if

I could schedule it. Hard to beat the combination—what else is both tiring and boring for two hours?

Actually, I could read or do limited VR while I was biking or rowing. It's kind of fun to row down the streets of New York or Paris. You do get run over a lot, but you get used to it.

Routine or no routine, the possibility of disaster is always in the back of your mind. But you always think in terms of something dramatic, like an explosion on board or a huge meteoroid collision. When it did happen, nobody knew but the pilot.

We had sprung a leak. On the cube, that would be air shrieking out, or at least whistling or hissing. Which would be kind of nice, because then you could find it and put a piece of duct tape over it. Ours was seeping out silently, and we didn't have too long to find the problem.

Paul put a message up on every screen, a strobing red exclamation point followed by WE ARE LOSING AIR! That got almost everybody's attention.

We were losing about a half of one percent a day. We were still four months away from Mars, so the oxygen would be getting pretty thin if we didn't fix it.

It was easy enough to find the general area of the leak. Every part of the ship could be closed off in case of emergency, so Paul just had us close up each section of the ship, one at a time, for about two hours. That was long enough to tell whether the pressure was still dropping.

First we closed off Pod A, where I lived, and I was relieved to find it wasn't there. It wasn't in Pod B, either, nor the solar-storm radiation shelter. It wasn't the zero-gee center room, which basically left the lander. That was bad news. As well as being the vehicle that would get us to the Martian surface, that was where all the pilot's instrumentation and controls were. We couldn't very well just close it off for the next three months, then refill it with air for the trip down.

In fact, though, we wound up doing a version of that. First, Paul tried to find the leak with a "punk"—not like Granddad's ancient music, but a stick of something that smoldered. The smoke should have led us to the leak. It didn't, though, which meant we didn't have a simple thing like a meteor ("micrometeoroid," technically) hole. A seam or something was leaking, maybe the port that the pilot looked through, or the air lock to the outside.

Of course there was also an inside air lock, between the lander and the rest of the ship, and that gave us the solution. Paul didn't have to live in the lander; he just checked things every now and then. In fact, he could monitor all the instruments with a laptop thing, from anywhere.

So although it made him nervous—not being able to run things from the pilot's chair—we closed off the lander and just let it leak. If Paul had to go in there every day or two, he could put on a space suit and go through the air lock.

It made some of us nervous, too, like being cargo in a ship without a rudder. Okay, that was irrational. But we'd already had one emergency. What if the next one called for immediate action, but Paul had to suit up, waiting for the air lock to cycle through? That took about two minutes.

In two minutes we covered almost a thousand miles. A lot could happen. And there weren't any space suits for the rest of us.

13

UIRTUAL FRIENDS AND FOES

I was not the most popular girl in my classes—I wasn't *in* class at all, of course, except as a face in a cube. As the time delay grew longer, it became impossible for me to respond in real time to what was going on. So if I had questions to ask, I had to time it so I was asking them at the beginning of class the next day.

That's a prescription for making yourself a tiresome know-it-all bitch. I had all day to think about the questions and look stuff up. So I was always thoughtful and relevant and a tiresome know-it-all bitch. Of course it didn't help at all that I was younger than most and a brave pioneer headed for another planet. The novelty of that wore off real fast.

Card wasn't having any such problems. But he already knew most of his classmates, some of them since grade school, and was more social anyhow. I've usually been the youngest in class, and the brain.

I was also a little behind my classmates socially, or a lot

behind. I had male friends but didn't date much. Still a virgin, technically, and when I was around couples who obviously weren't, I felt like I was wearing a sign proclaiming that fact.

That raised an interesting possibility. I never could see myself still a virgin five years from now. I might wind up being the first girl to lose her virginity on Mars—or on any other planet at all. Maybe someday they'd put up a plaque: "In this storage room on such-and-such a date . . ."

But with whom? I couldn't imagine Yuri tearing himself away from the keyboard long enough to get involved. Oscar and Murray seemed like such kids, though once they reached college age, that might be different.

There would be plenty of older men on Mars, who I'm sure would be glad to overlook my personality defects and lack of prominent secondary sexual characteristics. But thinking of an older man that way made me cringe.

Well, the next two ships would also be made up of families. Maybe I'd meet some nice Aussie or a guy from Japan or China. We could settle down on Mars and raise a bunch of weird children who ate calcium like candy and grew to be eight feet tall. Well, maybe not for a few generations.

Nobody talked about it much, but the idea of putting a breeding population of young men and women on Mars gave this project some of its urgency. After Kolkata and Gehenna, any nightmare was possible.

The mind veers away from it, but how much more sophisticated would the warriors have to be, to make the whole world into Gehenna? How much crazier would they have to be, to want it?

We got into that once on the climber, Dad doubting that it would be physically possible, at least for a long time, and also doubting that the most fanatical terrorist would be *that* crazy. To hate not just his enemies, but all of humanity, that much. Mother nodded, but she had her bland patient look:

I could argue, but won't. Card was kind of bored, familiar as he was with playing doomsday scenarios. Sometimes I think that nothing is really real to him, so why should doomsday be any different?

Time started passing really fast once we were settled into school, and most of our parents into their various research projects. It was more comfortable than you would expect, with all of us crammed into a space the size of a poverty-level tenement—but the parents and kids seemed to be giving each other more respect, more space.

Even the little kids calmed down. Mary Jefferson taught all four grades at once, in a partitioned-off part of B galley, and when they weren't in school or exercising, they played down in the zero-gee room, pretty far from anyone's work area, and usually respected the no-screaming rule.

(The idea of "Spaceship Earth" is such an old cliché that Granddad makes a face at it. But being constantly aware that we were isolated, surrounded by space, did seem to make us more considerate of one another. So if Earth is just a bigger ship, why couldn't they learn to be as virtuous as we are? Maybe they don't choose their crew carefully enough.)

Roberta was having more trouble than I was, making the transition from high school to college. For one thing, she's very social, and used to studying together with other girls and boys. That wasn't really possible on the ship, with us all going to different schools. Besides, she'd tested into advanced math and chemistry, while I was starting with calculus-for-dummies and general physical science. We both had English lit and philosophy, but of course with different textbooks.

Mother sometimes worried about my tendency to be a loner, but it turns out to be an advantage, studying when your classmates are millions of miles away.

I did coordinate my study hours with Roberta, so we

were both doing lit and philosophy homework at the same time, and she helped me over some humps in the math course. We also had exercise and meal hours together most of the time, along with Elspeth.

It was not much like anybody's picture of college life. No wicked fraternity parties, no experimenting with drugs and sex and finding out how much beer you can hold before overflowing. Maybe this whole Mars thing was a ruse my parents made up to keep me off campus. My education was going to be so incomplete!

That was actually a part of college I hadn't been looking forward to. Not "growing up too fast," as Mother repeatedly said, but looking foolish because I didn't know how to act when confronted with temptation. When do you politely decline and when should you be indignant?

And when should you say yes?

14

MIDWAY

At the midpoint of our voyage, Mars was a bright yellow beacon in front of us, Earth a bright blue star behind. It was an occasion to party, and the Mars Corporation had actually allotted a few kilograms' mass for a large plastic bottle of Rémy Martin cognac for that purpose.

Since several of the adults didn't drink, it proved enough to get the rest of them about as intoxicated as they wanted to be, or perhaps a little more. Like me.

We joked about the drinking age between planets, and my parents shrugged. Since there was no other alcohol aboard ship, I wasn't likely to become a drunkard. Which doesn't mean I couldn't get into trouble.

Paul had only one drink, mixed with water—the curse of being captain, he said wryly—but I had three before my parents went to bed, and maybe two afterward. It lowered my inhibitions, but I suppose I wanted them lowered.

The drinks were served in the galley, where there was

gravity to keep the booze in the glasses, but some of us moved into the zero-gee area to dance. Pretty strange, dancing without a floor. It was all kind of freestyle and rambunctious. We took turns asking the ship for music. A lot of it was old, jazz and ska and waterbug, or ancient like waltzes and rock, but there was plenty of city and sag.

Paul and I danced for a while, usually with each other, and I guess I started feeling glamorous, or at least sexy, dominating the captain's attentions. Not that there was much unmarried competition.

The zero-gee room goes to night-light from midnight till six, conserving power and giving people a reasonably private, or at least anonymous, place to have sex—or romance, but I don't think much of that was going on. There was no real privacy in the sleeping quarters, just a thin partition, which didn't prevent some people from embarrassing the rest of us. But most couples waited and met at one dark end or the other of the zero-gee room.

At midnight the only others in the zero-gee room were the Manchesters, who left us alone after a bit of obvious yawning and stretching.

Afterward, we agreed that we both had been sort of time bombs ticking, waiting for the midnight hour. If I hadn't wanted to be "seduced," I could have left while the lights were still on. But there was something desperate going on inside me, that wasn't just sexual desire or curiosity.

Our whispered conversation had gotten around to virginity, and my sort of in-between status, which I'd never told anyone about. But the booze loosened my tongue. When I was thirteen I was fooling around with a boy who had "borrowed" his sister's vibrator, and in the course of investigating how to use it, he was a little clumsy and popped me. It wasn't very painful, but it was the end of that relationship, right at the playing-doctor stage.

He didn't go to my school, so I didn't know whether any of the other boys knew about it, but I imagined they could all tell at a glance that I wasn't a virgin anymore. After about a year or so I realized that I still actually was.

I was unpopular and unattractive, or at least felt like it. Skipped a grade but then got it back after my parents took me out of school for a year to go overseas. They worked in London and Madrid, and I went back and forth, learning about enough Spanish to order a Coke in a restaurant.

From not speaking Spanish, it took only a few minutes for the conversation to get about to the difficulties of having sex in space, lack of privacy being only one of several problems, with the conservation of momentum and angular momentum high on the list. Difficult to describe, so I asked him to demonstrate, with our clothes on, of course.

That stage didn't last too long. We explored another problem, that of getting at least partially undressed while both of you had to hold on to a handle or go spinning apart.

We did manage to get our bottoms mostly removed. He looked kind of large, if smaller than my friend's sister's vibrator, but he was slow and gentle. As soon as he got it all the way in, he ejaculated, but we stayed together, and he recovered in a few minutes and did it again.

I'd been prepared for an ordeal, but in fact it was all pretty exciting and fun. I kept losing my grip, and he'd swim after me, while I groped for one of the handles. We wound up floating in midair, though, holding each other's shoulders, rotating slowly, then not slowly.

I didn't really have an orgasm until later, in the shower, but it was still overwhelming. Floating in space with Paul inside me, and me inside his arms. It took me a long time to fall asleep that night, and I woke up with the feeling still fresh. His face in the twilight, eyes closed, concentrating, then losing control. And me not a virgin anymore, not even technically.

❉

It was several days before we could find the privacy to talk about it. We were both in the galley for the last breakfast shift, and I killed some time cleaning up the microwave and prep area until the last people left.

He said it quickly, almost sotto voce: "Carmen, I'm sorry I took advantage of you."

"You didn't. I loved it."

"But you were drinking, and I really wasn't."

"Just to get up the courage." Not strictly true; I'm sure I would have had a couple no matter who was at the party. "Don't feel guilty." He was still sitting down; I leaned over and hugged him from behind. "Really, don't. You made me so happy."

I could tell he was trying not to squirm. "Made me happy, too," he said in an unhappy voice.

I sat down across from him. "What? What is it? Age difference?"

"No. That's part of it, but no." He leaned back. "It's my being pilot, which is to say captain." He visibly struggled, trying to find words. "I want to show you how I feel, but I can't. I can't *court* you; I can't treat you differently from anybody else."

"Of course not. I wouldn't expect—"

"But I want to! That night meant as much to me, maybe more, and I want to treat you like a lover. I can't even wink at you, not really. Let alone hold your hand, or . . ."

Or do it again, I realized. Even if we manufactured an opportunity. "Do you really think it's a secret? The Manchesters pretty obviously left to give us some privacy."

"You haven't told anybody?"

"No." Not in so many words. But Elspeth and Kaimei gave me big grins that were pretty clear.

"That's important. The ship runs on rumor as much as

hydrogen. People will whisper; they'll *know*, but as long as you and I keep it private, my . . . my authority isn't compromised."

His authority. And a devilish part of me wanted to tell everybody. *I'm a real woman—I'm fucking the captain.* "I can see that."

Somebody was coming down the ladder. He stood up.

It was my mother, coffee cup in hand.

"Oh . . . hello, Paul." Amazing how much she could communicate with two words.

"Morning, Laura. See you later, Carmen." He went up the ladder as soon as she let go.

She watched his retreating ass with a little smile. Then she got a spoonful of coffee and poured hot water on it. "I was younger than you," she said. "Seventeen, and no, it wasn't your father."

"You didn't meet until graduate school," I said inanely.

"He's eleven years older?"

"More like ten. He was born in February."

She put some sugar in the coffee, not normal for her. "Don't get too attached to him. He has a life on Mars, and he'll have to stay there."

"I might want to stay there, too." Even as I said the words, I couldn't believe they'd come out of my mouth.

"We all have the option, of course." She touched my shoulder. "He's a nice man. Don't forget there are a billion of them back on Earth."

She capped the coffee and swung up the ladder, back to her research station, without saying any motherly things like *Don't let him hurt you* or *Don't let your father know*, proving life is not a soap.

Of course Dad would know, along with everybody else. If the pilot had fucked any other innocent young thing, I suppose *I* would have known by breakfast.

I didn't feel particularly young or innocent. If everyone

knows, why not keep doing it? It wasn't as if I could get pregnant; with Delaze, I wouldn't start ovulating until after we'd landed on Mars, as he well knew. Even mighty space-pilot sperm wouldn't live that long.

After we reached the halfway mark, all of us young ones met our volunteer "Mars mentors," people who weren't teachers or parents but wanted to help us with our transition to their world.

My guy was "Oz," Dr. Oswald Penninger, a life scientist like Mother. He had a big smile and a salt-and-pepper beard.

Conversation was awkward, with an eight-minute delay between "How are you?" and "Fine," but we got used to it. It was kind of like really slow instant messaging. You ask a question, then do something else for a while, and he answers, then does something else for a while. We didn't normally use visual, unless there was something to show.

He was like everybody's favorite uncle, acknowledging the difference in our ages but then treating me like an equal who didn't know quite as much. I grew to like him better than I did most of the people on board, which I suppose was predictable. He was sixty-three, an African-American from Georgia, exobiologist and artist. They didn't have paper for drawing, of course, but he did beautifully intricate work on-screen that galleries in Atlanta and Oslo printed and sold.

Should an artist's pictures match his personality? Oz was a jolly plump man, given to sly wordplay and funny stories. But his art was dark and disturbing. He'd studied art in Norway for two years, and said his stuff was positively cheerful compared to the other people's in his studio. I'd have to see that to believe it.

He zapped me the software that he uses for drawing, but

I've never had much talent in that direction. He said he'll show me some tricks when we meet in person. Meanwhile, I've downloaded a beginner's text on cartooning and will try to learn enough to surprise him.

Funny to have a friend you've never touched or actually seen. I wonder whether we'll like each other in person.

15

SEXUAL DISORDER

About a week went by without Paul suggesting another tryst, if that's the right word. He seemed to be going out of his way to treat me like just another passenger, which was of course according to plan. But I was a little anxious because he was playing the part too well.

He wasn't avoiding me, but nobody on the ship was harder to get alone. I kept taking the last breakfast shift, and finally managed to corner him.

As I approached, he got a kind of resigned look, but reached out and took my hand. "I'm afraid I'm in trouble. With Mars."

"Because of me?"

He shrugged. "You're not in trouble. But somebody heard, and is whizzed at me for 'seducing one of the Earth children.'"

"I'm not a child! I'm nineteen, going on thirty."

"As I pointed out. They still say it was immature and unprofessional of me. Maybe they're right."

"It's not fair. We didn't really do anything wrong."

"Somebody thinks otherwise. Somebody here, who told somebody there."

"Who? Someone who has it in for you, or me?"

"I'm pretty sure who it is on Mars, but I don't know about here. It didn't have to start out malicious; just a juicy scrap of gossip." He took a sip of coffee that was probably cold. "I hope your parents don't find out this way."

"Oh, they know. At least Mother does, and she's okay with it."

He nodded slowly. "That's good. But I guess we'd better put it on ice for a while."

I tried to keep anger out of my voice. "I don't see why. What's done is done."

"The sexual part, yes. But now it would be insubordination as well. Which might be more serious. Would be."

"For your career."

"Not exactly. Nobody can *fire* me. But the colony's a small town, and I have to live there the rest of my life."

"If you . . ." I almost said something I would regret. "If you say so. But once we're on Mars?"

"Things will be different. People will get to know you, and accept you as an adult."

"Eventually. Guess I'll be one of the kids from Earth for a while."

"Not for long, I hope." He brightened. "Privacy isn't such an issue there, either, finding a time and place. My roommate wouldn't mind getting lost for a couple of hours, and you'll pick one you can trust."

Kaimei or Elspeth, for sure. "Unless they stick me with Card."

"They wouldn't be that cruel." He stood and hugged me and gave me a long kiss. "I'd better move along. You'll be okay?"

"Sure. I'm sorry. But I can wait." I didn't start crying until he was gone.

16

A NEW WORLD

Someday, I thought, maybe before I'm dead, Mars will have its own space elevator, but until then people have to get down there the old-fashioned way, in space-shuttle mode. It's like the difference between taking an elevator from the top floor of a building or jumping off with an umbrella and a prayer. Fast and terrifying.

We'd lived with the lander as part of our home for weeks, then as a mysterious kind of threatening presence, airless and waiting. Most of us weren't eager to go into it.

Before we'd made our second orbit of Mars, Paul opened the inner door, prepared to crack the air lock, and said, "Let's go."

We'd been warned, so we were bundled up against the sudden temperature drop when the air lock opened, and were not surprised that our ears popped painfully. It warmed up for an hour, and then we had to take our little metal suitcases and float through the air lock to go strap into our assigned seats, and try not to shit while we dropped like a rock to our doom.

From my studies I knew that the lander loses velocity by essentially trading speed for heat—hitting the thin Martian atmosphere at a drastic angle so the ship heats up to cherry red. What the diagrams in the physical science book don't show is the tooth-rattling vibration, the bucking and gut-wrenching wobble. If I'm never that scared again in my life, I'll be really happy.

All of the violence stopped abruptly when the lander decided to become a glider, I guess a few hundred miles from the landing strip. I wished we had windows like a regular airplane, but then realized that might be asking for a heart attack. It was scary enough just to squint at Paul's two-foot-wide screen as the ground rose up to meet us, too steep and fast to believe.

We landed on skis, grating and rumbling along the rocky ground. They'd moved all the big rocks out of our way, but we felt every one of the small ones. Paul had warned us to keep our tongues away from our teeth, which was a good thing. It could be awkward, starting out life on a new planet unable to speak because you've bitten off the tip of your tongue.

We hadn't put on the Mars suits for the flight down; they were too bulky to fit in the close-ranked seats—and I guess there wasn't any disaster scenario where we would still be alive and need them. So the first order of the day was to get dressed for our new planet.

We'd tested them several times, but Paul wanted to be supercautious the first time they were actually exposed to the Martian near vacuum. The air lock would only hold two people at once, so we went out one at a time, with Paul observing us, ready to toss us back inside if trouble developed.

We unpacked the suits from storage under the deck

and sorted them out. One for each person and two blobby general-purpose ones.

We were to leave in reverse alphabetical order, which was no fun, since it made our family dead last. The lander had never felt particularly claustrophobic before, but now it was like a tiny tin can, the sardines slowly exiting one by one.

At least we could see out, via the pilot's screen. He'd set the camera on the base, where all seventy-five people had gathered to watch us land, or crash. That led to some morbid speculation on Card's part. What if we'd crash-landed *into* them? I guess we'd be just as likely to crash into the base behind them. I'd rather be standing outside with a space suit on, too.

We'd seen pictures of the base a million times, not to mention endless diagrams and descriptions of how everything worked, but it was kind of exciting to see it in real time, to actually be here. The farm part looked bigger than I'd pictured it, I guess because the people standing around gave it scale. Of course the people lived underneath, because of radiation.

It was interesting to have actual gravity. I said it felt different, and Mom agreed, with a scientific explanation. Residual centripetal blah-blah-blah. I'll just call it real gravity, as opposed to the manufactured kind. Organic gravity.

A lot of people undressed on the spot and got into their Mars suits. I didn't see any point in standing around for an hour in the thing. I'm also a little shy, in a selective way. Paul had touched me all over, but he'd never seen me without a top. I waited until he was on the other side of the air lock before I revealed my unvoluptuous figure and barely necessary bra. Which I'd have to take off anyhow, for the skinsuit part of the Mars suit.

That part was like a lightweight body stocking. It fastened up the front with a gecko strip, then you pushed a button on your wrist and something electrical happened and it clasped your body like a big rubber glove. It could be sexy-looking if your body was.

The outer part of the Mars suit was more like lightweight armor, kind of loose and clanky when you put it on, but it also did an electrical thing when you zipped up, and fit more closely. Then clumsy boots and gloves and a helmet, all airtight. The joints would sigh when you moved your arms or legs or bent at the waist.

Card's suit had a place for an extension at the waist, since he could grow as much as a foot taller while we were here. Mine didn't have any such refinement, though there was room to put on a little weight if I loved Mars cooking.

Since we did follow strict anti-alphabetical order, Card got the distinction of being the last one out, and I was next to last. I got in the air lock with Paul, and he checked my oxygen tanks and the seals on my helmet, gloves, and boots. Then he pumped most of the air out, watching the clock, and asked me to count even numbers backward from thirty. (I asked him whether he had an obsession with backward lists.) He smiled at me through the helmet and kept his hand on my shoulder as the rest of the air pumped out and the door silently swung open.

The sky was brighter than I'd expected, and the ground darker. "Welcome to Mars," Paul said on the suit radio, sounding clear but far away.

We walked down a metal ramp to the sandy, rock-strewn ground. I stepped onto another planet.

How many people had ever done that?

Everything was suddenly different. This was the most real thing I'd ever done.

They could talk until they were blue in the face about how special this was, brave new frontier, leaving the cradle of Earth, whatever, and it's finally just words. When I felt the crunch of Martian soil under my boot it was suddenly all very plain and wonderful. I remembered an old cube—a movie—of one of the first guys on the Moon, jumping around like a little kid, and I jumped myself, and again, way high.

"Careful!" came Paul's voice over the radio. "Get used to it first."

"Okay, okay." While I walked, feather light, toward the other air lock, I tried to figure out how many people had actually done it, set foot on another world. A little more than a hundred, in all of history. And me one of them, now.

There were six of them waiting at the air-lock door; everyone else had gone inside. I looked around at the rusty desert and stifled the urge to run off and explore—I mean, for more than six months we hadn't been able to go more than a few dozen feet in any direction, and here was a whole new world. But there would be time. Soon!

Mother was blinking away tears, unable to touch her face behind the helmet, crying with happiness. The dream of her lifetime. I hugged her, which felt strange, both of us swaddled in insulation. Our helmets clicked together and for a moment I heard her muffled laugh.

While Paul went back to get Card, I just looked around. I'd spent hours there in virtual, of course, but that was fake. This was hard-edged and strange, even fearsome in a way. A desert with rocks. Yellow sky of air so thin it would kill you in a breath.

When Card got to the ground, he jumped higher than I had. Paul grabbed him by the arm and walked him over.

The air lock held five people. Paul and the two strangers gestured for us to go in when the door opened. It closed automatically behind us, and a red light throbbed for about a minute. I could hear the muffled clicking of a pump. Then a green light, and the inside door sighed open. "Home again," Paul said.

17

THE LAND OF OZ

We stepped into the greenhouse, a dense couple of acres of grain and vegetables and dwarf fruit trees. The air was humid and smelled of dirt and blossoms. A woman in shorts and a tee shirt, cut off under her breasts, motioned for us to take off our helmets.

She introduced herself as Emily. "I keep track of the air lock and suits," she said. "Follow me, and we'll get you square."

Feeling overdressed, we clanked down a metal spiral stair to a room full of shelves and boxes, the walls unpainted rock. One block of metal shelves was obviously for our crew, names written on bright new tape under shelves that held folded Mars suits and the titanium suitcases.

"Just come on through to the mess hall after you're dressed," she said. "Place isn't big enough to get lost. Not yet." They planned to more than double the underground living area while we were here.

I helped Mother out of her suit, and she helped me. I needed a shower and some clean clothes. My jumpsuit was wrinkled and damp with old sweat, fear sweat from the landing. I didn't smell like a petunia myself. But we were all in the same boat.

Paul and the two other men in Mars suits were rattling down the stairs as we headed for the mess hall. The top half of the corridor was smooth plastic that radiated uniform dim light, like the tubes that had linked the Space Elevator to the Hilton and the *John Carter*. The bottom half was numbered storage drawers.

I knew what to expect of the mess hall and the other rooms; the colony was a series of inflated half cylinders inside a large irregular tunnel, a natural pipe through an ancient lava flow. Someday the whole thing would be closed off and filled with air like the part we'd just left, but for the time being everyone lived and worked in the reinforced balloons.

We walked through a medical facility, bigger than anything we'd seen since the Hilton. No people, just a kind of medicated smell. Forty or fifty feet wide, it all seemed pretty huge after living in a spaceship. I don't suppose it would be that imposing if you went there directly from a town or a city on Earth.

The murmur of voices was pretty loud before we got to the mess hall. It sounded like a cocktail party, though the only thing to drink was water, and you don't dare spill a drop.

The mess hall was big enough for about two dozen people to eat at once, and now there were a hundred or so, sitting on the tables as well as the chairs, milling around saying hello. We twenty-six were the first new faces they'd seen in a year and a half—about one Martian year, one "are," pronounced air-ee. I'd better start thinking that way.

The room had two large false windows, like the ones on

the ship, looking out onto the desert. I assumed they were real-time. Nothing was moving, but then all the multicellular life on the planet was presumably right here.

You could see our lander sitting at the end of a pair of mile-long plowed grooves. I wondered whether Paul had cut it too close, stopping a couple of hundred feet away. He'd said the landing was mostly automatic, but I didn't see him let go of the joystick.

I saw Oz immediately and threaded my way over to him. We shook hands, then hugged. He was a little bit shorter than me, which was a surprise. He held me by both shoulders and looked at me with a bright smile, and then looked around the room. "It's pretty strange, isn't it? All these people."

Seventy-five new faces after seeing the same two dozen for months. "They look like a bunch of Martians."

He laughed. "Was the landing rough?"

"Pretty awful. But Paul seemed in control."

"He was my pilot, too. Good old 'Crash' Collins."

" 'Crash'?"

"Ask him about it someday."

An Asian woman a little taller than Oz came over, and he put his arm around her waist. "Josie, this is Carmen."

We shook hands. "I've seen your picture," she said. Josie Tang, Oz's lover. "Welcome to our humble planet."

I tapped my foot on the metal plate. "Nice to have real gravity."

"The same no matter where you go," Oz said. "I'll give you a tour after the formalities."

When Paul and the other two came into the room, an older woman started tapping on a glass with a spoon. Like many of them, men and women, she was wearing a belted robe made of some filmy material. She was pale and bony.

"Welcome to Mars. Of course I've spoken with most of you. I'm Dargo Solingen, current general administrator.

"The first couple of sols"—Martian days—"you are here, just settle in and get used to your new home. Explore and ask questions. We've assigned temporary living and working spaces to everyone, a compromise between the wish list you sent a couple of weeks ago and . . . reality." She shrugged. "It will be a little tight until the new modules are in place. We will start on that as soon as the ship is unloaded."

She almost smiled, though it looked like she didn't have much practice with it. "It is strange to see children. This will be an interesting social experiment."

"One you don't quite approve of?" Dr. Jefferson said.

"You probably know that I don't. But I was not consulted."

"Dr. Solingen," a woman behind her said in a tone of warning.

"I guess none of you were," Dr. Jefferson said. "It was an Earth decision, the Corporation."

"That's right," Solingen said. "This is an outpost, not a colony. They don't have families on Moonbase or even Antarctica."

Oz cleared his throat. "We were polled. Most of us were very much in favor." And most of them did call it "the colony," rather than Mars Base One.

The woman who had cautioned Solingen continued. "A hundred percent of the permanent party. Those of us who are not returning to Earth." She was either pregnant or the only fat person in the room. Looking more carefully, I saw one other woman who appeared to be pregnant.

You'd think that would have been on the news. Maybe it was, and I missed it, not likely. Mother and I exchanged significant glances. Something was going on.

(It turned out to be nothing more mysterious than a desire for privacy on the women's part, and everybody's desire to keep Earth out of their hair. When the first child was born, the Earth press would be all over them. Until then, there was no need for anyone to know the blessed event was nigh. So they asked that we not mention the pregnancies when writing or talking to home.)

Solingen went on to talk about work and living schedules. For those of us in school, study schedules would continue as on the *John Carter*, and we'd be assigned light duties "appropriate to our abilities." Probably fetch-and-carry or galley slave, as we called kitchen work on ship.

Then she introduced each new arrival, stating where they were from, what their specialties were, and lists of honors and awards, all from memory. It was an impressive performance. She even knew about us youngsters—Mike Manchester's national (Canadian) spelling bee, Yuri's solo with the St. Petersburg Orchestra, and my swimming medal, an extremely useful skill on this planet.

The way she looked at me left no doubt who it was who forbade Paul from being with me. I would try to stay out of her way.

People got together with friends or coworkers—almost everybody had been working along with one of the Martian teams en route—and moved toward the workstations and labs to talk. Oz and Josie took me and Card for a guided tour.

We'd already walked through the "hospital," an aid station about three meters wide by ten long. It was connected to the changing room by an automated air lock; if there was an accident with the main air lock, it would seal off the whole colony.

That was the standard size for most of the buildings, three by ten meters, but most of them were divided into smaller sections. The mess hall where we all met was about two-thirds that size, two hundred square meters for a hundred not-too-crowded people, the rest of the space a very compressed kitchen and pantry.

About half of the overall floor space was "cabins," more like walk-in closets, where people slept. Most of them were two meters long by a meter wide, three meters high, with upper and lower bunks for two people who had better be compatible. The bunks folded up to the wall, and desks for working or reading folded down. Four of the cabins were a half meter longer, for seven-footers.

The walls were colorful, in sometimes odd combinations. Each unit, twelve to thirty-two people, voted on a weekly color scheme. The walls glowed a comforting warm beige or cool blue most places, but there were bright yellows and moody purples and a Halloween orange.

We walked down the main corridor, about a meter wide, past six rows of cabins. The last bunch of sixteen had temporary partitions and improvised bunks, where most of us newcomer Earthlings would sleep. In normal times, that would be the recreation area, so people had real motivation to set up the new living areas we'd brought.

Then there were three large work areas, which besides labs and computer stations contained separate rooms for administration, power regulation, and environmental control—water, air, and heat. Finally, there was an air lock leading to the biosciences laboratory, where there were strict controls. We tried to be careful not to contaminate the Martian environment, and conversely, if there were dormant alien microorganisms in the rock and soil specimens, we didn't want to let even one of them into our air and water. The consensus was that it was unlikely Martian microbes could affect us, but who wanted to put it to the test? The whole area was kept at a slightly lower air pressure than the rest of the colony, discouraging leaks.

Here I was on a brand-new world, making history, and my phone beeped to remind me that I had a history paper due tomorrow. I thumbed that it would be a day late, 10 percent grade reduction.

Oz invited Card and me back to the cabin he shared with Josie. The four of us could sit comfortably on the lower bunk. He showed me how the desk worked, folding down with retractable arms, revealing a small high-definition screen. The work surface was flat but had a virtual keyboard. The arms were a clever parallelogram construction that let you position the desk at various heights.

The walls were covered with pictures, only two his own work. From art history class I recognized Rembrandt, Pollack, and Wyeth paintings; the others were by Scandinavian artists I'd never heard of.

A public-address system called all "new colonists" to dinner. It was fantastic, after months of ship rations. Salad with fresh greens and tomatoes, hot corn bread, fried tilapia.

After the meal, we were invited to come up and look at the farm. Those tilapia weren't the happiest-looking fish I'd ever seen, crowded into a small tank of murky water with agricultural waste (their food) floating on top.

Most of the crops had supplemental lights over their beds, Martian sunlight being pretty thin. It was easy to recognize stands of corn and apple trees, tomato plants, and beds of lettuce and cabbage. I didn't know what rice looked like, but it was probably different on Earth anyhow; not enough water here for paddies. Kaimei laughed when she saw it.

We went back down to get our assigned sleeping areas straight and get on the shower roster. There were two showers, and you could sign up for a twenty-minute interval for the female one. (The men only had fifteen minutes; there were more of them.) There was a complicated list of instructions in the small dressing room.

We were allowed one hundred sixty minutes per month, two showers a week. The twenty shower minutes you had included ten for undressing and dressing. The ten minutes you were actually in the shower included only five minutes of actual running water: get wet, then soap and shampoo, then try to rinse off.

All of us newbies were penciled in for showers if we wanted them—*if!* I had one scheduled for 1720, and waited outside the door for ten minutes. Mrs. Washington came out, radiantly clean, and I slipped in to undress and wait for Kaimei to finish, behind the shower curtain. The dressing room was the same size as the shower, about a meter square, and, unsurprisingly, smelled like a girls' locker room on Earth.

I chatted with Kaimei through the curtain when her water stopped and she switched to the dryer. No towels, just a hot-air machine. She came out, looking all new and shiny, and I moved my sweaty corpus in to be sluiced.

It was an odd sensation. The water that sprayed from the handheld nozzle was warm enough, but the rest of your body got really cold, the water on your skin evaporating fast in the thin air.

The amber liquid that served as both soap and shampoo was watery and weak, probably formulated more for its recycling efficiency than its cleaning power. But I did get pretty clean, much cleaner than I'd ever felt on the ship. I used the last thirty seconds of rinse time letting the warm water roll down my tired back.

There was a fixed dryer about four feet off the ground, somewhat aimable, to get your back and butt dry, and a handheld thing like a powerful hair dryer for the rest. The heat was welcome, and I felt pretty wonderful when I pulled the curtain.

Dargo Solingen stood there naked, bony and parchment pale. She marched by me without a word. I managed, "Hello?"

I dressed quickly and looked at the roster. There had been someone else's name after mine, someone unfamiliar, but now it was Dargo Solingen. I supposed she could butt in line anytime she wanted, pulling rank. But it was an odd coincidence. Did she want to see the sexy body that seduced her pilot? As if you would have to be a great beauty to appeal to a guy who's been celibate for three months. I think "nominally female" would fill the bill.

18

MARSWALK

I shared a small temporary space with Elspeth and Kaimei—
an air mattress on the floor and a bunk bed. We agreed to
rotate, so everyone would have a bed two-thirds of the time.

No romantic trysts for a while. I could ask the girls to
look the other way, but Paul might feel inhibited.

Hanging sheets for walls and only one desk, with a small
screen and a clunky keyboard and an old VR helmet with a
big dent on the side. The timing for that worked out okay,
since Elspeth had classes seven hours before Eastern time,
and Kaimei three hours later. We drew up a chart and taped
it over the desk. The only conflict was my physical science
class versus Kaimei's history of Tao and Buddhism. Mine
was mostly equations on the board, so I used the screen and
let her have the helmet.

Our lives were pretty regimented the first couple of
weeks, because we had to coordinate classes with the work
roster here, and leave a little time for eating and sleeping.

Everybody was impatient to get the first new module set up, but it wasn't just a matter of unloading and inflating it. First there was a light exoskeleton of spindly metal rods that became rigid when they were all pulled together. Then floorboards to bear the weight of the things and people inside. Then the connection to the existing base, through an improvised air lock, until they were sure the module wouldn't leak.

I enjoyed working on that, at first outdoors, unloading the ship and sorting and preassembling some parts; then later, down in the cave, attaching the new to the old. I got used to working in the Mars suit and using the "dog," a wheeled machine about the size of a large dog. It carried backup oxygen and power.

About half the time, though, my work roster put me inside, helping the younger ones do their lessons and avoid boredom. "Mentoring," they called it, to make it sound more important than babysitting.

I hardly ever saw Paul. It was as if whoever was in charge of the work details—guess who—took a special effort to keep us apart. One day, though, while I was just getting off work detail, he found me and asked whether I'd like to go exploring with him. What, skip math? I got fresh oxygen and helped him check out one of the dogs, and we went for a walk.

The surface of Mars might look pretty boring to an outsider, but it's not at all. It must be the same if you live in a desert on Earth: you pretty much have the space around your home memorized, every little mound and rock—and when you venture out, it's "Wow! A different rock!"

He took me off to the left of Telegraph Hill, walking at a pretty good pace. The base was below the horizon in less than ten minutes. We were still in radio contact as long as we could see the antenna on top of the hill, and if we wanted to go farther, the dog had a collapsible booster antenna that went up ten meters, which we could leave behind as a relay.

We didn't need it for that, but Paul clicked it up into place when we came to the edge of a somewhat deep crater he wanted to climb into, then cross to the hill in the middle, its "central peak."

"Be really careful," he said. "We have to leave the dog behind. If we both were to fall and be injured, we'd be in deep shit."

I followed him, watching carefully as we picked our way to the rim. Once there, he turned around and pointed.

It's hard to express how strange the sight was. We weren't that high up, but you could see the curvature of the horizon. The dog behind us looked tiny but unnaturally clear, in the near vacuum. To the right of Telegraph Hill, the pad where the *John Carter* had been raised to stand on its tail, waiting for the synthesizer to slowly make fuel from the Martian air.

Paul was carrying a white bag, now a little rust-streaked from the dust. He pulled out a photomap of the crater, unfolded it, and showed it to me. There were twenty X's, with numbers from one to twenty, starting on the top of the crater rim, where we must have been standing, then down the incline, and across the crater floor to its central peak.

"Dust collecting," he said. "How's your oxygen?"

I chinned the readout button. "Three hours forty minutes."

"That should be plenty. Now you don't have to go down if you—"

"I do! Let's go!"

"Okay. Follow me." I didn't tell him that my impatience wasn't all excitement, but partly anxiety at having to talk and pee at the same time. Peeing standing up, into a diaper, trying desperately not to fart. "Funny as a fart in a space suit" probably goes back to the beginning of spaceflight, but there's nothing real funny about it in reality. I'd taken two antigas tablets before I came out, and they still seemed to be working.

Keeping your footing was a little harder, going downhill. And it had been some years since I'd walked with a wet diaper. I was out of practice.

Paul had the map folded over so it only showed the path down the crater wall; every thirty or forty steps he would fish through the bag, take out a prelabeled plastic vial, and scrape a sample of dirt into it.

On the floor of the crater I felt a little shiver of fear at our isolation. Looking back the way we'd come, though, I could see the tip of the dog's antenna.

The dust was deeper than I'd seen anyplace else, I guess because the crater walls kept out the wind. Paul took two samples as we walked toward the central peak.

"You better stay down here, Carmen. I won't be long." The peak was steep, and he scrambled up it like a monkey. I wanted to yell *Be careful*, but kept my mouth shut.

Looking up at him, the sun sinking under the crater's rim, I could see Earth gleaming blue in the ochre sky. How long had it been since I had thought of Earth, other than as "the place where school is"? I guess I hadn't been here long enough to feel homesickness. Nostalgia for Earth— crowded place with lots of gravity and heat.

It might be the first time I seriously thought about staying. In five years I'd be twenty-four, and Paul would still be in his early thirties. I didn't feel as romantic about him as I had on the ship. But I liked him and he was funny. That would put us way ahead of a lot of marriages I'd observed.

But then how did I really feel about him? Up there being heroic and competent and, admit it, sexy.

Turn down the heat, girl. He's only twelve years younger than your father. Probably sterile from radiation, too. I didn't think I wanted children, but it would be nice to have the option.

Meanwhile, he would be fun to practice with.

He collected his samples and tossed the bag down. It drifted slowly, rotating, and landed about ten feet away. I was enough of a Martian to be surprised to hear a faint click when it landed, the soles of my boots picking the noise up, conducted through the rock of the crater floor.

He worked his way down slowly, which was a relief. I was holding the sample bag; he took it and made the hand signal for *Turn off your communicator.* I did, and he stepped over close enough to touch helmets. His face close enough to kiss. He spoke, and his voice was a faraway whisper. "Can you come sleep with me tonight?"

"Yes! Oh, yes."

"My roommate's putting in an extra half shift, from 1800 to 2300. Are you free during that time?"

"Class till 1900, but then, sure."

He gave me an awkward squeeze. Hard to be intimate in a Mars suit, but I could feel his gloves on my shoulders, the welcome pressure of his chest.

He turned his comm back on and gave me a mischievous wink. I followed him back the way we had come.

At the top of the crater wall, he stopped and looked back. "Can't see it from here," he said. "I'll show you."

"What?"

"My greatest triumph," he said, and started down. "You'll be impressed."

He didn't offer any further explanation on the ground. He picked up the dog's handle and proceeded to walk around to the other side of the crater.

It was a dumbo, an unpiloted supply vehicle. Its rear end was tilted up, the nose down in a small crater.

"I brought her in like that. I was not the most popular man on Mars." As we approached it, I could see the ragged hole someone had cut in the side with a torch or a laser. "Landed it right on the cargo-bay door, too."

So that was how he'd become "Crash" Collins. "Wow. I'm glad you weren't hurt."

He laughed. "It was remote control; I landed it from a console inside the base. Harder than being aboard, actually." We turned around and headed back to the base.

"It was a judgment call. There was a lot of variable wind, and it was yawing back and forth." He made a hand motion like a fish swimming. "I was sort of trying not to hit the base or Telegraph Hill. But I overdid it."

"People could understand that."

"Understanding isn't forgiving. Everybody had to stop their science and become pack animals." I could see the expression on Solingen's face, having to do labor, and smiled.

She really did have something against me. I had to do twice as much babysitting as Elspeth or Kaimei—and when I suggested that the boys ought to do it, too, she said the "personnel allocation" was *her* job, thank you. And when my person got allocated to an outside job, it would be something boring and repetitive, like taking inventory of supplies. (That was especially useful, in case there were actual Martians sneaking in at night to steal nuts and bolts.)

When we got back, I went straight to the john and recycled the diaper and used a couple of towelettes from my allotment. No shower for eighteen hours, but I was reasonably fresh, and Paul wouldn't be that critical.

At the console there was a blinking note from the Dragon herself, noting that I had missed math class, saying she wanted a copy of my homework. Did she monitor anybody else's VR attendance?

I'd had the class recorded, of course, the superexciting chain rule for differentiation. I fell asleep twice, hard to do in VR, and had to start over. Then I had a problem set with fifty chains to differentiate. Wrap me in chains and throw me in the differential dungeon, but I had to get a nap before going over to Paul's. I set a beeper for 1530, ninety minutes, then got the air mattress partly inflated and flopped onto it without undressing.

At 1800 I tried to concentrate on a physical science lecture about the conservation of angular momentum. Sexy dancers and skaters spinning around. The lecturer reminded me of Paul. Probably any male would have.

Went to the john and freshened up here and there. Then walked up to 4A—no way to be discreet about it—and tapped quietly on the door. Paul opened it and sort of pulled me in.

We hugged and kissed and undressed each other in a kind of two-person riot. He was extremely erect; I played with it for a minute, but he said that might prove counterproductive, and carried me to the bed and caressed me all over, and with his hands and tongue brought me to orgasm twice, my jaws clenched, trying not to make too much noise.

Then he showed me a picture of a frieze in India, and I copied it, putting my arms around his neck and clasping his hips with my legs while he entered me. Probably a lot easier on Mars than in India. It was a pleasant sensation but odd, since he completely filled me, his penis bumping the top of my vagina with every thrust.

Maybe in the future there will be advertisements: come to Mars and fuck like an Indian goddess. Maybe not.

I didn't have a third orgasm in me, but his was plenty for both of us. Then we lay in his narrow bunk, spoon fashion, dozing, until his erection came back and we did it again, in that position. Nicely intimate but not too stimulating, which he took care of afterward with his fingers.

An hour or so of dreamless sleep, and he woke me with a hand on my shoulder. He was fully dressed. "Jerry wouldn't mind walking in on you like this," he said, "but you might be startled."

I dressed quickly and kissed him good night. There was nobody in his corridor, but I did pass a couple on the main way, including Jerry, who gave me an arched eyebrow and a little wave.

I slipped into our temporary room and undressed quietly without turning on the lights.

"So how was our pilot?" Kaimei murmured in the dark. When I didn't say anything, she continued. "A simple deduction, Sherlock. You don't exactly smell like you've been riding a bicycle."

"I'm sorry . . ."

"I didn't say I didn't like it. Sweet dreams."

In fact, my dream was odd, and disturbing. I was trying to find a party, but every door opened onto an empty room. The last door opened onto the sea.

Not delivering my homework like a good little girl got me into a special corner of Dargo Hell. I had to turn over my notes and homework in math every day to Ana Sitral, who obviously didn't have time for checking it. She must have done something to piss off the Dragon herself.

Then I had to take on over half of the mentoring hours that Kaimei and Elspeth had been covering, and was not allowed any outside time. The extra babysitting time came out of my ag hours, working on the farm upstairs, which most of us considered a treat, as Dargo well knew.

I had been selfish, she said, tiring myself out on a silly lark, using up resources that might be needed for real work. So I had the temerity to suggest that part of my real work was getting to know Mars, and she really blew up about that. It was not up to me to make up my own training schedule.

Okay, part of it was that she didn't like young people. But part was also that she didn't like *me*, the sex kitten who'd distracted her pilot. She didn't bother to hide that from anybody. I complained to Mother, and she didn't disagree, but said I had to learn to work with people like that. Especially here, where there wasn't much choice.

I didn't bother complaining to Dad. He would make a Growth Experience out of it. I should try to see the world her way. Sorry, Dad. If I saw the world her way and cast my weary eyes upon Carmen Dula, wouldn't that be self-loathing? That would not be a positive Growth Experience.

19

FISH OUT OF WATER

After a month, I was able to put a Mars suit on again, but I
didn't go up to the surface. There was plenty of work down
below, inside the lava tube that protected the base from cosmic and solar radiation.

There's plenty of water on Mars, but most of it is in the
wrong place. If it was ice on or near the surface, it had to
be at the north or south pole. We couldn't put bases there
because they were in total darkness a lot of the time, and
we needed solar power.

But there was a huge lake hidden a few hundred meters
below the base. It was the easiest large one to get to on
all of Mars, we learned from some kind of satellite radar,
which was why the base was put here. One of the things
we'd brought on the *John Carter* was a drilling system de-
signed to tap it. (The drills that came with the first ship and
the third broke, though, the famous Mars Luck.)

I worked with the team that set the drill up, nothing

more challenging than fetch-and-carry, but a lot better than trying to mentor kids when you wanted to slap them instead.

For a while we could hear the drill through our boots, a faint sandpapery sound that was conducted through the rock. Then it was quiet, and most of us forgot about it. A few weeks later, though, it broke through. It was Sagan 12, which from then on would be Water Day.

We put on Mars suits and walked down between the wall of the lava tube and the base's exterior wall. It was kind of creepy, just suit lights, less than a meter between the cold rock and the inflated plastic you weren't supposed to touch.

Then there was light ahead, and we came out into swirling madness—it was a blizzard! The drill had struck ice, liquefied it, and sent it up under pressure, dozens of liters a minute. When it hit the cold vacuum it exploded into snow.

It was ankle deep in places, but of course it wouldn't last; the vacuum would evaporate it eventually. But people were already working with lengths of pipe, getting ready to fill the waiting tanks up in the hydroponics farm. One of them had already been dubbed the swimming pool. That was how the trouble started.

I got on the work detail that hooked up the water supply to the new pump. That was to go in two stages: emergency and "maintenance."

The emergency stage worked on the reasonable assumption that the pump wasn't going to last very long. So we wanted to save every drop of water we could, while it still did work.

This was the "water boy" stage. We had collapsible insulated water containers that held fifty liters each. That's about 110 pounds on Earth, about my own weight, awkward but not too heavy to handle on Mars.

All ten of the older kids alternated a couple of hours on, a couple off, doing water boy. We had wheelbarrows, three of them, so it wasn't too tiring. You fill the thing with water, which takes eight minutes, then turn off the valve and get away fast, so not too much pressure builds up before the next person takes over. Then trundle the wheelbarrow up a ramp and around to the air lock, leave it there, and carry or drag the water bag inside and across the farm to the storage tanks. Dump in the water—a slurry of ice by then—and go back to the pump with your wheelbarrow and empty bag.

The work was boring as dust, and would drive you insane if you didn't have music. I started out being virtuous, listening to classical pieces that went along with my textbook on the history of music. But as the days droned by, I listened to more and more city and even sag.

You didn't have to be a math genius to see that it was going to take three weeks at this rate to fill the first tank, which was two meters tall and eight meters wide, bigger than most backyard pools in Florida.

The water didn't stay icy; they warmed it up to above room temperature. We all must have fantasized about diving in there and paddling around. Elspeth and Kaimei and I even planned for it.

There was no sense in asking permission from the Dragon. What we were going to do was coordinate our showers so we'd all be squeaky clean—so nobody could say we were contaminating the water supply—and come in the same time, off shift, and see whether we could get away with a little skinny-dip. Or see how long we could do it before somebody stopped us.

At two weeks, the engineers sort of forced our hand. They'd been working on a direct link from the pump to this tank and the other two.

Jordan Westling, Barry's inventor dad, seemed to be in charge of that team. We always got along pretty well. He was old but always had a twinkle in his eye.

He and I were alone by the tank while he fiddled with some tubing and gauges. I lifted the water bag with a groan and poured it in.

"This ought to be the last day you have to do that," he said. "We should be on line in a few hours."

"Wow." I stepped up on a box and looked at the water level. It was more than half-full, with a little layer of red sediment at the bottom. "Dr. Westling . . . what would happen if somebody went swimming in this?"

He didn't look up from the gauge. "I suppose if somebody washed up first and didn't pee in the pool, nobody would have to know. It's not exactly distilled water. Not that I would endorse such an activity."

When I went back to the water point, I touched helmets with Kaimei—always assuming the suit radio was monitored—and we agreed we'd do it at 02:15, just after the end of the next shift. She'd pass the word on to Elspeth, who came on at midnight. That would give her time to have a quick shower and smuggle a towel up to the tank.

I got off at 10 and VR'ed a class on Spinoza, better than any sleeping pill. I barely stayed awake long enough to set the alarm for 1:30.

Two and a half hours' sleep was plenty. I awoke with eager anticipation and, alone in the room, put on a robe and slippers and quietly made my way to the shower. The roster was almost empty at this hour.

Kaimei had already bathed, and was sitting outside the shower with a reader. I took my shower and, while I was drying, Elspeth came in from work, wearing skinsuit and socks.

After she showered, the three of us tiptoed past the work/study area—a couple of people were working there, but a hanging partition kept them from being distracted by passersby.

The mess hall was deserted. We went up through the changing room and the air-lock foyer and slipped into the farm.

There were only dim maintenance lights at this hour. We padded our way to the swimming pool tank—and heard whispered voices!

Oscar Jefferson, Barry Westling, and my idiot brother had beat us to it!

"Hey, girls," Oscar said. "Look—we're out of a job." A faucet in the side was gurgling out a narrow stream.

"My father said we could quit," Barry said, "so we thought we'd take a swim to celebrate."

"You didn't tell him," I said.

"Do we look like idiots?" No, they looked like naked boys. "Come on in. The water's not too cold."

I looked at the other two girls, and they shrugged okay. Spaceships and Mars bases don't give you a lot of room for modesty.

I sort of liked the way Barry looked at me anyhow, when I stepped out of my robe and slippers. When Kaimei undressed, his look might have been a little more intense.

I stepped up on the box and had one leg over the edge of the tank, not the most modest posture, when the lights snapped on full.

"Caught you!" Dargo Solingen marched down the aisle between the tomatoes and the squash. "I *knew* you'd do this." She looked at me, one foot on the box and the other dangling in space. "And I know exactly who the ringleader is."

She stood with her hands on her hips, studying. Elspeth was only half-undressed, but the rest of us were obviously ready for some teenaged sex orgy. "Get out, now. Get dressed and come to my office at 0800. We will have a disciplinary hearing." She stomped back to the door and snapped off the bright lights on her way out.

"I'll tell her it wasn't you," Card said. "We just kind of all decided when Barry's dad said the thing was working."

"She won't believe you," I said, stepping down. "She's been after my ass all along."

"Who wouldn't be?" Barry said. He was a born romantic.

All of our parents were crowded into the Dragon's office at 0800. That was not good. My parents were both working the shift from 2100 to 0400, and needed their sleep. The parents were on one side of the room, and we were on the other, with a large video screen in the middle.

Without any preamble, Dargo Solingen made the charge: "Last night your children went for a swim in the new Water Tank One. Tests on the water reveal traces of coliform bacteria, so it cannot be used for human consumption without boiling or some other form of sterilization."

"It was only going to be used for hydroponics," Dr. Westling said.

"You can't say that for certain. At any rate, it was an act of extreme irresponsibility, and one that you encouraged." She pointed a hand control at the video screen and clicked. I saw myself talking to him.

"What would happen if somebody went swimming in this?" He answered that nobody would have to know—not that he would endorse such a thing. He was restraining a smile.

"You're secretly recording me?" he said incredulously.

"Not you. Her."

"She didn't do it!" Card blurted out. "It was my idea."

"You will speak when spoken to," she said with ice in her voice. "Your loyalty to your sister is touching, but misplaced." She clicked again, and there was a picture of me and Kaimei at the water point, touching helmets.

"Tonight has to be skinny-dipping night. Dr. Westling says they'll be on line in a few hours. Let's make it 02:15, right after Elspeth gets off." You could hear Kaimei's faint agreement.

"You had my daughter's suit bugged?" my father said.

"Not really. I just disabled the OFF switch on her suit communicator."

"That is so . . . so illegal. On Earth they'd throw you out of court, then—"

"This isn't Earth. And on Mars, there is nothing more important than water. As you would appreciate more if you had lived here longer." Oh, sure, like living in a spaceship doesn't count. I think you could last longer without water than without air.

"Besides, it was improper for the boys and girls to be together naked. Even if they hadn't planned any sexual misbehavior—"

"Oh, please," I said. "Excuse me for speaking out of turn, Dr. Solingen, but there was nothing like that. We didn't even know the boys would be there."

"Really. The timing was remarkable, then. And you weren't acting surprised about them when I turned on the lights. Nor modest." Card was squirming, and put up his hand, but the Dragon ignored it. She turned to the parents. "I want to discuss with you what punishment might be appropriate."

"Twenty laps a day in the pool," Dr. Westling said, almost snarling. He didn't like her anyhow, I'd noticed, and spying on him apparently had been the straw that broke the camel's back. "They're just kids, for Chris'sake."

"You're going to say they didn't mean any harm. They have to learn that Mars doesn't recognize intent as an excuse.

"An appropriate punishment, I think, would start with not allowing them to bathe for a month. I would also reduce the amount of water they be allowed to drink, but that is difficult to control. And I wouldn't want to endanger their health." God, she was so All Heart.

"For that month, I would also deny them recreational use of the cube and VR, and no exploring on the surface. Double that for the instigator, Ms. Dula"—and she turned back to face us—"and her brother as well, if he insists on sharing the responsibility."

"I *do*!" he snapped.

"Very well. Two months for both of you."

"It seems harsh," Kaimei's father said. "Kaimei told me that the girls did take the precaution of showering before entering the water."

"Intent means nothing. The bacteria are there."

"Harmless to plants," Dr. Westling repeated. "Probably to people."

She looked at him for a long second. "Your dissent is noted. Are there any other objections to this punishment?"

"Not the punishment," my mother said, "but Dr. Dula and I both object to the means of acquiring evidence."

"I am perfectly willing to stand on review for that." The old-timers would probably go along with her. The new ones might still be infected by the Bill of Rights, or the laws of Russia and France.

There were no other objections, so she reminded the parents that they would be responsible for monitoring our VR and cube use, but even more, she would rely on our sense of honor.

What were we supposed to be "honoring," though? The now-old-fashioned sanctity of water? Her right to spy on us? In fact, her unlimited authority?

I would find a way to get back at her.

20

NIGHTWALK

After one day of steaming over it, I'd had enough. I don't
know when I made the decision, or whether it even *was* a
decision, rather than a kind of sleepwalking. It was sometime before three in the morning. I was still feeling so angry
and embarrassed I couldn't get to sleep.

So I got up and started down the corridor to the mess
hall, to nibble on something. But I walked on past.

It looked like no one else was up. Just dim safety lights.
I wound up in the dressing room and realized what I was
doing.

The air lock had a WARNING OVERRIDE button that you
could press so the buzzer wouldn't go on and on if you had
to keep the inner door open. Card had shown me how you
could keep the button stuck down with the point of a pencil
or a pen.

With the air-lock buzzer disabled, a person could actually go outside alone, undetected. Card had done it with

Barry for a few minutes early one morning, just to prove it could be done. So I could just be by myself for an hour or two, then sneak back in.

And did I ever want to be by myself.

I went through the dress-up procedure as quietly as possible. Then before I took a step toward the air lock, I visualized myself doing a safety check on another person and did it methodically on myself. It would be so pathetic to die out there, breaking the rules.

I went up the stairs silently as a thief. Well, I *was* a thief. What could they do, deport me?

For safety's sake, I decided to take a dog, even though it would slow me down a bit. I actually hesitated and tested carrying two extra oxygen bottles by themselves, but that was awkward. *Better safe than sorry,* I said to myself in Mother's voice, and ground my teeth while saying it. But going out without a dog and dying would be pathetic. Archcriminals are evil, not pathetic. I clicked the OVERRIDE button down and jammed it with the point of a penstick.

The evacuating pump sounded loud, though I knew you could hardly hear it in the changing room. It rattled off into silence, then the red light glowed green and the door swung open into darkness.

I stepped out, pulling the dog, and the door slid shut behind it.

I decided not to turn on the suit light, and stood there for several minutes while my eyes adjusted. Walking at night just by starlight—you couldn't do that any other place I've lived. It wouldn't be dangerous if I was careful. Besides, if I turned on a light, someone could see me from the messhall window.

The nearby rocks gave me my bearings, and I started out toward Telegraph Hill. On the other side of the hill I'd be invisible from the base, and vice versa—alone for the first time in months.

Seeing the familiar rock field in this ghostly half-light brought back some of the mystery and excitement of the first couple of days. The landing and my first excursion with Paul.

If he knew I was doing this—well, he might approve, secretly. He wasn't much of a rule guy, except for safety.

Thinking that, my foot turned on a small rock and I staggered, getting my balance back. Keep your eyes on the ground while you're walking. It would be—what is the word I'm looking for?—*pathetic* to trip and break your helmet out here.

It took me less than a half hour to get to the base of Telegraph Hill. It wasn't all that steep, but the dog's traction wasn't really up to it. A truly adventurous person would leave the dog behind and climb to the top with her suit air alone, and although I do like adventure, I'm also afflicted with pathetico-phobia. The dog and I could go around the mountain rather than over it. I decided to walk in a straight line for one hour, see how far I could get, and walk back, following the dog's track in the dust.

That was my big mistake. One of them, anyhow. If I'd just gone to the top, taken a picture, and headed straight back, I might have gotten away with the whole thing.

I wasn't totally stupid. I didn't go into the hill's "radio shadow," and I cranked the dog's radio antenna up all the way, since I was headed for the horizon, and knew that any small depression in the ground could hide me from the colony's radio transceiver.

The wind picked up a little. I couldn't feel or hear it, of course, but the sky showed it. Jupiter was just rising, and its bright pale yellow light had a halo, and was slightly dimmed, by the dust in the air. I remembered Dad pointing out Jupiter, then Mars, the morning we left Florida, and had a delicious shiver at the thought that I was standing on that little point of light now.

The area immediately around the colony was as well explored as any place on Mars, but I knew from rock-hounding with Paul that you could find new stuff just a couple of hundred meters from the air-lock door. I went four or five kilometers and found something really new.

I had been going for fifty-seven minutes, about to turn back, and was looking for a soft rock that I could mark with an X or something—maybe scratch SURRENDER PUNY EARTHLINGS on it, though I suspected people would figure out who had done it.

There was no noise. Just a suddenly weightless feeling, and I was falling through a hole in the ground—I'd broken through something like a thin sheet of ice. But there was nothing underneath it!

I was able to turn on the suit light as I tumbled down, but all I saw was a glimpse of the dog spinning around beside and then above me.

It seemed like a long time, but I guess I didn't fall for more than a few seconds. I hit hard on my left foot and heard the sickening sound of a bone cracking, just an instant before the pain hit me.

I lay still, bright red sparks fading from my vision while the pain amped up and up. Trying to think, not scream. It was dark again.

My ankle was probably broken, and at least one rib on the left side. I breathed deeply, listening—Paul told me about how he had broken a rib in a car wreck, and he could tell by the sound that it had punctured his lung. This did hurt, but didn't sound different—then I realized I was lucky to be breathing at all. The helmet and suit were intact.

But would I be able to keep breathing long enough to be rescued?

I clicked the suit-light switch over and over, and nothing happened. If I could find the dog, and if it was intact, I'd have an extra sixteen hours of oxygen. Otherwise, I probably had two, two and a half hours.

I didn't suppose the radio would do any good, underground, but I tried it anyway. Yelled into it for a minute, and then listened. Nothing.

These suits ought to have some sort of beeper to trace people with. But then I guess nobody was supposed to wander off and disappear.

It was about four. How long before someone woke up and noticed I was gone? How long before someone got worried enough to check and see that the suit and dog were missing?

I tried to stand, and it wasn't possible. The pain was intolerable, and the bone made an ominous sound. I couldn't help crying but stopped after a minute. Pathetic.

Had to find the dog, with its oxygen and power. I stretched out and patted the ground back and forth, and scrabbled around in a circle, feeling for it.

It wasn't anywhere nearby. But how far could it have rolled after it hit?

I had to be careful, not just crawl off in some random direction and get lost. I remembered feeling a large, kind of pointy, rock off to my left—good thing I hadn't landed on it—and could use it as a reference point.

I found it and moved up so my foot was touching it. Visualizing an old-fashioned clock with me as the hour hand, I went off in the 12:00 direction, measuring four body lengths inchworm style. Then crawled back to the pointy rock and did the same thing in the opposite, 6:00, direction. Nothing there, nor at 9:00 or 3:00, and I tried not to panic.

In my mind's eye I could see the areas where I hadn't been able to reach, the angles midway between 12:00 and 3:00, 3:00 and 6:00, and so on. I went back to the pointy rock and started over. On the second try, my hand touched one of the dog's wheels, and I smiled in spite of my situation.

It was lying on its side. I uprighted it and felt for the switch that would turn on its light. When it came on, I was looking straight into it and it dazzled me blind.

Facing away from it, after a couple of minutes I could see some of where I was. I'd fallen into a large underground cavern, maybe shaped like a dome, though I couldn't see as far as the top. I guessed it was part of a lava tube that was almost open to the surface, worn so thin that it couldn't support my weight.

Maybe it joined up with the lava tube that we lived in! But even if it did, and even if I knew which direction to go, I couldn't crawl the four kilometers back. I tried to ignore the pain and do the math, anyhow—sixteen hours of oxygen, four kilometers, that means creeping 250 meters per hour, dragging the dog along behind me . . . no way. Better to hope they would track me down here.

What were the chances of that? Maybe the dog's tracks, or my boot prints? Only in dusty places, if the wind didn't cover them up before dawn.

If they searched at night, the dog's light might help. How close would a person have to come to the hole to see it? Close enough to crash through and join me?

And would the dog's power supply last long enough to shine all night and again tomorrow night? It wouldn't have to last any longer than that.

The ankle was hurting less, but that was because of numbness. My hands and feet were getting cold. Was that a suit malfunction, or just because I was stretched out on this cold cave floor? Where the sun had never shone.

With a start, I realized the coldness could mean that my suit was losing power—it should automatically warm up the gloves and boots. I opened my mouth wide and with my chin pressed the switch that ought to project a technical readout in front of my eyes, with "power remaining," and nothing came up.

Well, the dog obviously had power to spare. I unreeled the recharge cable and plugged its jack into my LSU.

Nothing happened.

I chinned the switch over and over. Nothing.

Maybe it was just the readout display that was broken; I was getting power, but it wasn't registering. Trying not to panic, I wiggled the jack, unplugged and replugged it. Still nothing.

I was breathing, though; that part worked. I unrolled the umbilical hose from the dog and pushed the fitting into the bottom of the LSU. It made a loud pop and a sudden breeze of cold oxygen blew around my neck and chin.

So at least I wouldn't die of that. I would be frozen solid before I ran out of air; how comforting. Acid rush of panic in my throat; I choked it back and sucked on the water tube until the nausea was gone.

Which made me think about the other end, and I clamped up. I was not going to fill the suit's emergency diaper with shit and piss before I died. Though the people who deal with dead people probably have seen that before. And it would be frozen solid, so what was the difference. Inside the body or outside.

I stopped crying long enough to turn on the radio and say good-bye to people, and apologize for my stupidity. Though it was unlikely that anyone would ever hear it. Unless there was some kind of secret recorder in the suit, and someone stumbled on it years from now. If the Dragon had anything to say about it, there would be.

I wished I had Dad's zen. If Dad were in this situation, he would just accept it, and wait to leave his body.

I tipped the dog up on end, so its light shone directly up toward the hole I'd fallen through, still too high up to see.

I couldn't feel my feet or hands anymore and was

growing heavy-lidded. I'd read that freezing to death was the least painful way to go, and one of my last coherent thoughts was "Who came back to tell them?"

Then I hallucinated an angel, wearing red, surrounded by an ethereal bubble. He was incredibly ugly.

PART 2

FIRST CONTACT

I

GUARDIAN ANGEL

I woke up in some pain, ankle throbbing and hands and feet burning. I was lying on a huge inflated pillow. The air was thick and muggy, and it was dark. A yellow light was bobbing toward me, growing brighter. I heard lots of feet.

It was a flashlight, or rather a lightstick like you wear, and the person holding it . . . wasn't a person. It was the red angel from my dream.

Maybe I was still dreaming. I was naked, which sometimes happens in my dreams. The dog was sitting a few feet away. My broken ankle was splinted between two pieces of what felt like wood. On Mars?

This angel had too many legs, like four, sticking out from under the red tunic thing. His head, if that's what it was, looked like a potato that had gone really bad. Soft and wrinkled and covered with eyes. Maybe they *were* eyes, lots of them, or antennae. He was almost as big as a small horse. He seemed to have two regular-sized arms and two little ones. For an angel, he smelled a lot like tuna fish.

I should have been terrified, naked in front of this monster, but he definitely was the one who had saved me from freezing to death. Or he was dressed like that one.

"Are you real?" I said. "Or am I still dreaming, or dead?"

He made some kind of noise, sort of like a bullfrog with teeth chattering. Then he whistled, and the lights came on, dim but enough to see around. The unreality of it made me dizzy.

I was taking it far too calmly, maybe because I couldn't think of a thing to do. Either I was in the middle of some complicated dream, or this was what happened to you after you died, or I was completely insane, or, least likely of all, I'd been rescued by a Martian.

But a Martian wouldn't breathe oxygen, not this thick. He wouldn't have wood for making splints. Though this one might know something about ankles, having so many of them.

"You don't speak English, do you?"

He responded with a long speech that sounded kind of threatening. Maybe it was about food animals not being allowed to talk.

I was in a circular room, a little too small for both me and Big Red, with a round wall that seemed to be several layers of plastic sheeting. He had come in through slits in the plastic. The polished stone floor was warm. The high ceiling looked like the floor, but there were four bluish lights embedded in it, that looked like cheap plastic decorations.

It felt like a hospital room, and maybe it was one. The pillow was big enough for one like him to lie down on it.

On a stone pedestal over by the dog was a pitcher and a glass made of something that looked like obsidian. He poured me a glass of something and brought it over.

His hand, also potato brown, had four long fingers without nails and lots of little joints. The fingers were all the same length, and it looked like any one of them could be the thumb. The small hands were miniature versions of the big ones.

The stuff in the glass didn't smell like anything and tasted like water, so I drank it down in a couple of greedy gulps.

He took the glass back and refilled it. When he handed it to me, he pointed into it with a small hand, and said, "Ar." Sort of like a pirate.

I pointed, and said, "Water?" He answered with a sound like "war," with a lot of extra R's.

He set down the glass and brought me a plate with something that looked remarkably like a mushroom. No, thanks. I read that story.

(For a mad moment I wondered whether that could be it—I *had* eaten, or ingested, something that caused all this, and it was one big dope dream. But the pain was too real.)

He picked the thing up delicately and a mouth opened up in his neck, broad black teeth set in grisly red. He took a small nibble and replaced it on the plate. I shook my head no, though that could mean yes in Martian. Or some mortal insult.

How long could I go without eating? A week, I supposed, but my stomach growled at the thought.

He heard the growling and pointed helpfully to a hole in the floor. That took care of one question, but not quite yet, pal. We've hardly been introduced, and I don't even let my *brother* watch me do that.

I touched my chest and said, "Carmen." Then I pointed at his chest, if that's what it was.

He touched his chest and said, "Harn." Well, that was a start.

"No." I took his hand—dry, raspy skin—and brought it

over to touch my chest. "Car-men," I said slowly. Me Jane, you Tarzan. Or Mr. Potato Head.

"Harn," he repeated, which wasn't a bad Carmen if you couldn't pronounce C or M. Then he took my hand gently and placed it between his two small arms and made a sputtering sound no human could do, at least with the mouth. He let go, but I kept my hand there, and said, "Red. I'll call you Red."

"Reh," he said, and repeated it. It gave me a shiver. I was communicating with an alien. Someone put up a plaque! But he turned abruptly and left.

I took advantage of being alone and hopped over to the hole and used it, not as easy as that sounds. I needed to find something to use as a crutch. This wasn't exactly Wal-Mart, though. I drank some water and hopped back to the pillow and flopped down.

My hands and feet hurt a little less. They were red, like bad sunburn, which I supposed was the first stage of frostbite. I could have lost some fingers and toes—not that it would matter much to me, with lungs full of ice.

I looked around. Was I inside of Mars or was this some kind of a spaceship? You wouldn't make a spaceship out of stone. We had to be underground, but this stone didn't look at all like the petrified lava of the colony's tunnel. And it was warm, which had to be electrical or something. The lights and plastic sheets looked pretty high-tech, but everything else was kind of basic—a hole in the floor? (I hoped it wasn't somebody else's ceiling!)

I mentally reviewed why there can't be higher forms of life on Mars, least of all technological life: no artifacts—we've mapped every inch of it, and anything that looked artificial turned out to be natural. Of course there's nothing to breathe, though I seemed to be breathing. Same thing with water. And temperature.

There are plenty of microscopic organisms living underground, but how could they evolve into big bozos like Red? What is there on Mars for a big animal to eat? Rocks?

Red was coming back with his lightstick, followed by someone only half his size, wearing bright lime green. Smoother skin, like a fresher potato. I decided she was female and called her Green. Just for the time being; I might have it backward. They had seen me naked, but I hadn't seen them—and wasn't eager to, actually. They were scary enough this way.

Green was carrying a plastic bag with things inside that clicked softly together. She set the bag down carefully and exchanged a few noises with Red.

First she took out a dish that looked like pottery, and from a plastic bag shook out something that looked like an herb, or pot. It started smoking immediately, and she thrust it toward me. I sniffed it; it was pleasant, like mint or menthol. She made a gesture with her two small hands, a kind of shooing motion, that I interpreted to mean "Breathe more deeply," and I did.

She took the dish away and brought two transparent disks, like big lenses, out of the bag and handed one to me. While I held it, she pressed the other one against my forehead, then chest, then the side of my leg. She gently lifted up the foot with the broken ankle, and pressed it against the sole. Then she did the other foot. She put the lenses back in her bag and stood motionless, staring at me like a doctor or scientist.

I thought, Okay, this is where the alien sticks a tube up your ass, but she must have left her tube back at the office.

She and Red conferred for a while, making gestures with their small arms while they made noises like porpoises and machinery. Then she reached into the bag and pulled out a small metal tube, which caused me to cringe away, but she gave it a snap with her wrist and it ratcheted out to about six feet long. She mimicked using it as a cane, which looked really strange, like a spider missing four legs, and handed it to me, saying, "Harn."

Guess that was my name now. The stick felt lighter than aluminum, but when I used it to lever myself up, it was rigid and strong.

She reached into her bag of tricks and brought out a thing like her tunic, somewhat thicker and softer and colored gray. There was a hole in it for my head, but no sleeves or other complications. I put it on gratefully and draped it around so I could use the stick. It was agreeably warm.

Red stepped ahead, and with a rippling gesture of all four hands, indicated, *Follow me*. I did, with Green coming behind me.

It was a strange sensation, going through the slits in those plastic sheets, or whatever they were. It was like they were alive, millions of feathery fingers clasping you, then letting go all at once, to close behind you with a snap.

When I went through the first one, it was noticeably cooler, and cooler still after the second one, and my ears popped. After the fourth one, it felt close to freezing, though the floor was still warm, and the air was noticeably thin; I was almost panting, and could see my breath.

We stepped into a huge dark cavern. Rows of dim lights at about knee level marked off paths. The lights were all blue, but each path had its own kind of blue, different in shade or intensity. Meet me at the corner of bright turquoise and dim aquamarine.

I tried to remember our route, left at this shade of blue, then right at *this* one, but I was not sure how useful the knowledge would be. What, I was going to escape? Hold my breath and run back to the colony?

We went through a single sheet into a large area, at least as well lit as my hospital room, and almost as warm. It had a kind of barnyard smell, not unpleasant. There were things that had to be plants all around, like broccoli but brown and gray with some yellow, sitting in water that you could hear was flowing. A little mist hung near the ground, and my face felt damp. It was a hydroponic farm like ours, but without greens or the bright colors of tomatoes and peppers and citrus fruits.

Green leaned over and picked something that looked like a cigar, or something even less appetizing, and offered it to me. I waved it away; she broke it in two and gave half to Red.

I couldn't tell how big the place was, probably acres. So where were all the people it was set up to feed? All the Martians.

I got a partial answer when we passed through another sheet, into a brighter room about the size of the new pod we'd brought. There were about twenty of the aliens arranged along two walls, standing at tables or in front of things like data screens, but made of metal rather than plastic. There weren't any chairs; I supposed quadrupeds didn't need them.

They all began to move toward me, making strange noises, of course. If I'd brought one of them into a room, humans would have done the same thing, but nevertheless I felt frightened and helpless. When I shrank back, Red put a protective arm in front of me and said a couple of bullfrog syllables. They all stopped about ten feet away.

Green talked to them more softly, gesturing toward me. Then they stepped forward in an orderly way, by colors—two in yellow-tan, three in green, two in blue, and so forth—each standing quietly in front of me for a few seconds. I wondered if the color signified rank. None of the others wore red, and none was as big as Big Red. Maybe he was the alpha male, or the only female, like bees.

What were they doing? Just getting a closer look, or taking turns trying to destroy me with thought waves?

After that presentation, Red gestured for me to come over and look at the largest metal screen.

Interesting. It was a panorama of our greenhouse and the other parts of the colony that were aboveground. The picture might have been from the top of Telegraph Hill. Just as I noticed that there were a lot of people standing around—too many for a normal work party—the *John Carter* came sliding into view, a rooster tail of red dust fountaining out behind her. A lot of the people jumped up and down and waved.

Then the screen went black for a few seconds, and a red rectangle opened slowly . . . It was the air-lock light at night, as the door slid open. I was looking at myself, just a little while ago, coming out and pulling the dog behind me.

The camera must have been like the flying bugs that Homeland Security spies use. I certainly hadn't seen anything.

When the door closed, the picture changed to a ghostly blue, like moonlight on Earth. It followed me for a minute or so. Stumbling and then staring at the ground as I walked more cautiously.

Then it switched to another location, and I knew what was coming. The ground collapsed and the dog and I disappeared in a shower of dust, which the wind swept away in an instant.

The bug, or whatever it was, drifted down through the hole to hover over me as I writhed around in pain. A row of glowing symbols appeared at the bottom of the screen. There was a burst of white light when I found the dog and switched it on.

Then Big Red floated down—this was obviously the speeded-up version—wearing several layers of that wall plastic, it seemed; riding a thing that looked like a metal sawhorse with two sidecars. He put me in one and the dog in the other. Then he floated back up.

Then they skipped all the way to me lying on that pillow, naked and unlovely, in an embarrassing posture—I blushed, as if any of them cared—and then moved in close to my ankle, which was blue and swollen. Then a solid holo of a human skeleton, obviously mine, in the same position. The image moved in the same way as before. The fracture line glowed red, and then my foot, below the break, shifted slightly. The line glowed blue and disappeared.

Just then I noticed it wasn't hurting anymore.

Green stepped over and gently took the staff away from me. I put weight on the foot, and it felt as good as new.

"How could you do that?" I said, not expecting an answer. No matter how good they were at healing themselves, how could they apply that to a human skeleton?

Well, a human vet could treat a broken bone in an animal she'd never seen before. But it wouldn't heal in a matter of hours.

Two of the amber ones brought out my skinsuit and Mars suit, and put them at my feet.

Red pointed at me, then tapped on the screen, which again showed the surface parts of the colony. You could hardly see them for the dust, though; there was a strong storm blowing.

He made an up-and-down gesture with his small arms, then his large ones, obviously meaning "Get dressed."

So with about a million potato eyes watching, I took off the tunic and got into the skinsuit. The diaper was missing, which made it feel kind of baggy. They must have thrown it away—or analyzed it, ugh.

The creatures stared in silence while I zipped that up, then climbed and wiggled into the Mars suit. I secured the boots and gloves and clamped the helmet into place, and automatically chinned the switch for an oxygen and power readout, but of course it was still broken. I guess that would be asking too much—you fixed my ankle, but you can't fix a simple space suit? What kind of Martians *are* you?

It was obvious I wasn't getting any air from the backpack, though. I'd need the dog's backup supply.

I unshipped the helmet and faced Green, and made an exaggerated pantomime of breathing in and out. She didn't react. Hell, they probably breathed by osmosis or something.

I turned to Red and crouched over, patting the air at the level of the dog. "Dog," I said, and pointed back the way we'd come.

He leaned over and mimicked my gesture, and said, "Nog." Pretty close. Then he turned to the crowd and croaked out a speech, which I think had both "Harn" and "nog" in it.

He must have understood, at least partly, because he made that four-armed "Come along" motion at me, and went back to the place where we'd entered. I went through the plastic and looked back. Green was leading four others; it looked like one of each color, following us.

Red in the lead, we all went back by what seemed the same path we'd come. I counted my steps, so that when I told people about it I'd have at least one actual concrete number. The hydroponics room, or at least the part we cut through, was 185 steps wide; then it was another 204 steps from there to the "hospital" room. I get about 70 centimeters to a step, so the trip covered about 270 meters, allowing for a little dogleg in the middle. Of course it might go on for miles in every direction, but at least it was no smaller than that.

We went into the little room and they watched while I unreeled the dog's umbilical and plugged it in. The cool air coming through the neck fitting was more than a relief. I put my helmet back on. Green stepped forward and did a pretty good imitation of my breathing pantomime.

I sort of didn't want to go. I was looking forward to coming back and learning how to communicate with Red and Green. We had other people more qualified, though. I should have listened to Mother when she got after me to take a language in school. If I'd known this was going to happen, I would have taken Chinese and Latin and Body Noises.

The others stood away from the plastic, and Red gestured for me to follow. I pulled the dog along through the four plastic layers; this time we turned sharply to the right and started walking up a gently sloping ramp.

After a few minutes I could look down and get a sense of how large this place was. There was the edge of a lake—an immense amount of water even if it was only a few inches deep. From above, the buildings looked like domes of clay, or just dirt, with no windows, just the pale blue light that filtered through the door layers.

There were squares of different sizes and shades that were probably crops like the mushrooms and cigars, and one large square had trees that looked like six-foot-tall broccoli, which could explain the wooden splints.

We came to a level place, brightly lit, that had shelves full of bundles of the plastic stuff. Red walked straight to one shelf and pulled off a bundle. It was his Mars suit. Bending over at a strange angle, bobbing, he slid his feet into four opaque things like thick socks. His two large arms went into sleeves, ending in mittens. Then the whole thing seemed to come alive and ripple up and over him, sealing together, then inflating. It didn't have anything that looked like an oxygen tank, but air was coming from somewhere.

He gestured for me to follow, and we went toward a dark corner. He hesitated there, and held out his hand to me. I took it, and we staggered slowly through dozens of layers of the stuff, toward a dim light.

It was obviously like a gradual air lock. We stopped at another flat area, which had one of the blue lights, and rested for a few minutes. Then he led me through another long series of layers, where it became completely dark—without him leading me, I might have gotten turned around—and then it lightened slightly, the light glowing pink this time.

When we came out, we were on the floor of a cave; the light was coming from a circle of Martian sky. When my eyes adjusted, I could see there was a smooth ramp leading uphill to the cave entrance.

I'd never seen the sky that color. We were looking up through a serious dust storm.

Red pulled a dust-covered sheet off his sawhorse-shaped vehicle. I helped him put the dog into one of the bowl-like sidecars, and I got in the other. There were two things like stubby handlebars in front, but no other controls that I could see.

He backed onto the thing, straddling it, and we rose off the ground a foot or so, and smoothly started forward.

The glide up the ramp was smooth. I expected to be buffeted around by the dust storm, but as impressive as it looked, it didn't have much power. My umbilical tube did flap around in the wind, which made me nervous. If it snapped, a fail-safe would close off the tube so I wouldn't immediately die. But I'd use up the air in the suit pretty fast.

I couldn't see more than ten or twenty feet in any direction, but Red, I hoped, could see farther. He was moving very fast. Of course, he was unlikely to hit another vehicle, or a tree.

I settled down into the bowl—there wasn't anything to see—and was fairly comfortable. I amused myself by imagining the reaction of Dargo Solingen and Mother and Dad when I showed up with an actual Martian.

It felt like an hour or more before he slowed down, and we hit the ground and skidded to a stop. He got off his perch laboriously and came around to the dog's side. I got out to help him lift it and was knocked off balance by a gust. Four legs were a definite advantage here.

He watched while I got the umbilical untangled, then pointed me in the direction we were headed. Then he made a shooing motion.

"You have to come with me," I said, uselessly, and tried to translate it into arm motions. He pointed and shooed again, and then backed onto the sawhorse and took off in a slow U-turn.

I started to panic. What if I went in the wrong direction? I could miss the base by twenty feet and just keep walking on into the desert.

And maybe I wasn't even near the base. Maybe Red had left me in the middle of nowhere, for some obscure Martian reason.

That wouldn't make sense. Human sense, anyhow.

I stood alone in the swirling dust and felt helplessness turning into terror.

2

HOMECOMING

I took a few deep breaths. The dog was pointed in the right direction. I picked up its handle and looked straight ahead as far as I could see, through the swirling gloom. I saw a rock, directly ahead, and walked to it. Then another rock, maybe ten feet away. After the fourth rock, I looked up and saw I'd almost run into the air-lock door. I leaned on the big red button and the door slid open immediately. It closed behind the dog and the red light on the ceiling started blinking. It turned green and the inside door opened on a wide-eyed Emily.

"Carmen! You found your way back!"

"Well, um . . . not really . . ."

"Got to call the search party!" She bounded down the stairs, yelling for Howard.

I wondered how long they'd been searching for me. I would be in shit up to my chin.

I put the dog back in its place—there was only one other

parked there, so three were out looking for me. Or my body.

Card came running in when I was half out of my skinsuit. "Sis!" He grabbed me and hugged me, which was moderately embarrassing. "We thought you were—"

"Yeah, okay. Let me get dressed? Before the shit hits the fan?" He let me turn around and step out of the skinsuit and into my coverall.

"What, you went out for a walk and got lost in that dust storm?"

For a long moment, I thought of saying yes. Who was going to believe my story? I looked at the clock and saw that it was 1900. If it was the same day, seventeen hours had passed. I *could* have wandered around that long without running out of air, using up the dog reserves.

"How long have I been gone?"

"You can't remember? All foogly day, man. Were you derilious?"

"Delirious." I kneaded my brow and rubbed my face hard with both hands. "Let me wait and tell it all when Mother and Dad get here."

"That'll be hours! They're out looking for you."

"Oh, that's great. Who clsc?"

"I think it was Paul the pilot."

"Well," said a voice behind me. "You decided to come back after all."

It was Dargo Solingen, of course. There was a quaver of emotion in her voice that I'd never heard. I think rage.

"I'm sorry," I said. "I don't know what I was thinking."

"I don't think you were thinking at *all*. You were being a foolish *girl*, and you put more lives than your own into danger."

About a dozen people were behind her. "Dargo," Dr. Jefferson said. "She's back; she's alive. Let's give her a little rest."

"Has she given *us* any rest?" she barked.

"I'm *sorry*! I'll do anything—"

"You will? Isn't that pretty. What do you propose to do?"

Dr. Estrada put a hand on her shoulder. "Please let me talk to her." Oh, good, a shrink. I needed a xenologist. But she would listen better than Solingen.

"Oh . . . do what you want. I'll deal with her later." She turned and walked through the small crowd.

Some people gathered around me, and I tried not to cry. I wouldn't want *her* to think she had made me cry. But there were plenty of shoulders and arms for me to hide my eyes in.

"Carmen." Dr. Estrada touched my forearm. "We ought to talk before your parents get back."

"Okay." A dress rehearsal. I followed her down to the middle of A.

She had a large room to herself, but it was her office as well as quarters. "Lie down here"—she indicated her single bunk—"and just try to relax. Begin at the beginning."

"The beginning isn't very interesting. Dargo Solingen embarrassed me in front of everybody. Not the first time, either. Sometimes I feel like I'm her little project. Let's drive Carmen crazy."

"So in going outside like that, you were getting back at her? Getting even in some way?"

"I didn't think of it that way. I just had to get out, and that was the only way."

"Maybe not, Carmen. We can work on ways to get away without physically leaving."

"Like Dad's zen thing, okay. But what I did, or why, isn't really important. It's what I *found*!"

"So what did you find?"

"Life. Intelligent life. They saved me." I could hear my voice, and even I didn't believe it.

"Hmm," she said. "Go on."

"I'd walked four kilometers or so and was about to turn around and go back. But I stepped on a place that wouldn't support my weight. Me and the dog. We fell through. At least ten meters, maybe twenty."

"And you weren't hurt?"

"I *was*! I heard my ankle break. I broke a rib, maybe more than one, here."

She pressed the area, gently. "But you're walking."

"They fixed . . . I'm getting ahead of myself."

"So you fell through and broke your ankle?"

"Then I spent a long time finding the dog. My suit light went out when I hit the ground. But finally I found it, found the dog, and got my umbilical plugged in."

"So you had plenty of oxygen."

"But I was freezing. The circuit to my gloves and boots wasn't working. I really thought that was it."

"But you survived."

"I was rescued. I was passing out and this, uh, this *Martian* came floating down; I saw him in the dog's light. Then everything went black, and I woke up—"

"Carmen! You have to see that this was a dream. A hallucination."

"Then how did I get here?"

Her mouth set in a stubborn line. "You were very lucky. You wandered around in the storm and came back here."

"But there *was* no storm when I left! Just a little wind. The storm came up while I was . . . well, I was underground. Where the Martians live."

"You've been through so much, Carmen . . ."

"This was *not* a dream!" I tried to stay calm. "Look. You can check the air left in the tanks. My suit and the dog. There will be *hours* unaccounted for. I was breathing the Martians' air."

"Carmen . . . be reasonable . . ."

"No, *you* be reasonable. I'm not saying anything more until—" There was one knock on the door, and Mother burst in, followed by Dad.

"My baby," she said. When did she ever call me that? She hugged me so hard I could barely breathe. "You found your way back."

"Mother . . . I was just telling Dr. Estrada . . . I didn't find my way back. I was brought."

"She had a dream about Martians. A hallucination."

"*No!* Would you just listen?"

Dad sat down cross-legged, looking up at me. "Start at the beginning, honey."

I did. I took a deep breath and started with taking the suit and the dog and going out to be alone. Falling and breaking my ankle. Waking up in the little hospital room. Red and Green and the others. Seeing the base on their screen. Being healed and brought back.

There was an uncomfortable silence after I finished. "If it wasn't for the dust storm," Dad said, "it would be easy to verify your . . . your account. Nobody could see you from here, though, and the satellites won't show anything, either."

"Maybe that's why he was in a rush to bring me back. If they'd waited for the storm to clear, they'd be exposed."

"Why would they be afraid of that?" Dr. Estrada asked.

"Well, I don't know. But I guess it's obvious that they don't want anything to do with us—"

"Except to rescue a lost girl," Mother said.

"Is that so hard to believe? I mean, I couldn't say three words to them, but they seemed to be friendly and good-hearted."

"It just sounds so fantastic," Dad said. "How would you feel in our position? By far the easiest explanation is that you were under extreme stress and—"

"*No!* Dad, do you really think I would do that? Come up with some elaborate lie?" I could see on his face that he did indeed. Maybe not a lie, but a fantasy. "There's objective proof. Look at the dog. It has a huge dent where it hit the ground in the cave."

"Maybe so; I haven't seen it," he said. "But being devil's advocate, aren't there many other ways that could have happened?"

"What about the *air*? The air in the dog! I didn't use enough of it to have been out so long."

He nodded. "That would be compelling. Did you dock it?"

Oh hell. "Yes. I wasn't thinking I'd have to *prove* anything." When you dock the dog it automatically starts to refill air and power. "There must be a record. How much oxygen a dog takes on when it recharges."

They all looked at each other. "Not that I know of," Dad said. "But you don't need that. Let's just do an MRI of your ankle. That'll tell if it was recently broken."

"But they *fixed* it. The break might not show."

"It will show," Dr. Estrada said. "Unless there was some kind of . . . magic involved."

Mother's face was getting red. "Would you both leave? I need to talk to Carmen alone." They both nodded and went out.

Mother watched the door close. "I know you aren't lying. You've never been good at that."

"Thanks," I said. Thanks for nothing.

"But it was a stupid thing to do, going off like that, and you know it."

"I do, I *do*! And I'm sorry for all the trouble I—"

"But look. I'm a scientist, and so is your dad, after a fashion, and so is almost everybody else who's going to hear this story today. You see what I'm saying?"

"Yeah, I think so. They're going to be skeptical."

"Of course they are. They don't get paid for believing things. They get paid for questioning them."

"And you, Mother. Do you believe me?"

She stared at me with a fierce intensity I'd never seen before in my life. "Look. Whatever happened to you, I believe one hundred percent that you're telling the truth. You're telling the truth about what you remember, what you believe happened."

"But I might be nuts."

"Well, wouldn't you say so? If I came in with your story? You'd say, 'Mom's getting old.' Wouldn't you?"

"Yeah, maybe I would."

"And to prove that I wasn't crazy, I would take you out and show you something that couldn't be explained any other way. You know what they say about extraordinary claims?"

"They require extraordinary evidence."

"That's right. Once the storm calms down, you and I are going out to where you say . . . to where you fell through to the cave." She put her hand on the back of my head and rubbed my hair. "I so much want to believe you. For my sake as well as yours. To find life here."

3

THE DRAGON LADY

Paul was so sweet when he came in from his search. He hugged me so hard I cried out, from the rib, and then laughed. I'll always remember that. Me laughing and him crying, with his big grin.

For hours he had pictured me out there dead. Prepared himself for finding my body.

It was his for the asking. At least that hadn't changed.

Mother wanted to call a general assembly, so I could tell everybody the complete story, all at once, but Dargo Solingen wouldn't allow it. She said that children did stunts like this to draw attention to themselves, and she wasn't going to reward me with an audience. Of course she was an expert about children, never having had any herself. Good thing. They'd be monsters.

So it was like the whisper game, where you sit in a circle and whisper a sentence to the person next to you, and she whispers it to the next, and so on. When it gets back to you, it's all wrong, sometimes in a funny way.

This was not particularly funny. People would ask if I was really going around on the surface without a Mars suit, or think the Martians stripped me naked and interrogated me, or they broke my ankle on purpose. I put a detailed account on my Web site, but a lot of people would rather talk than read.

The MRI didn't help much, except for people who wanted to believe I was lying. Dr. Jefferson said it looked like an old childhood injury, long ago healed. Mother was with me at the time, and she told him she was absolutely sure I'd never broken that ankle. To people like Dargo Solingen that was a big shrug; so I'd lied about that, too. I think we won Dr. Jefferson over, though he was inclined to believe me anyhow. So did most of the people who came over on the *John Carter* with us. They were willing to believe in Martians before they'd believe I would make up something like that.

Dad didn't want to talk about it, but Mother was fascinated. I went to talk with her at the lab after dinner, where she and two others were keeping a twenty-four-hour watch on an experiment.

"I don't see how they could be actual Martians," she said, "in the sense that we're Earthlings. I mean, if they evolved here as oxygen-water creatures similar to us, then that was three billion years ago. And, as you said, a large animal isn't going to evolve alone, without any other animals. Nor will it suddenly appear, without smaller, simpler animals preceding it. So they must be like us."

"From Earth?"

She laughed. "I don't think so. None of the eight-limbed creatures on Earth has very high technology. I think they have to have come from yet another planet. Unless we're completely wrong about areology, about the history of conditions on this planet, they can't have come from here."

"What if they used to live on the surface?" I said. "Then moved underground as the planet dried up and lost its air?"

She shook her head. "The time scale. No species more complicated than a bacterium has survived for billions of years."

"None on Earth," I said.

"Touché." She laughed. A bell chimed, and she went to the other side of the room and looked inside an aquarium, or terrarium. Or ares-arium, here, I suppose. She looked at the things growing inside and typed some numbers onto her clipboard.

"So they went underground three billion years ago with the technology to duplicate what sounds like a high-altitude Earth environment. And stayed that way for three billion years." She shook her head. "The record in Earth creatures is a bacterium that's symbiotic with aphids. Genome hasn't changed in fifty million years."

She laughed. "This would be sixty times longer? For such a complex organism? And I still want to know where the fossils are. Maybe they dug them all up and destroyed them, just to confuse us?"

"But it's not like we've looked everywhere. Paul says it may be that life wasn't distributed uniformly, and we just haven't found any of the islands where things lived. The dinosaurs or whatever."

"Well, you know it didn't work that way on Earth. Fossils everywhere, from the bottom of the sea to the top of the Himalayas. Crocodile fossils in Antarctica."

"Okay. That's Earth."

"It's all we have. Coffee?" I said no, and she poured herself half a cup. "You're right that it's weak to generalize from one example. Paul could very well be right, too; there's no evidence one way or the other.

"But look. We know all about one form of life on Mars: you and me and the others. We have to live in an artificial bubble that contains an alien environment, maintained by high technology, because we *are* the aliens here. So you stumble on eight-legged potato people who also live in a bubble that contains an alien environment, evidently maintained by high technology. The simplest explanation is that they're aliens, too. Alien to Mars."

"Yeah, I don't disagree. I know about Occam's razor."

She smiled at that. "What's fascinating to me, one of many things, is that you spent hours in that environment and felt no ill effects. Their planet's very Earth-like."

"What if it *was* Earth?"

That stopped her. "Wouldn't we have noticed?"

"I mean a long time ago. What if they lived only on mountaintops, and developed high technology thousands and thousands of years ago? Then they all left."

"It's an idea," she said. "But it's hard to believe that every one of them would be willing and able to leave—and that there would be no trace of their civilization, ten or even a hundred thousand years later. And where are their genetic precursors? The eight-legged equivalent of apes?"

"You don't really believe me."

"Well, I do; I do," she said seriously. "I just don't think there's an easy explanation."

"Like Dargo Solingen's? The Figment of Imagination Theory?"

"Especially that. People don't have complex consistent hallucinations; they're *called* hallucinations because they're fantastic, dreamlike.

"Besides, I saw the dog; you couldn't have put that dent in it with a lead-lined baseball bat. And she can't explain the damage to your Mars suit, either, without positing that you leaped off the side of a cliff just to give yourself an alibi." She was getting worked up. "And I'm your *mother*, even if I'm not a model one. I would goddamn remember if you had ever broken your ankle! That healed hairline fracture is enough proof for me—and for Dr. Jefferson and Dr. Milius and anybody else in this goddamned hole who didn't convict you before you opened your mouth."

"You've been a good mother," I said.

She suddenly sat up and awkwardly hugged me across the table. "Not so good. Or you wouldn't have done this."

She sat down and rubbed my hand. "But if you hadn't done it"—she laughed—"how long would it have been before we stumbled on these aliens? They're watching us, but don't seem eager to have us see them."

The window on the wall was a greenboard of differential equations. She clicked on her clipboard and it became a real-time window. The storm was still blowing, but it had thinned out enough so I could see a vague outline of Telegraph Hill.

"Maybe tomorrow we'll be able to go out and take a look. If Paul's free, he'd probably like to come along; nobody knows the local real estate better than him."

I stood up. "I can hardly wait. But I *will* wait; promise."

"Good. Once is enough." She smiled up at me. "Get some rest. Probably a long day tomorrow."

Actually, I was up past midnight catching up on schoolwork, or not quite catching up. My brain wouldn't settle down enough to worry about Kant and his Categorical Imperative. Not with aliens out there waiting to be contacted.

4

BAD COUGH

Paul was free until 1400, so right after breakfast we suited up and equipped a dog with extra oxygen and climbing gear. He'd done a lot of climbing and caving on both Earth and Mars. If we found the hole—*when* we found the hole—he was going to approach it roped up, so if he broke through the way I had, he wouldn't fall far or fast.

I'd awakened early with a slight cough, but felt okay. I got some cough-suppressant pills from the first-aid locker, chewed one, and put two in my helmet's tongue-operated pill cache.

We went through the air lock and weren't surprised to see that the storm had covered all my tracks, and everyone else's—including Red's; I was hoping that his sawhorse thing might have gouged out a distinctive mark when it stopped.

We still had a good chance of finding the hole, thanks to the MPS built into the suit and its inertial compass. I'd started counting steps, going west, when I set out from Telegraph Hill, and was close to five thousand when I fell through. That's about four kilometers, maybe an hour's walk in the daytime.

"So we're probably being watched," Mother said, and waved to the invisible camera. "Hey there, Mr. Red! Hello, Dr. Green! We're bringing back your patient with the insurance forms."

I waved, too, both arms. Paul put up both his hands palm out, showing he wasn't armed. Though what it would mean to a four-armed creature, I wasn't sure.

No welcoming party appeared, so we went to the right of Telegraph Hill and started walking and counting. A lot of the terrain looked familiar. Several times I had us move to the left or right when I was sure I had been closer to a given formation.

We walked a half kilometer or so past Paul's wrecked dumbo. I hadn't seen it in the dark.

Suddenly I noticed something. "Wait! Paul! I think it's just ahead of you." I hadn't realized it, walking in the dark, but what seemed to be a simple rise in the ground was actually rounded, like an overturned shallow bowl.

"Like a little lava dome, maybe," he said. "That's where you fell through." He pointed at something I couldn't quite see from my angle and height. "Big enough for you and the dog, anyhow."

He unloaded his mountaineering stuff from the dog, then took a hammer and pounded into the ground a long piton, which is like a spearpoint with a hole for the rope. Then he did another one about a foot away. He passed an end of the rope through both of them and tied it off.

He pulled on the rope with all his weight. "Carmen, Laura, help me test this." We did, and it still held. He looped most of the rope over his shoulder and took a couple of turns under his arms, and then clamped it through a metal thing he called a crab. It's supposed to keep you from falling too fast, even if you let go.

"This probably isn't all necessary," he said, "since I'm just taking a look down. But better safe than dead." He backed up the slight incline, checking over his shoulder, then got on his knees to approach the hole.

I held my breath as he took out a big flashlight and leaned over the edge. I didn't hear Mother breathing, either.

"Okay!" he said. "There's the side reflector that broke off your dog. I've got a good picture."

"Good," I tried to say, but it came out as a cough. Then another cough, and then several, harder and harder. I felt faint and sat down and tried to stay calm. Eyes closed, shallow breathing.

When I opened my eyes, I saw specks of blood on the inside of my helmet. I could taste it inside my mouth and on my lips. "Mother, I'm sick."

She saw the blood and knelt down next to me. "Breathe. Can you breathe?"

"Yes. I don't think it's the suit." She was checking the oxygen fitting and meter on the back.

"How long have you felt sick?"

"Not long . . . well, *now* I do. I had a little cough this morning."

"And didn't tell anybody."

"No, I took a pill and it was all right."

"I can see how all right it was. Do you think you can stand?"

I nodded and got to my feet, wobbling a little. She held on to my arm. Then Paul came up and held the other.

"I can just see the antenna on Telegraph Hill," he said. "I'll call for the jeep."

"No, don't," I pleaded. "I don't want to give the Dragon the satisfaction."

Mother gave a nervous laugh. "This is way beyond that, sweetheart. Blood in your lungs? What if I let you walk back, and you dropped dead?"

"I'm not going to *die*." But saying that gave me a horrible chill. Then I coughed a bright red string onto my faceplate. Mother eased me back down, and awkwardly sat with my helmet in her lap while Paul shouted, "Mayday!" over the radio.

"Where did they come up with that word?" I asked Mother.

"Easy to understand on a radio, I guess. 'Mo dough' would work just as well." I heard the click as her glove touched my helmet. Trying to smooth my hair.

I didn't cry. Embarrassing to admit, but I guess I felt kind of important, dying and all. Dargo Solingen would feel like shit for doubting me. Though the cause-and-effect link there wasn't too clear.

I lay there trying not to cough for maybe twenty minutes before the jeep pulled up, driven by Dad. One big happy family. He and Mother lifted me into the back, and Paul took over the driving, leaving the dog and his climbing stuff behind.

It was a fast and rough ride back. I got into another coughing spasm and spattered more blood and goop on the faceplate.

Mother and Dad carried me into the air lock like a sack of grain, and then were all over each other trying to get me out of the Mars suit. At least they left the skinsuit on while they hurried me through the corridor and mess area to Dr. Jefferson's aid station.

He asked my parents to step outside, set me on the examination table, and stripped off the top of the skinsuit, to listen to my breathing with a stethoscope. He shook his head.

"Carmen, it sure sounds as if you've got something in your lungs. But when I heard you were coming in with this, I looked at the whole-body MRI we took yesterday, and there's nothing there." He clicked on his clipboard and asked the window for my MRI, and there I was in all my transparent glory.

"Better take another one." He pulled the top up over my shoulders. "You don't have to take anything off; just lie down here." The act of lying down made me cough sharply, but I caught it in my palm.

He took a tissue and gently wiped my hand, and looked at the blood. "Damn," he said quietly. "You aren't a smoker. I mean on Earth."

"Just twice. Once tobacco and once pot. Just one time each."

He nodded. "Now take a really deep breath and try to hold it." He took the MRI wand and passed it back and forth over my upper body. "Okay. You can breathe now.

"New picture," he said to the window. Then he was quiet for too long.

"Oh my. What . . . what could that be?"

I looked, and there were black shapes in both of my lungs, about the size of golf balls. "What is . . . What are they?"

He shook his head. "Not cancer, not an infection, this fast. Bronchitis wouldn't show up black, anyhow. Better call Earth." He looked at me with concern and something else, maybe puzzlement. "Let's get you into bed in the next room, and I'll give you a sedative. Stop the coughing. And then maybe I'll take a look inside."

"Inside?"

"Brachioscopy, put a little camera down there. You won't feel anything."

❄

In fact, I didn't feel anything until I woke up several hours later. Mother was sitting by the bed, her hand on my forehead.

"My nose . . . The inside of my nose feels funny."

"That's where the tube went in. The brachioscope."

"Oh, yuck. Did he find anything?"

She hesitated. "It's . . . not from Earth. They snipped off some of it and took it to the lab. It's not . . . It doesn't have DNA."

"I've got a Martian disease?"

"Mars, or wherever your potato people are from. Not Earth, anyhow; everything alive on Earth has DNA."

I prodded where it ached, under my ribs. "It's not organic?"

"Well, it is. Carbon, hydrogen, oxygen. Nitrogen, phosphorus, sulfur—it has amino acids and proteins and even something like RNA. But that's as far as it goes."

That sounded bad enough. "So they're going to have to operate? On both of my lungs?"

She made a little noise and I looked up and saw her wiping her eyes. "What is it? Mother?"

"It's not that simple. The little piece they snipped off, it had to go straight into the glove box, the environmental isolation unit. That's the procedure we have for any Martian life we discover, because we don't know what effect it might have on human life. In your case . . ."

"In my case, it's already attacked a human."

"That's right. And they can't operate on you in the glove box."

"So they're just going to leave it there?"

"No. But Dr. Jefferson can't operate until he can work in a place that's environmentally isolated from the rest of the base. They're working on it now, turning the far end of Unit B into a little self-contained hospital. You'll move in there tomorrow or the next day, and he'll take out the stuff. Two operations."

"Two?"

"The first lung has to be working before he opens the second. On Earth, he could put you on a heart-lung machine, I guess, and work on both. But not here."

I felt suddenly cold and clammy, and I must have turned pale. "It's not that bad," Mother said quickly. "He doesn't have to open you up; he'll be working through a small hole in your side. It's called thorascopy. Like when I had my knee operated on, and I was just in and out. And he'll have the best surgeons on Earth looking over his shoulder, advising him."

With a half-hour delay, I thought. What if their advice was "No—don't do *that*!" Oops.

I thought of an old bad joke: politicians cover their mistakes with money; cooks cover their mistakes with mayonnaise; doctors cover theirs with dirt. I could be the first person ever buried on Mars. What an honor.

"Wait," I said. "Maybe *they* could help."

"The Earth doctors? Sure—"

"No! I mean the aliens."

"Honey, they couldn't—"

"They fixed my ankle just like that, didn't they?"

"Well, evidently they did. But that's sort of a mechanical thing. They wouldn't have to know any internal medicine . . ."

"But it wasn't medicine at all, not like we know it. Those big lenses, the smoking herbs. It was kind of mumbo-jumbo, but it worked!"

There was one loud rap on the door, and Dr. Jefferson opened it and stepped inside, looking agitated. "Laura, Carmen—things have gone from bad to worse. The Parienza kids started coughing blood; they've got it. So I put my boy through the MRI, and he's got a mass in one of his lungs, too.

"Look, I have to operate on the Parienzas first; they're young, and this is hitting them harder . . ."

"That's okay," I said. By all means, get some practice on someone else first.

"Laura, I want you to assist me in the surgery along with Selene." Dr. Milius. "So far, this is only infecting the children. If it gets into the general population, if *I* get it—"

"Alf! I'm not a surgeon—I'm not even a doctor!"

"If Selene and I get this and die, you are a doctor. You are *the* doctor. You at least know how to use a scalpel."

"Cutting up animals that are already dead!"

"Just . . . calm down. The machine's not that complicated. It's a standard waldo interface, and you have real-time MRI to show you where you're going."

"Can you hear yourself talking, Alphonzo? I'm just a biologist."

There was a long moment of silence while he looked at her. "Just come and pay attention. You might have to do Carmen."

"All right," Mother said. She looked grim. "Now?"

He nodded. "Selene's preparing them. I'm going to operate on Murray while she watches and assists; then she'll do Roberta while I observe. Maybe an hour and a half each."

"What can I do?" I said.

"Just stay put and try to rest," he said. "We'll get to you in three or four hours. Don't worry . . . You won't feel anything." Then he and Mother were gone.

Won't feel anything? I was already feeling pretty crappy. I get pissed off and go for a walk and bring back the Plague from Outer Space?

I touched the window, and said, "Window outside." It was almost completely dark, just a faint line of red showing the horizon. The dust storm was over.

The whole plan crystallized then. I guess I'd been thinking of parts of it since I knew I'd be alone for a while.

I just zipped up my skinsuit and walked. The main corridor was almost deserted, people running along on urgent errands. Nobody was thinking of going outside—no one but me.

If the aliens had had a picture of me leaving the base at two in the morning, before, then they probably were watching us all the time. I could signal them. Send a message to Red.

I searched around for a pencil to disable the air-lock buzzer. Even while I was doing it, I wondered whether I was acting sanely. Was I just trying to escape being operated on? Mother used to say, "Do something, even if it's wrong." There didn't seem to be anything else to do other than sit around and watch the situation deteriorate.

If the aliens were watching, I could make Red understand how serious it was. Whether he and Green could do anything, I didn't know. But what else was there? Things were happening too fast.

I didn't run into anyone until I was almost there. Then I nearly collided with Card as he stepped out of the mess-hall bathroom.

"What you doing over here?" he said. "I thought you were supposed to be in sick bay."

"No, I'm just—" Of course I started coughing. "Let me by, all right?"

"No! What are you up to?"

"Look, microbe. I don't have time to explain." I pushed by him. "Every second counts."

"You're going outside again! What are you, crazy?"

"Look, look, look—for once in your life, don't be a . . ." I had a moment of desperate inspiration, and grabbed him by the shoulders. "Card, listen. I need you. You have to trust me."

"What, this is about your crazy Martian story?"

"I can prove it's not crazy, but you have to come help me."

"Help you with what?"

"Just suit up and step outside with me. I think they'll come, the Martians, if I signal them, and they might be able to help us."

He was hesitant. I knew he only half believed me—but at least he did half believe me. "What? What do you want me to do outside?"

"I just want you to stand in the door, so the air lock can't close. That way the Dragon can't come out and froog the deal."

That did make him smile. "So what you want is for me to be in as deep shit as you are."

"Exactly! Are you up for it?"

"You are so easy to see through, you know? You could be a window."

"Yeah, yeah. Are you with me?"

He glanced toward the changing room, then back down the hall. "Let's go."

We must have gotten me into my suit in ninety seconds flat. It took him an extra minute because he had to strip and wiggle into the skinsuit first. I kept my eye on the changing-room door, but I didn't have any idea what I would say if someone walked in. Just a little incest?

My faceplate was still spattered with dried blood, which was part of the vague plan: I assumed they would know that the blood meant trouble, and their bug camera, or whatever it was, would be on me as soon as I stepped outside. I had a powerful flashlight, and would turn that on my face, with no other lights. Then wave my arms, jump around, whatever.

We rushed through the safety check, and I put two fresh oxygen bottles into the dog I'd bashed up. Disabled the buzzer, and we crowded into the air lock, closed it, and cycled it.

We'd agreed not to use the radio. Card signaled for me to touch helmets. "How long?"

"An hour, anyhow." I could walk past Telegraph Hill by then.

"Okay. Watch where you step, clumsy." I hit his arm.

The door opened and I stepped out into the darkness. There was a little light, actually; the sun had just gone down.

Card put one foot out on the sand and leaned back against the door. He pantomimed looking at his watch.

I closed my eyes and pointed the light at my face. Bright red through my eyelids; I knew I'd be dazzled blind for a while after I stopped. So after I'd given them a minute of the bloody faceplate, I just stood in one place and shined the light out over the plain, waving it around in fast circles, which I hoped would mean "Help!"

I wasn't sure how long it had taken Red to bring me from their habitat level to the cave where he was parked, and then on to here. Maybe two hours? I hadn't been tracking too well. Without a dust storm it might be faster. I pulled on the dog and headed toward the right of Telegraph Hill.

The last thing I expected to happen was this: I hadn't walked twenty yards when Red came zooming up on his weird vehicle and stopped in a great spray of dust, which sparkled in the last light of dusk.

Card broke radio silence with a justifiable *"Holy shit!"*

Red helped me put the dog on one side, and I got into the other, and we were off. I looked back and waved at Card, and he waved back. The base shrank really fast and slipped under the horizon.

I looked forward for a moment, then turned away. It was just a little too scary, screaming along a few inches over the ground, missing boulders by a hair. The steering must have been automatic. Or maybe Red had inhuman reflexes. Nothing else about him was all that human.

Except the need to come back and help. He must have been waiting nearby.

It seemed no more than ten or twelve minutes before the thing slowed down and drifted into the slanted cave I remembered. Maybe he had taken a roundabout way before, to hide the fact that they were so close.

We got out the dog and I followed him back down the way we had come a couple of days before. I had to stop twice with coughing fits, and by the time we got to the place where he shed his Mars suit, there was a scary amount of blood.

An odd thing to think, but I wondered whether he would take my body back if I died here. Why should I care?

We went on down, and at the level where the lake was visible, Green was waiting, along with two small ones dressed in white. We went together down to the dark floor and followed blue lines back to what seemed to be the same hospital room where I'd first awakened after the accident.

I slumped down on the pillow, feeling completely drained and about to barf. I unshipped my helmet and took a cautious breath. It smelled like a cold mushroom farm, exactly what I expected.

Red handed me a glass of water and I took it gratefully. Then he picked up my helmet with his two large arms and did a curiously human thing with a small one: he wiped a bit of blood off the inside with one finger, and then lifted it to his mouth to taste it.

"Wait!" I said. "That could be poison to you!"

He set the helmet down. "How nice of you to be concerned," he said, in a voice like a British cube actor.

I just shook my head. After a few seconds I was able to squeak, "What?"

"Many of us can speak English," Green said, "or other of your languages. We've been listening to your radio, television, and cube for two hundred years."

"But . . . before . . . you . . ."

"That was to protect ourselves," Red said. "When we saw you had hurt yourself, and I had to bring you here, it was decided that no one would speak a human language in your presence. We were not ready to make contact with humans. You are a dangerous, violent race that tends to destroy what it doesn't understand."

"Not all of us," I said.

"We know that. We were considering various courses of action when we found out you were ill."

"We monitor your colony's communications with Earth," one of the white ones said, "and saw immediately what was happening to you. We all have that breathing fungus soon after we're born. But with us it isn't serious. We have an herb that cures it permanently."

"So . . . you can fix it?"

Red spread out all four hands. "We are so different from you, in chemistry and biology. The treatment might help you. It might kill you."

"But this crap is sure to kill me if we don't do anything!"

The other white-clad one spoke up. "We don't know. I am called Rezlan, and I am . . . of a class that studies your people. A scientist, or philosopher.

"The fungus would certainly kill you if it continued to grow. It would fill up your lungs, and you couldn't breathe. But we don't know; it never happens to us. Your body may learn to adapt to it, and it would be . . . illegal? Immoral, improper . . . for us to experiment on you. If you were to die . . . I don't know how to say it. Impossible."

"The cure for your *cheville*? Your . . . ankle was different," Green said. "There was no risk *à sa vie* . . . to your life."

I coughed and stared at the spatter of blood on my palm.

"But if you don't treat me, and I die? Won't that be the same thing?"

All four of them made a strange buzzing sound. Red patted my shoulder. "Carmen, that's a wonderful joke. 'The same thing.'" He buzzed again, and so did the others.

"Wait," I said. "I'm going to *die*, and it's funny?"

"No no *non*," Green said. "Dying itself isn't funny." Red put his large hands on his potato head and waggled it back and forth, and the others buzzed.

Red tapped his head three times, which set them off again. A natural comedian. "If you have to explain a joke, it isn't funny."

I started to cry, and he took my hand in his small scaly one and patted it. "We are so different. What is funny . . . is how we here are caught. We don't have a choice. We have to treat you even though we don't know what the outcome will be." He buzzed softly. "But that's not funny to you."

"*No!*" I tried not to wail. "I can see this part. There's a paradox. You might kill me, trying to help me."

"And that's not funny to you?"

"No, not really. Not at all, really."

"Would it be funny if it was somebody else?"

"Funny? *No!*"

"What if it was your worst enemy? Would that make you smile?"

"No. I don't have any enemies that bad." Maybe one.

He said something that made the others buzz. I gritted my teeth and tried not to cry. My whole chest hurt, like both lungs held a burning ton of crud, and here I was trying not to barf in front of a bunch of potato-head aliens. "Red. Even if I don't get the joke. Could you do the treatment before I foogly die?"

"Oh, Carmen. It's being prepared. This is . . . It's a way of dealing with difficult things. We joke. You would say laughing instead of crying." He turned around, evidently looking back the way we had come, though it's hard to tell which way a potato is looking. "It is taking too long, which is part of why we have to laugh. When we have children, it's all at one time, and so they all need the treatment at the same time, a few hundred days later, after they bud. We're trying to grow . . . It's like trying to find a vegetable out of season? We have to make it grow when it doesn't want to. And make enough for the other younglings in your colony."

"The adults don't get it?"

He did a kind of shrug. "We don't. Or rather, we only get it once, as children. Do you know about mumps and measles?"

"You-sels?"

"Measles and mumps used to be diseases humans got as children. Before your parents' parents were born. We heard about them on the radio, and they reminded us of this."

A new green-clad small one came through the plastic sheets, holding a stone bowl. She and Red exchanged a few whistles and scrapes. "If you are like us when we are small," he said, "this will make you excrete in every way. So you may want to undress."

How wonderful. Here comes Carmen, the stark naked shitting pissing farting burping barfing human sideshow. Don't forget snot and earwax. I got out of the Mars suit and unzipped the skinsuit and stepped out of that. I was cold, and every orifice clenched up tight. "Okay. Let's go."

Red held my right arm with his two large ones, and Green did the same on the left. Not a good sign. The new green one spit into the bowl and it started to smoke.

She brought the smoking herb under my nose and I tried to get away, but Red and Green held me fast. It was the worst-smelling crap you could ever imagine. I barfed through mouth and nose and then started retching and coughing explosively, horribly, like a cat with a hairball. It did bring up the two fungus things, like small, furry, rotten fruit. I would've barfed again if there had been anything left in my stomach, but I decided to pass out instead.

5

INVASION FROM EARTH

I half woke up, I don't know how much later, with Red tugging gently on my arm. "Carmen," he said, "do you live now? There is a problem."

I grunted something that meant yes, I am alive, but no, I'm not sure I want to be. My throat felt like someone had pulled something scratchy and dead up through it. "Sleep," I said, but he picked me up and started carrying me like a child.

"There are humans from the colony here," he said, speeding up to a run. "They do not understand. They're wrecking everything." He blew through the plastic sheets into the dark hall.

"Red . . . it's hard to breathe here." He didn't respond, just ran faster, a rippling horse gait. His own breath was coming hard, like sheets of paper being ripped. "Red. I need . . . suit. Oxygen."

"As we do." We were suddenly in the middle of a crowd—

hundreds of them in various sizes and colors—surging up the ramp toward the surface. He said three short words over and over, very loud, and the crowd stopped moving and parted to let us through.

When we went through the next set of doors I could hear air whistling out. On the other side my ears popped with a painful *crack*, and I felt cold, colder than I ever had been. "What's happening?"

"You . . . humans . . . have a . . . thing." He was wheezing before each word. "A tool . . . that . . . tears . . . through."

He set me down gently on the cold rock floor. I shuddered out of control, teeth chattering. No air. Lungs full of nothing but pain. The world was going white. I was starting to die but instead of praying or something I just noticed that the hairs in my nose had frozen and were making a crinkly sound when I tried to breathe.

Red was putting on the plastic layers that made up his Mars suit. He picked me up and I cried out in startled pain—the skin on my right forearm and breast and hip had frozen to the rock—and he held me close with three arms while the fourth did something to seal the plastic. Then he held me with all four arms and crooned something reassuring to weird creatures from another planet. He smelled like a mushroom you wouldn't eat, but I could breathe again.

I was bleeding some from the ripped skin and my lungs and throat still didn't want to work, and I was being hugged to death by a nightmarish singing monster, so rather than put up with it all, my body just passed out again.

I woke up to my lover fighting with Red, with me in between. Red was trying to hold on to me with his small arms while Paul was going after him with some sort of pipe, and he was defending himself with the large arms. "No!" I screamed. "Paul! No!"

Of course he couldn't hear anything in the vacuum, but I

guess anyone can lip-read the word "no." He stepped back with an expression on his face that I had never seen. Anguish, I suppose, or rage. Well, here was his lover, naked and bleeding, in the many arms of a gruesome alien, looking way too much like a movie poster from a century ago.

Taka Wu and Mike Silverman were carrying a spalling laser. "Red," I said, "watch out for the guys with the machine."

"I know," he said. "We've seen you use it underground. That's how they tore up the first set of doors. We can't let them use it again."

It was an interesting standoff. Four pretty big aliens in their plastic-wrap suits. Paul and my father and mother and nine other humans in Mars suits, armed with tomato stakes and shovels and one laser, the humans looking kind of pissed off and frightened. The Martians probably were, too. A good thing we hadn't brought any guns to this planet.

Red whispered, "Can you make them leave the machine and follow us?"

"I don't know . . . They're scared." I mouthed, "Mother, Dad," and pointed back the way we had come. "Fol-low us," I said with slow exaggeration. Confined as I was, I couldn't make any sweeping gestures, but I jabbed one forefinger back the way we had come.

Dad stepped forward slowly, his hands palm out. Mother started to follow him. Red shifted me around and held out his hand, and my father took it, and held his other one out for Mother. She took it and we went crabwise through the dark layers of the second air lock. Then the third and the fourth, and we were on the slope overlooking the lake.

The crowd of aliens we'd left behind was still there, perhaps a daunting sight for Mother and Dad. But they held on, and the crowd parted to let us through.

I noticed ice was forming on the edge of the lake. Were we going to kill them all?

"Pardon," Red muttered, and held me so hard I couldn't breathe, while he wiggled out of his suit and left it on the ground, then set me down gently.

It was like walking on ice—on *dry* ice—and my breath came out in plumes. But he and I walked together along the blue line paths, followed by my parents, down to the sanctuary of the white room. Green was waiting there with my skinsuit. I gratefully pulled it on and zipped up. "Boots?"

"Boots," she said, and went back the way we'd come.

"Are you all right?" Red asked.

My father had his helmet off. "These things speak English?"

Red sort of shrugged. "And Chinese, in my case. We've been eavesdropping on you since you discovered radio."

My father fainted dead away.

Green produced this thing that looked like a gray cabbage and held it by Dad's face. I had a vague memory of it being used on me, sort of like an oxygen source. He came around in a minute or so.

"Are you actually Martians?" Mother said. "You can't be."

Red nodded in a jerky way. "We are Martians only the same way you are. We live here. But we came from somewhere else."

"Where?" Dad croaked.

"No time for that. You have to talk to your people. We're losing air and heat, and have to repair the door. Then we have to treat your children. Carmen was near death."

Dad got to his knees and stood up, then stooped to pick up his helmet. "You know how to fix it? The laser damage."

"It knows how to repair itself. But it's like a wound in the body. We have to use stitches or glue to close the hole. Then it grows back."

"So you just need for us to not interfere."

"And help, by showing where the damage is."

He started to put his helmet on. "What about Carmen?"

"Yeah. Where's my suit?"

Red faced me. I realized you could tell that by the little black mouth slit. "You're very weak. You should stay here."

"But—"

"No time to argue. Stay here till we return." All of them but Green went bustling through the air lock.

"So," I said to her. "I guess I'm a hostage."

"My English is not good," she said. *"Parlez-vous français?"* I said no. *"Nihongo de hanashimasu ka?"*

Probably Japanese, or maybe Martian. "No, sorry." I sat down and waited for the air to run out.

6

ZEN FOR MORONS

Green put a kind of black fibrous poultice on the places where my skin had burned off from the icy ground, and the pain stopped immediately. That raised a big question I couldn't ask, having neglected both French and Japanese in school. But help was on its way.

While I was getting dressed after Green had finished her poulticing, another green one showed up.

"Hello," it said. "I was asked here because I know English. Some English."

"I—I'm glad to meet you. I'm Carmen."

"I know. And you want me to say my name. But you couldn't say it yourself. So give me a name."

"Um . . . Robin Hood?"

"I am Robin Hood, then. I am pleased to meet you."

I couldn't think of any pleasantries, so I dove right in: "How come your medicine works for us? My mother says we're unrelated at the most basic level, DNA."

"Am I 'DNA' now? I thought I was Robin Hood."

This was not going to be easy. "No. Yes. You're Robin Hood. Why does your medicine work on humans?"

"I don't understand. Why shouldn't it? It's medicine."

So much for the Enigmatic Superior Aliens theory. "Look. You know what a molecule is?"

"I know the word. Very small. Too small to see." He took his big head in two large-arm hands and wiggled it, the way Red did when he was agitated. "Forgive me. Science is not my . . . There is no word. I can't know science. I don't think any of us can, really. But especially not me."

I gestured at everything. "Then where did *this* all come from? It didn't just *happen*."

"That's right. It didn't happen. It's always been this way."

I needed a scientist, and they sent me a philosopher. Not too bright, either. "Can you ask her?" I pointed to Green. "How can her medicine work when we're chemically so different?"

"She's not a 'her.' Sometimes she is, and sometimes she's a 'he.' Right now she's a 'what.' "

"Okay. Would you please ask it?"

They exchanged a long series of wheedly-poot-rasp sounds.

"It's something like this," Robin Hood said. "Curing takes intelligence. With Earth humans, the intelligence comes along with the doctor, or scientists. With us, it's in the medicine." He touched the stuff on my breast, which made me jump. "It knows you are different, and works on you differently. It works on the very smallest level."

"Nanotechnology," I said.

"Maybe smaller than that," he said. "As small as chemistry. Intelligent molecules."

"You do know about nanotechnology?"

"Only from TV and the cube." He spidered over to the

bed. "Please sit. You make me nervous, balanced there on two legs." I obliged him. "This is how different we are, Carmen. You know when nanotechnology was discovered."

"End of the twentieth century sometime."

"There's no such knowledge for us. This medicine has always been. Like the living doors that keep the air in. Like the things that make the air, concentrate the oxygen. Somebody made them, but that was so long ago, it was before history. Before we came to Mars."

"Where *did* you come from? When?"

"We would call it Earth, though it's not your Earth, of course. Really far away, really long ago." He paused. "More than ten thousand ares."

A hundred centuries before the Pyramids. "But that's not long enough ago for Mars to be inhabitable. Mars was Mars a million ares ago."

He made an almost human gesture, all four hands palms up. "It could be much longer. At ten thousand ares, history becomes mystery. Our faraway Earth could be a myth, and the Others who created us. There aren't any spaceships lying around.

"What deepens the mystery is that we could never live on Mars, on the surface, but we *could* live on Earth, your Earth. So why did the Others bring us many light-years just to leave us on the wrong planet?"

I thought about what Red had said. "Maybe because we're too dangerous."

"That's a theory. Or it might have been the dinosaurs. They looked pretty dangerous."

Dinosaurs. I took a deep breath. "Robin Hood. Have you, have your people, actually been on Mars that long? I mean, dinosaurs were on Earth a *long* time before people."

He wiggled his head again, with his big hands. "I don't *know*! You have to ask the story family, the history family. The yellow people?"

I remembered the two dressed in amber in that room where I was taken for inspection. "Okay. I'll ask a yellow person. So what do green people do? Are you doctors?"

"Oh, no." He pointed at the other. "It's green, and it's a doctor. But why would you think that all of us greens are doctors? Every human I ever saw wears white, but I don't think therefore that you all have the same function."

Good grief. Was I the first cross-species racist? "I'm sorry. What is it that you do, then?"

He shuffled forward and back like a nervous spider. "I'm not a 'do.' " He put a small hand on my knee. "I'm more a 'be.' You humans . . ." He touched his head with both large hands but didn't wiggle it. "You are all about what you *do*. Like, what do you *do*, Carmen?"

"I'm a student. I study things."

"But that's not a 'do' at all! That's a *be*, like me."

I was either out of my depth or into a profound shallowness. "So while you're . . . being, what do you . . . be? What do you be that's different from what others be?"

"You see? You see?" He emitted a sound like a thumbnail scraping across a comb. " 'What do you *be*?'—you can't even *say* it!"

"Robin Hood. Look. I'm both a do and a be—my 'be' is I'm a human being, female, American, whatever—it's what I am when I'm just standing here. But then I can go *do* something, like get a drink of water, and that doesn't change my *be* at all."

"But it *does*! It always does. Don't you see?"

Ontology, meet linguistics. Go to your corners and come out swinging. "You're right, Robin. You're absolutely right. We just don't put things quite that way."

"Put things?"

"We don't *say* it quite that way." I took a deep breath. "Tell me about these Others. They lived very far away?"

"Yes, very far. We used to call it something like the

'heaven' some humans talk about, but since we got TV and the cube, we know it's just really far away. Some other star."

"But you don't know which one."

"No, not which and not how long ago. But very far and very long. The story family says it was a time before time had meaning. The builder family says it must be so far away that light takes ares to get from that star to here. Because there are no stars any closer."

"That's interesting. You don't have telescopes and things, but you figured that out?"

"We don't need telescopes. We get that kind of knowledge from you humans, from the cube."

"Before the cube, though. They were up in heaven?"

"I guess so. We also learned about gods from you. The Others are sort of gods; they created us. But they actually exist."

Red suddenly appeared to rescue me from Sunday school. "Carmen, if you feel able, we'd like to have you up where we're working. The humans are not understanding us too well."

My experience with Robin Hood didn't make me too hopeful. But I could do "pick this up and put it there." I stepped into my suit and chinned the heat up all the way, and followed him up to the cold.

7

SUFFER THE LITTLE CHILDREN

The damage from the laser was repaired in a few hours, and I was bundled back to the colony to be rayed and poked and prodded and interviewed by doctors and scientists. They couldn't find anything wrong with me, human or alien in origin.

"The treatment they gave you sounds like primitive arm-waving," Dr. Jefferson said. "The fact that they don't know why it works is scary."

"They don't know why *anything* works over there. It sounds like it's all hand-me-down science from thousands of years ago. Ares."

He nodded and frowned. "You're the only data point we have. If the disease were less serious, I'd try to introduce it to the kids one at a time, and monitor their progress. But there's no time. And everyone may have it already."

Rather than try to take a bunch of sick children over there, they invited the Martians to come to us. It was Red

and Green, logically, with Robin Hood and an amber one
following closely behind. I was outside, waiting for them,
and escorted Red through the air lock.

Half the adults in the colony seemed crowded into the
changing room for a first look at the aliens. There was a lot
of whispered conversation while Red worked his way out
of his suit.

"It's hot," he said. "The oxygen makes me dizzy. This is
less than Earth, though?"

"Slightly less," Dr. Jefferson said. He was in the front of
the crowd. "Like living on a mountain."

"It smells strange. But not bad. I can smell your
hydroponics."

"Where are *les enfants*?" Green said as soon as she was
out of the suit. "No time talk." She held out her bag of
herbs and chemicals and shook it.

The children had been prepared with the idea that these
"Martians" were our friends, and had a way to cure them.
There were pictures of them and their cave. But a picture
of an eight-legged potato-head monstrosity isn't nearly as
distressing as the real thing—especially to a room full of
children who are terribly ill with something no one can explain but which they know is Martian in origin. So their
reaction when Dr. Jefferson walked in with Dargo Solingen
and Green was predictable—screaming and crying and,
from the ambulatory ones, escape attempts. Of course the
doors were locked, with people like me spying in through
the windows, looking in on the chaos.

Everybody loves Dr. Jefferson, and almost everybody
is afraid of Dargo Solingen, and eventually the combination worked. Green just quietly stood there like Exhibit A,
which helped. It takes a while not to think of giant spiders
when you see them walk.

They had talked about the possibility of sedating the
children, to make the experience less traumatic, but the

only data they had about the treatment was my description, and they were afraid that if the children were too relaxed, they wouldn't cough forcefully enough to expel all the crap. Without sedation, the experience might haunt them for the rest of their lives, but at least they would *have* lives.

They wanted to keep the children isolated, and both adults would have to stay in there for a while after the treatment, to make sure they hadn't caught it, the Martians' assurances notwithstanding.

So the only thing between the child who was being treated and the ones who were waiting for it was a sheet suspended from the ceiling, and after the first one, they all had heard what they were in for. It was done in age order, youngest to oldest, and at first there was some undignified running around, grabbing the victims and dragging them to behind the sheet, where they volubly did the hairball performance.

But the children all seemed to sleep peacefully after the thing was over, which calmed most of the others—if they were like me, they hadn't been sleeping much. Card, one of the oldest, who had to wait the longest, pretended to be unconcerned and sleep before the treatment. I know how brave that was of him; he doesn't handle being sick well. As if I did.

The rest of us were mostly crowded into the mess hall, talking with Red and Robin Hood. The other one asked that we call him Fly-in-Amber, and said that it was his job to remember, so he wouldn't be saying much.

Red said that his job, his function, was hard to describe in human terms. He was sort of like a mayor, a local leader or organizer. He also did things that called for a lot of muscular strength.

Robin Hood said he was being modest; for 140 ares he had been a respected leader. When their surveillance device showed that I was in danger of dying, they all looked to Red to make the decision, then act on it.

"It was not a hard decision," he said. "Ever since humans landed, we knew that a confrontation was inevitable. I took this opportunity to initiate it, so it would be on our terms. I couldn't know that Carmen would catch this thing, which you call a disease, and bring it back home with her."

"You don't call it a disease?" one of the scientists asked.

"No . . . I guess in your terms it might be called a 'phase,' a developmental phase. You go from being a young child to being an older child. For us, it's unpleasant but not life-threatening."

"It doesn't make sense," the xenologist Howard Jain said. "It's like a human teenager who has acne, transmitting it to a trout. Or even more extreme than that—the trout at least has DNA."

"And you and the trout have a common ancestor," Robin Hood said. "We have no idea what we might have evolved from."

"Did you get the idea of evolution from us?" he asked.

"No, not as a practical matter. We've been crossbreeding plants and fungi for a long time. But Darwinism, yes, from you. From your television programs back in the twentieth century."

"Wait," my father said. "How did you build a television receiver in the first place?"

There was a pause, and then Red spoke: "We didn't. It's always been there."

"What?"

"It's a room full of metal spheres, about as tall as I am. They started making noises in the early twentieth century—"

"Those like me remembered them all," Fly-in-Amber said, "though they were just noises at first."

"—and we knew the signals were from Earth because we only got them when Earth was in the sky. Then the spheres started showing pictures in midcentury, which gave us visual clues for decoding human language. Then when the cube was developed, they started displaying in three dimensions."

"Always been there . . . How long is 'always'?" Howard Jain asked. "How far back does your history go?"

"We don't have history in your sense," Fly-in-Amber said. "Your history is a record of conflict and change. We have neither, in the normal course of things. A meteorite damaged an outlying area of our home 4,359 ares ago. Otherwise, not much has happened until your radio started talking."

"You have explored more of Mars than we have," Robin Hood said, "with your satellites and rovers, and much of what we know about the planet, we got from you. You put your base in this area because of the large frozen lake underground; we assume that's why we were put here, too. But that memory is long gone."

"Some of us have a theory," Red said, "that the memory was somehow suppressed, deliberately erased. What you don't know you can't tell."

"You can't erase a memory," Fly-in-Amber said.

"*We* can't. The ones who put us here obviously could do many things we can't do."

"You are not a memory expert. I am."

Red's complexion changed slightly, darkening. It probably wasn't the first time they had had this argument. "One thing I do remember is the 1950s, when television started."

"You're that old!" Jain said.

"Yes, though I was young then. That was during the war between Russia and the United States, the Cold War."

"You have told us this tale before," Robin Hood said. "Not all of us agree."

Red pushed on. "The United States had an electronic network it called the 'Distant Early Warning System,' set up so they would know ahead of time, if Russian bombers were on their way." He paused. "I think that's what we are."

"Warning whom?" Jain said.

"Whoever put us here. We call them the Others. We're on Mars instead of Earth because the Others didn't want you to know about us until you had spaceflight."

"Until we posed a threat to them," Dad said.

"That's a very human thought." Red paused. "Not to be insulting. But it could also be that they didn't want to influence your development too early. Or it could be that there was no profit in contacting you until you had evolved to this point."

"We wouldn't be any threat to *them*," Jain said. "If they could come here and set up the underground city we saw, thousands and thousands of years ago, light-years from home, it's hard to imagine what they could do now. What they could do to us."

The uncomfortable silence was broken by Maria Rodriguez, who came down from the quarantine area. "They're done now. It looks like all the kids are okay." She looked around at all the serious faces. "I said they're okay. Crisis over."

Actually, it had just begun.

8

AMBASSADOR

Which was how I would become an ambassador to the Martians. Everybody knows they didn't evolve on Mars, but what else are you going to call them?

Red, whose real name is Twenty-one Leader Leader Lifter Leader, suggested that I would be a natural choice as a go-between. I was the first human to meet them, and the fact that they risked exposure by saving my life would help humans accept their good intentions.

On Earth, there was a crash program to orbit a space station, Little Mars, that duplicated the living conditions the aliens were used to. Before my five-year residence on Mars was over, I would be sent back there with Red and Green, along with four friends, who would be coordinating research, and Dargo Solingen, I guess because she was the only bureaucrat available on Mars.

Nobody wanted to bring the Martians all the way down to Earth quite yet. A worldwide epidemic of the lung crap wouldn't improve relations, and nobody could say whether they might harbor something even more unpleasant.

So as well as an ambassador, I became sort of a lab animal, under quarantine and constant medical monitoring, maybe for life. But I'm also the main human sidekick for Red and Green. Leaders come up from Earth to make symbolic gestures of friendship, even though it's obviously more about fear than brotherhood. If and when the Others show up, we want to have a good report card from the Martians.

We thought that would be decades or centuries or even millennia—unless they had figured a way around the speed-of-light speed limit.

Or unless they were closer.

PART 3

SECOND CONTACT

I

SETTING THE STAGE

Red says that Americans in the middle of the twentieth century used to call this sort of thing a "crash program," which sounds ominous. Like when America had to build an atomic bomb to end World War II, or when Russia had to beat America into space, to prove that communism worked.

Whatever, the effort to build Little Mars in orbit was the biggest and fastest piece of space engineering in this century, severely denting the economies of the eight countries and multinationals who banded together to get it done. It made the orbital Hilton look like a roadside motel.

The size and complexity were partly due to the ground rules driven by fear of contagion. The lung crap, Martian pulmonary cyst, proved that diseases could move from the Martians to us, through a mechanism that couldn't yet be explained. So for a period of some years, no one who had been exposed to the Martians could come in direct contact with humans who had not. Some said five years, and some said ten, and a significant minority opted for forever.

I had to admit that the argument for forever was pretty strong. Our getting the lung cysts from the Martians was less likely than getting Dutch Elm disease from a tree. More outlandish, actually, since I was part of the disease vector—it was like getting Dutch Elm disease from a person who had touched a tree that had once had the disease. But it *had* happened, and until scientists figured out how, anyone who had been exposed to the Martians had to be biologically isolated from the rest of the human race. That meant all of the 101 people who lived on Mars at the time of the Martian "invasion" of our living space—103, counting the unborn—and especially the fourteen of us who'd been infected.

(I was not the most popular woman in the world, whether that world was Mars or Earth, since if I'd had the decency to die for disobeying orders, none of this would have happened. There were people on Earth who thought I should be imprisoned or even put to death for being a traitor to the human race. But we would have run into the Martians in a few years no matter what, and the lung cysts would have followed.)

So Little Mars was two orbiting space habitats, physically joined, but biologically independent from one another. We had separate life-support systems, with different environments.

It was as if you had two large houses filling a couple of acres of land, which had separate entrances and shared an interior wall with no doors and only two windows.

Their actual shape, viewed from space, was a pair of conventional toroids, like two doughnuts stuck together. They rotated fast enough to produce the illusion of normal Martian gravity. Two extensions, like pencils stuck on either side of the top doughnut, gave Earth-normal gravity for our exercise rooms, and a little more oxygen. Otherwise, our toroid—the "Mars side"—matched the conditions in the Martians' underground city, though the humans' rooms were kept warmer.

I'd never been to the Earth side, and might never be allowed there, but I knew it was sort of like the Hilton, but bigger and more spartan. It might have as many as a hundred people, maybe thirty of them more or less permanent staff. The others were visiting scientists and scholars and dignitaries. Fewer dignitaries as the novelty wore off.

The Mars side was half farm, raising a selection of mushroomy crops, tended mostly by the four Martians who eventually lived with us. Sometimes we'd pitch in and help with the planting and gathering, but that was largely a symbolic gesture. Their food practically grew itself, sort of like mold or mildew, and we weren't going to share it with them.

We humans lived on a combination of simple rations and the most expensive carryout in history, box lunches from the Hilton, which floated less than a mile away, across from the Space Elevator.

The Mars side and the Earth side had only two panes of glass separating them, but they were literally worlds apart. Everything living in our little world came from Mars; all of theirs was an extension of Earth. And the twain would not meet for five or ten years, or ever.

The fact that going to Mars or to our side of Little Mars meant exile from Earth didn't stop people from volunteering. Lots of scientists were willing, or even eager, to make that sacrifice in order to study the Martians close-up, here or on Mars. It gave our small population some variety, people staying with us for some months before going on to Mars.

Little Mars took three years to build, during which time I finished my bachelor's degree, a hodgepodge of course work and directed research and reading that added up to a triple degree in linguistics, literature, and philosophy, with a strong minor in xenology. My lack of facility with mathematics kept me from pursuing biology and xenobiology to any depth, but I took all the elementary courses I could.

The trip from Mars was interesting. The life support in both the lander and the zero-gee middle of the ship was adjusted to effect a compromise between human and Martian needs and comfort levels. The two living areas were kept warmer for the humans and colder for the Martians. They weren't closed by air locks, just doors, so I could go visit Red at his home if I bundled up.

Getting to LMO, Low Mars Orbit, had been a challenge. The Martians, mostly through Red and me, worked with engineers on Earth to develop modifications to the acceleration couches so they would work with four-legged creatures who couldn't actually sit down.

There was no easy way to estimate how much acceleration the Martians could handle. The return ship would normally reach 3.5 gees soon after blasting off from the Martian surface. That was more than nine times Martian gravity.

Humans can tolerate four to six gees without special equipment and training, but there was no reason to generalize from that observation—keeping the acceleration down to six times Martian gravity. Much less, though, and we wouldn't be able to make orbit.

We were learning a lot about their anatomy and physiology; they didn't mind being scanned and prodded. But we couldn't wave a magic wand and produce a centrifuge, to test their tolerance for gee force.

Red wasn't worried. In the first place, he was physically one of the strongest Martians, and in the second place, he said if he died, he just died, and one would later be born to replace him.

(That was something we hadn't figured out, and they couldn't explain—after fifty or sixty of them had died, about the same number became female and fertile, to give birth, or make buds, about a year later. The ones who were born would be in the same families as the ones who had died.)

So we went ahead with it, with some trepidation, as soon as Little Mars was up and running. We only took two Martians on the first flight, Red and Green, and six humans, Oz and Josie and me and a married pair of xenologists, Meryl Sokolow and "Moonboy" Levitus, and Dargo Solingen, I supposed for ballast. A lot of the mass going up was Martian food plus cuttings, seeds, and such, for getting crops established in their new home.

Paul was going to take us up to the new ship, the *Tsiolkovski*, waiting in orbit, and help transfer us and the luggage. Then he would take the *John Carter* back to the colony, and Jagrudi Pakrash would be our pilot for the eight-month trip back. She was pleasant and no doubt expert, but I did want my own personal pilot, with all his useful accessories.

My good-bye to Paul was a physical and emotional trial for both of us. The sex didn't work, no surprise, and there wasn't much to talk about that we hadn't gone over. Over and over. There was no getting around the fact that the radiation exposure limit kept him from ever coming to Earth again, and it would be many years before I could ever return to Mars. If ever.

Fortunately, we'd timed our tryst so I would leave early enough for him to get eight hours of sleep. I doubt that I got two. I stayed up late with my parents and Card, reminiscing about Earth.

It was hardest on Mother. We'd drawn ever closer since First Contact, when she seemed to be the only one who believed me. She was my protector and mentor, and in many ways my best friend.

Aristotle said that was a single soul dwelling in two bodies. But in physical fact we were one body, my part separated at birth.

It was not good-bye forever, or at least we were determined to maintain that illusion. I would be rotated back to Mars; she and any or all of them might eventually be assigned to Little Mars; we might all be allowed to go back to Earth, if contact with Martians proved to be safe.

That was a big "if." How many years of uneventful co-existence with the Martians would be enough? If I were living on Earth, I might suggest a few hundred. Just to be on the safe side.

As it turned out, the launch was easier on the Martians than the humans. Oz, Josie, Meryl, and Moonboy had been on Mars for eight or ten ares, Dargo for twelve, and they nearly suffocated under 3.5 gees; I had some trouble myself. Red and Green said it was like carrying a heavy load, but both of them routinely carried more than their own weight, tending crops.

Red enjoyed it immensely, in fact, the experience of space travel. He was budded in 1922, and had watched the human space program from its infancy to its current adolescence. He knew more about it than I did.

He and a couple of dozen others were especially well prepared for dealing with humans. Ever since the Mars colony's planning stages, they'd known that contact was inevitable. Out of a natural sense of caution, they wanted to put it off for as long as possible, but they would come to that meeting well prepared. Even the charade of not being able to speak human languages had been rehearsed since before my father was born.

Human languages were easy to them, and not just because each one was already at least bilingual. The yellow, white, green, and blue families all had different languages—not dialects, but unique unrelated languages—and they all spoke a single communal language as well, to communicate across family lines.

But they didn't have to *learn* those languages! They were born with innate ability and a pretty large vocabulary in both the consensus language and the family-oriented one. Red understood them all and, weirdly enough, his own language, which no other living Martian knew. He had spent much of his youth learning it, so he could read messages left by his predecessors, and so he could send advice up to the future, essentially in a secret "leader's" code.

Red's language was the only one with a written version. The others were all completely aural—why write things down if the yellows remember everything?—and so weirdly inflected that they defied translation into human languages.

My accident had moved up the Martians' timetable for meeting humans, but not by all that much. Our satellite radar had shown the presence of water in their location, so eventually it would have been explored.

Another thing the accident did was turn a human into a relative of a Martian. They have a thing called *beghnim*, or at least that's a rough transliteration. It's a relationship, but also the word for a person—I was Red's *beghnim* because he had saved my life, which gave him a responsibility for my future. He said there used to be a similar custom among humans, in old Japan.

On the way to Little Mars, we spent a lot of time talking with Red and Green—the others more than me, since I was finishing up my last year of graduate work at Maryland. In fact, I was in a kind of nonstop study mode; when I wasn't doing schoolwork I was going over the notes that the others made from their conversations with the Martians. Moonboy was trying to study the general Martian language, and basic bits of the green one, but he hadn't made much headway, and I didn't try to follow his progress. Red's written language was as complex as an opera score—words, music, and dynamics.

My own daily round was interesting but tiring, the scheduling more regimented than it had ever been under Dargo's ministrations on Mars. Besides the schoolwork, and colloquy with Red and Green, I kept in contact with Paul and my family. Paul was understanding, and timed his calls around my schedule. As the time lag increased, our romantic conversations took on a surreal aspect. He would say something endearing and I would reply, then click open a textbook and study plant physiology for seven and a half minutes, then listen to his response and reply again, and go back to adenosine triphosphate decomposition for another seven and a half minutes—and of course he was doing something similar on his side. Not the most passionate situation.

There was also a period of two hours for exercise each day, in one of the two one-gee extensions. One side rowing, one side cycling, both plus the resistance machine. It wasn't too unpleasant; my only time for light reading or casual VR. I think we all looked forward to the two hours' guaranteed alone-time.

The eight months' transit went by pretty fast, a lot faster to me than the six months going to Mars, four years before. (Two and a fraction ares. We decided to switch to Earth units at the halfway point.) I guess subjective distance is usually that way: when you take a trip to a new place, it feels longer than the return will seem. And we had plenty to occupy ourselves with.

I met twice a week, Monday and Thursday, in VR with the Mars Project Corporation Board of Trustees. That was pretty excruciating at first, with the time lag. When the lag was several minutes, it was less a conversation than an exchange of set speeches. Each of the four or five—there were twenty-four on the Board, but not everybody attended the meetings—would have his or her say, and I would respond. It was anything but spontaneous, since most of them e-mailed me their text hours before the meeting, for which I was grateful.

Sometimes Dargo joined in, which didn't help.

Red couldn't take part directly; it would be years before we could know enough about the Martians' nervous system to attempt VR with them. So I'd normally go talk with him just before the meeting, even if there wasn't anything that directly needed his input.

I enjoyed talking with him, even in the dim fungoid chill of his quarters. (He said he didn't mind coming to my side, but he was much more expansive in his own environment.) In a curious way, he was more "human" to me than many of the Board members and professors with whom I had regular contact, and even one of my fellow passengers.

More than an are before launch, we'd learned that Red was unique—in a sense, the only one of his family. He would live hundreds of ares, and when he died, that would precipitate the fertilization frenzy, and another Red would be budded.

"I'm a Renaissance Martian," he said. "I'm supposed to know everything, be able to duplicate any other family's functions, understand all of their languages. The one who preceded me was the last who could literally know everything, though. Contact with the human race, radio and television, made that impossible.

"Those like Fly-in-Amber remember everything, but they don't have to make sense of it. I do. Somewhere between general relativity and Jack Benny, that became impossible." Jack Benny, I found out, was not a scientist.

He might have been obsolete, what with all that information overload, but he was still the logical one to go rescue the first Earthling alien they made contact with. He might not have been the Renaissance Martian anymore, but he still was Hawking and Superman and the pope all rolled into one.

I asked him why, if the budding process could result in one individual like him every couple of centuries, why only one? Why didn't every Martian have his capabilities?

He said he didn't know: "That may be the one thing it is impossible for me to know." He referred me to Gödel's Incompleteness Theorem, which of course made everything crystal clear.

Red and I had a lot of dramatic shared history, but there was another level of connectedness that was almost human, as if he were a favorite uncle. We were halfway to Earth before it dawned on me that on his side, it was necessarily planned and artificial—he'd been studying the human race for more than a century before we met, and he knew how to act, to form a family-like bond with someone like me. When I confronted him with that, he was both amused and a little upset: it was true, but he thought I'd been aware of that all along, and was doing the same thing with him. There was also the *beghnim* factor, which of course could not have been planned.

He and Green also felt a degree of *beghnim* toward the other thirteen young humans they'd cured of the lung cysts, although it was philosophically complicated, since Martians were the source of the problem as well as its solution.

Our friendship grew over the eight months, perhaps in ways that the other humans couldn't share, although the four researchers spent more time with him than I did.

Dargo never warmed to either of the Martians, but she was hardly a ray of sunshine with the humans, either.

I couldn't believe it when I found out that she was going along. Maybe there really is a God, and for my disbelief, he was getting back at me. The colony administrators were a more likely target for blame, though. Paul was sure she was just getting kicked upstairs, very literally; promoted to get her out of the way.

You could make a good case for her qualifications objectively. She had more years of experience in administration than anyone else off Earth, with the exception of Conrad Hilton IV, who was really just an ancient figurehead, living in orbit to keep his heart thumping while others tended the store.

But I couldn't really see how running the Mars "outpost," which she wouldn't call a colony, made her that qualified for administering our odd mix of humans and Martians. Who decided our small group needed some kind of hierarchal structure, anyhow? A chief who wasn't really one of the Indians.

I supposed there had to be some third party, someone who was not involved with the actual work with the Martians, to evaluate proposals and be the naysayer. If we tried to work on every proposal the Corporation generously approved, there wouldn't be time to eat or sleep.

The argument was that decisions had to be made by someone who was not herself a specialist, so she wouldn't give preferential treatment to xenoanatomy or linguistics or whatever. Martian cuisine. I could agree in principle, but as a practical matter, I would rather trust Oz or Josie—or even Moonboy, odd as he was—to make objective choices.

But then *I* was hardly objective about Dargo.

Anyhow, a lot of people were not sorry to see her go, and many of the same ones were just as glad that I was leaving on the same boat. A kind of poetic justice, that she should be locked up in orbit with her troublemaker nemesis.

Our orbital elements had been manipulated so we would arrive at Little Mars on the Fourth of July, two cheers for the U.S.A. But it was convenient for me, because my last master's exams were a month before that. So my life could be simplified for the last few weeks, before it became complicated in a different way.

In those last few weeks, Earth grew from a bright blue spark to a dot, to a button, and finally to the size of a classroom globe. We moved into the lander and strapped in, but matching orbits with Little Mars was agreeably gentle, almost boring.

We didn't know what boring was. We were about to find out.

2

FORMALITIES

It wasn't just a matter of shaking hands with the president through a feelie glove. The president doesn't come up the Space Elevator without his staff filling up the rest of it. Then there were leaders of all the other seven countries and corporate entities that had built Little Mars, none of whom came up alone, either, and the Corporation trustees, and another fifteen or so who had contributed to the Mars Project in some important way.

There were more people in orbit than at any other time in history. One hundred and fifteen were stuffed into the Earth side of Little Mars, and the Hilton was as crowded as a Bombay slum. Less interesting food, probably.

They all had to talk to us, and they all said the same things. After a while I could have used dark glasses to hide my drooping eyes, but settled for synthetic coffee and drugs. Red was very patient, though of course it was impossible to tell whether he was awake at any given time.

That's an advantage to sleeping standing up, and having eyes like a potato's.

The French delegation had a champagne reception that was pretty amusing, since there's no way you can open a bottle of champagne at our reduced air pressure without it spraying all over. They sent us a bottle, too, through the complicated biohazard air lock, and there was enough left after the initial fountain for us each to have a glass. The Martians use ethyl alcohol as a cleaning fluid, but it's toxic to them. Josie and Jagrudi don't drink, and Dargo declined, so we three had enough to get a little buzz.

Jag would be with us for six months, before piloting the next Mars shuttle, as it was now called. She planned to do three and a half more round-trips, and then stay on Mars as a colonist, stuck by radiation limit as well as quarantine.

I was prematurely, or proactively, jealous of her, an unbeatable rival for Paul's affections. In the short time they'd been together in Mars orbit, they had been all business, but I suspected that would evolve into monkey business. She was pretty and well built—her figure reminded me of the idealized women on the erotic Indian frieze that Paul had shown me—and she was closer to Paul's age, and would share his radiation-forced isolation.

The ceremonial silliness faded after about a week, and we settled down to business.

There were fifty-eight scientists and other investigators living in the Earth side, and after discussing it with Red and Green, we set up a simple schedule: they were both independently available for interview for two hours in the morning and two hours in the afternoon. I would be there with Red all the time, and Meryl (who was fluent in French) with Green. We let the Earth-side people haggle among themselves as to how to split up those eight hours. If they wanted to be democratic, that was close to an hour a week apiece, even with every tenth day a holiday.

(Half of my tenth-day "holiday" was a trial, hooked up to a robot doctor who took obscene liberties with my body, though I was allowed to sleep through the worst, the brachioscopy. My reward for being the only one in orbit who'd survived expelling the lung cysts.)

The interviews went both ways, the Martians studying the humans as intensely as the humans were the Martians. It made the situation more interesting, more dynamic, as a question asked to a Martian could provoke an analogous question from the Martian, and vice versa. Hundreds of researchers on Earth were monitoring the whole exchange, of course, and sometimes their suggestions filtered up.

Red and Green worked hard. When they weren't dealing with the researchers on the other side of the glass, they had to deal with us, who could not only ask them questions but literally prod them for answers. Oz and Meryl were trying to understand their anatomy and physiology; they also monitored us humans for signs of Dutch Elm disease. While Moonboy tried to decode the logic and illogic of their language. He said it was like trying to climb a Teflon wall.

Three of the people who would be going on to Mars with Jag came up early—Franz De Haven and Terry and Joan Magson. Terry and Joan were new to xenology, coming out of successful careers in archeology and architecture; they had gotten permission to live in and study the Martian city. Franz was an expert on human immune response; he was going to Mars to study the human population.

It was interesting to have our own population almost double. Terry and Joan were an old married couple, Joan the famous one. Their status as a prominent lesbian pair might have helped their chances in the "lottery"—or maybe not; they weren't going to have any children to add to the Martian population boom, without outside help.

Franz was a darkly handsome man in his midtwenties.

Jag was obviously interested in him, which stimulated in me a kind of primal jealousy—she would have him for seven months on the ship; I should be allowed to get in a lick or two, so to speak, while I was 50 percent of the available female population.

I mentioned that jokingly to Paul in my morning e-mail, and he responded with unexpected force: I should definitely do it while I had the chance; he never expected me to be a nun for five years, or seven or ten or forever. He even quoted Herrick to me, the romantic old areologist. Okay, I would gather my rosebud.

Men are not very mysterious when it comes to sex. A touch, a raised eyebrow, and there we were, wrestling in his cabin.

He was actually better at it than Paul, but that was just technique, and maybe size. But I suppose it's better to have a clumsy man you love than an expert acquaintance. Or maybe I felt a little guilt in spite of Paul having given permission. I didn't mention it in my letters until Franz was safely gone.

I was only getting half my rosebud's pollen, anyhow. Jag was kind enough to share.

I did talk about it with Red, who straightaway had asked whether I was having sex with the new male. Was it that obvious, even to a centenarian potato head? He pointed out that he'd read bushels of novels and seen thousands of movies and cubes, and the young girl falling for the dark stranger passing through town was a pretty common pattern.

Trying to be objective, I explained the difference between this and my relationship with Paul, and of course that was familiar to him as well, sometimes in the same books and movies and cubes.

He admitted to being jealous of humans for having that level of complexity in their daily lives. He had been fertile four times, and successfully budded in three of them, but there were dozens of other individuals involved in the buddings, and no one of them had a relationship like lover or father of the bud. "Gather ye rosebuds while ye may" would be an obscure joke to him.

Their reproduction did involve a combination of genetic materials, but it was sort of like a shower, or a fish swimming through milt. Six or more of them would engage in something that looked kind of like four-armed arm wrestling, and after all of them were exhausted, the one who had tested out strongest would become nominally female, and the others would sort of roll around with her, covering her with sweatlike secretions that contained genetic code. The female would bud to replace all the ones who had recently died.

It was weird enough. In terran terms, Red was definitely an alpha male, a big strong natural leader—which meant that he was often pregnant.

Terry and Joan were a lot of fun to talk with. I was used to the company of the colony's scientists and engineers, so it was a novelty to exchange ideas with an architect and an archeologist. They picked my brains for everything I could recall about the Martians' city—their research had been exhaustive, but we were the first people they'd met who had actually been there.

They'd been together fifteen years. Joan, the famous architect, was forty-five and Terry was thirty-five, so they'd been about the same age as Paul and me when they'd started out. It was Terry who'd had the lifelong interest in xenology and Mars; when we "discovered" the Martians, they'd both bent their considerable energies toward qualifying for a ticket.

When I sent Dad a picture of them he said they were a real "Mutt and Jeff" couple, I guess from some old movie about homosexuals. Joan was short and dark; Terry was taller than me and blond. They bickered all the time, but it was obviously affectionate.

Selfishly, I was glad to have some rich and famous people on our side of the quarantine. That much more pressure to lower it when we came to the five-year or ten-year mark.

The three of us talked with Red a few times. Terry was fascinated and frustrated by their lack of actual history.

"There've been preliterate societies who didn't have a sense of history going back very far," she said after one such meeting. "People might memorize their genealogies, and they might have traditions about which tribes were friend or foe, but without writing, after a few generations, memory merges into myth and legend. Though the Martians claim incredible memory power." It wasn't just a claim—they were born with language ability and most of the vocabulary they would naturally use.

"No conflict, no history," Joan said. "Nobody owns anything or anybody. One generation is just like the previous one, so why bother keeping track of anything? At least until our radios started talking to them."

"They do record some things," I said. "Fly-in-Amber knew exactly when a meteorite had hit, over four thousand ares ago. But I asked him how many had died, and he just said new ones were born."

"If they were human, I'd say they were in a culture-wide state of denial about death," Terry said. "They obviously have individual personalities, individual identity, but they act as if there's no difference between existing and not existing. Even Red."

"But they know how *we* feel about death. Red could have left me to die when I had that accident. And they were quick to volunteer to help our young people with the lung cysts."

We were talking in the galley. Dargo had come in to get a drink, and listened silently for a minute.

"You're too anthropomorphic with them," she said. "I wouldn't carelessly assign them human motivation."

"You do have to wonder," Joan said. "Where would their altruism come from? In humans and some animals there's survival value in regarding the safety of the group over the individual's—but the Martians don't have any natural enemies to band together against."

"Maybe they did have, in their prehistory," Terry said. "Their home planet might be full of predators."

"For which they would be ill prepared," said Dargo. "No natural armor, delicate hands with no claws."

"Unimpressive teeth, too," I said. "Something like humans." Dargo gave me a weary look.

"Both Red and Green are adamant, insisting they didn't evolve," Joan said. "That the Others created them ab initio."

"A lot of Americans still believe that of the human race," I said. "With only one Other, a lot more recent than the Martians' master race."

It was interesting that otherwise the Martians didn't have anything like religion. Some of them studied human religions with intense curiosity, but so far none had expressed a desire to convert.

From my own skepticism I could see why religion would face an uphill battle trying to win converts among Martians. They were a race with no other races to fear, no concept of wealth or even ownership, no real family, and sex as impersonal as a trip down to the gene shop. Which of the Ten Commandments could they break?

And yet they seemed so weirdly human in so many ways. That was partly our seeing them through a human-colored filter, interpreting their actions and statements in anthropomorphic ways—give the devil her due—a fallacy long familiar to students of anthropology and animal behavior.

But we actually had changed them profoundly, if indirectly, in a human direction, over the past couple of hundred years. Red was sure there weren't any Martians left alive who could remember life before the radio machines started talking. And although at first they couldn't understand the noises coming from them, individuals like Fly-in-Amber recorded them all. The noises were obviously important and resembled speech.

There wasn't a single Rosetta stone for understanding human language, but two things combined to make it possible. One was television, which allowed them to connect words with objects, and the other was SETI, the twentieth-century Search for Extraterrestrial Intelligence, where scientists tried to communicate with aliens via binary-coded radio signals that started with simple arithmetic and moved up, by making diagrams, through mathematics, physics, and astronomy, and finally into biology and human affairs.

The translation was easier for the Martians than it would be for someone farther away—they not only got the messages, but they could watch TV programs explaining about the messages in English.

We talked with Red about that. Maybe the Others had been listening to us, too, but if they were far away, they'd be years behind the Martians in understanding us. He didn't think so, and gave a reasonable relativistic argument—if they were light-years away, traveling toward us at close to the speed of light, then as they approached the solar system, the information would pile up in an increasingly concentrated way, and of course by the time they got here, they'd be totally caught up. Assuming they were infinitely smart.

It turned out otherwise.

3

SPEAKING IN TONGUES

When Jagrudi took my rosebud Franz off to Mars, along with Terry and Joan and another twenty-three, she was also carrying a cargo of special interest to Paul, an experimental drug called Primo-L. If it worked, it could revolutionize space travel, as well as other aspects of modern life: it was an antidote to radiation poisoning, at least from the low-dose, long-term kind of exposure that grounded space pilots and killed people who lived too close to places like the ruins of Kolkata.

They wouldn't let him just take it, since there would be years of human trials before it could be approved. He volunteered to be one of the "lab rats," but they turned him down, since he wouldn't be taking it under clinically controlled conditions. They'd only sent it along in case an emergency arose that required him to drive the shuttle if the other two pilots were unavailable.

It happened. A few months later, in November, Jagrudi

was out on the surface, working on the *Tsiolkovski* prior to launch, and a piece flew off a power tool and ripped open her helmet. They got an emergency patch on it and had her down in the clinic in a few minutes, but she had pulmonary embolisms, and her eyes and ears were damaged. She might be all right in a couple of months, but that was way past the launch window. The third pilot was in the *Schiaparelli*, four months out, so Paul got the job.

It was a course of ten shots over two weeks, and he admitted they caused a little nausea and dizziness, but said it went away after the tenth, so he took off with his payload of two Martians and a bunch of stuff from their city.

Scientists couldn't wait to get their hands on the Martian hovercraft and the communication sphere that had connected them to Earth. But those engineering marvels paled in significance, compared to something the Martians didn't even know they were bringing.

The engineering team came up to Little Mars three weeks before rendezvous, two of them joining us on the Mars side—a married couple who would eventually emigrate to Mars—and seven who joined the permanent party on the Earth side.

Our couple, Elias and Fiona Goldstein, were practically bouncing off the walls with infectious enthusiasm. Only a little older than me, they both had fresh doctorates, in mechanical engineering and systems theory, tailored for this mysterious job—analyzing self-repairing machines that had worked for centuries or millennia with no obvious source of power. Would they even work, this far from Mars? If they didn't, Elias and Fiona were prepared to continue their investigations in the field, which is to say the Martians' city.

They'd brought miniature tennis rackets and rubber balls with them, and we improvised a kind of anarchic racquetball game up in Exercise A, scheduling it while no one was on the machines. It was great to work up a sweat *doing* something rather than sitting there in VR pedaling or rowing.

Of course, my own favorite way of working up a sweat was only weeks away, and never far from my thoughts.

Planning for our reunion was fun. I had eight months and quite a bit of money, with a good salary and no living expenses.

Shipping nonessential goods on the Space Elevator came to about $200 per kilogram, and I tried to spend it wisely. I ordered fine sheets and pillows from Egypt, caviar from the Persian coalition, and wine from France. I could have bought it directly from the Hilton, but found that I could have more and better wine if I managed it myself. I wound up buying a mixed case of vintage Bordeaux, of which I took half, the other six bottles financed by Oz and Josie, who in turn sold two to Meryl and Moonboy.

As the *Tsiolkovski* approached, there of course was less and less time delay, messaging, and Paul and I were able to converse almost in real time. We coordinated our schedules and made half-hour "dates" every day, just chatting, catching up on each other's life over the past couple of years. I have to admit that his obvious eagerness to talk was a relief. A lot could have happened to either of us during two and a half years, but a lot more could have happened to *him*—one of the few single young men on a whole planet.

He had admitted to a fling with Jag, which was about as surprising as gravity. But it didn't really work, partly because she was having reservations about living on Mars, which was rather less exciting than her native Seattle. If the quarantine was lifted before radiation kept her out of space, she probably would exercise her option to go back to the ground the next time she returned to Earth orbit. The scary accident made her even less enthusiastic about staying.

Paul was committed to Mars; it had been his planet since he signed up years ago. To him, the place where I lived was a suburb of Mars, though it happened to orbit another planet. That was my own attitude, though in my case it was more resignation than affirmation.

I knew I wouldn't be able to just drag him off the ship and down to my room—but the leer he gave me when he stepped out of the air lock said that was on his mind, too. He had to supervise the unloading and disposition of his cargo, which took two hours, with Dargo breathing down his neck. Then say hello to Red and Green and get Fly-in-Amber and Snowbird established in the Martian quarters, and meet the new members of the Mars-side human team.

Dargo offered to introduce him to the people on the Earth side, but he pled fatigue and let me guide him by the elbow on a tour of the Mars side, which got as far as my room.

He didn't show any sign of fatigue over the next half hour, though at first he sweetly suppressed his own urgency to attend to mine. I did have the impression that it had been all carefully rehearsed in his mind, but what else was he going to do for eight months, locked up with a couple of Martians?

It was much better for me, for whatever reasons, than aboard the *John Carter* or in his shared room in the colony. My own territory, I guess, with my own lock on the door. Egyptian sheets and pillowcases might have helped.

The wine bottles had corks made of actual cork, which I should have foreseen. I quickly dressed and slipped down to the galley unobserved—almost everybody was over in the Martian environment with the new arrivals—and got a thin-bladed knife that served the purpose.

I undressed when I got back, because it would be silly to drink wine with a naked man otherwise. The wine was amazing, bottled the year I was born. The caviar was kind of like salty fish eggs to me, but Paul went crazy for it. Well, after years of Martian food and ship rations, anything different would be ambrosia.

He said it tasted something like me, which made me feel oh-so-feminine and scaly.

We each had a couple of glasses, which left me light-headed and giggly, and him, light-headed and horny. We got out of bed and did it that Indian way, my arms around his neck and legs clasping him, and it was even more intense than the first time.

We collapsed on the bunk and held each other tightly for a while. I think it was the first time I'd ever produced actual tears of joy. I hadn't been able to admit to myself how much I'd missed him and how much I feared losing him.

Of course, I'd been missing *it*, too, ever since Jag took Franz away.

We eased into sleep intertwined, Egyptian cotton wicking away our sweat while French wine weighed down our eyelids. A most international coma, and interplanetary, the man from Mars holding the girl from Florida.

My phone started pinging, and after about four pings I managed to pry one eye open, then sort through the pile of clothes for the pinger. One problem with living inside a tin can is that you can't ignore the phone and then say, "I was out," like taking a stroll through the afternoon vacuum.

It was Oz. I pushed NO VISION, and then remembered that my standby picture this week was a little movie of pandas copulating.

"What's up, Oz?" I said quietly.

"I don't suppose Paul is there."

"He's sleeping. It was a long trip."

"I guess it can wait. When he gets up, tell him he's not the biggest news story anymore."

"Hey, Oz." Paul was up on one elbow, blinking. "What do you mean?"

"It's weird, Paul. The timing. Just about the same time you docked here, astronomers in Hawaii recorded a strong blinking beam of coherent light from Neptune. Apparently a laser, blinking on and off."

"I don't understand. We don't have anything out there, do we?"

"Nope. They're falling over each other, trying to find a natural explanation. Lased light aimed toward Earth? It's brighter than the planet itself."

"Maybe China? They can do some weird shit."

"Come on, Paul. That'd cost more than Little Mars and the Hilton combined. Get a big laser out there.

"Anyhow, there's a news conference at 1900. We'll all be watching it over at Earth A."

"Okay, we'll be there."

"Bye . . . Loverboy."

He smiled and raised his eyebrows. "I do believe Dr. Oswald is jealous."

"E-ew. That would almost be incest."

"Like incest doesn't happen. How much time we have?"

I checked my wrist tattoo. "Forty-two minutes." He got out of bed and stretched. He was becoming erect again. "Oh, put that thing away and let's go get a cup of coffee." He pouted, so I amused him for a few minutes. We did have time to go by the galley and get a cup on the way to Earth A.

※

Earth A was the largest room on the Mars side; it was where we met, or "met," various presidents and prime ministers and CEOs, pressing palms through a feelie glove. The room had enough seating for twice our human population, and a raised platform behind that was big enough for a dozen Martians.

All four of them were there—Red, Green, Fly-in-Amber, and Snowbird—chattering and chirping and buzzing. Red raised a large arm and waved hello.

Most of the humans were already in place, in the first two rows of theater-style seats. Paul and I sat alone in the third row.

The walls were an intense blue. "The color of Neptune," Paul said.

"Did they name it Neptune because it was the color of the sea?"

"I don't know. Sounds logical."

Some weird music started. "Holst, of course," I said.

"What?"

"Didn't you ever take music appreciation?"

"I was an engineer, sweetheart. Did you take Fourier transforms?"

"Don't give me any trouble." I pinched his leg. "Gustav Holst wrote a suite called *The Planets*, which had eight parts. This is the last one, Neptune. It's kind of famous because it was the first orchestral piece written that ends by fading to silence." I put a hand over my mouth. "Chattering. Sorry."

"Chatter anytime," he said softly.

A face appeared in the cube, vaguely familiar. "Who's that?"

"Raymo Sebastian. He's the default science explainer for BBC/Fox."

"Good evening," he said, in round announcer tones. He was famous enough that he didn't have to identify himself.

"This is a special brief report—brief because so little is yet known—about the strange phenomenon astronomers noticed a few hours ago in the vicinity of Neptune."

His image faded to the image of a blue ball with faint dark markings and a white smear. Just next to it, a red light was blinking regularly, five or six times a second. It was so bright it made me squint.

"The red light is coherent," Sebastian said off camera, "and its wavelength suggests—it almost requires—a ruby laser. The same kind used for commercial scanning since the last century, but trillions of times more powerful. Viewed from Earth, it's as bright as the planet itself."

Behind us, there was a thud, and a quiet susurrus of Martian talking. I turned and saw that Fly-in-Amber had fallen over and was twitching. Paul and I ran up the aisle to their raised platform.

Green was going out the door. Red and Snowbird were kneeling by Fly-in-Amber, who was lying on the floor, twitching. It was an unnatural sight, even for people used to seeing Martians, since they didn't lie down to rest. I remembered seeing a picture of a cow on Earth that some pranksters had tipped over on its side; he looked as odd as that.

"What happened?" I asked Red.

"I've never seen it before, except as a joke." He was gently bending one of Fly-in-Amber's legs. "It looked as if these two legs suddenly collapsed, and the other pair, at the same time, pushed hard, as if jumping." He said something in Martian, loudly, but Fly-in-Amber didn't respond.

Most of the other humans were right behind us. "Maybe it is some kind of odd joke?" Moonboy asked. "A practical joke?"

"I don't think so. It's childish. Fly-in-Amber is too stiff for that. Yellow is a dignified family." Red faced Paul. "Did he act strangely during the crossing?"

"Forgive me, Red," Paul said, "but to me you all act strange, all the time."

He made his little buzz sound. "You should talk, Two-legs. I mean, did his behavior or conversation suddenly change?"

"He talked a lot more during the last couple of days, approaching Earth. But we were all excited, ready to get off the ship."

"Of course. You were eager to mate with Carmen. Did that happen yet?"

I had to smile. "It was fine, Red."

"That's good. Green has gone to Mars C, to send a message to the other healers at home. She'd never seen this, either."

"Nor have I," said Snowbird. "Nor have I heard of it, ever, except children playing. It's painful."

"Should we pull him back upright?" I asked.

"Not yet," Red and Snowbird said at the same time. "Wait until we hear from—"

Fly-in-Amber started talking, a quiet uninflected warble. Snowbird moved close to listen.

"Is this being recorded?" Paul said.

"Of course," Dargo Solingen snapped.

"What is he saying?" I asked.

"It sounds like nonsense to me." Red shook his head, ponderously, a gesture that he'd learned to copy from us. "Perhaps code? I've never heard anything like it."

"You can't make any sense of it?"

"No, not yet. But it doesn't seem . . . It isn't random. He is saying something, and repeating it."

Fly-in-Amber stopped with a noise like a sneeze. Then a long monotone, like a sung sigh. Snowbird said something in Martian, and after a pause, Fly-in-Amber answered a couple of halting syllables.

He started to rise but hesitated. Red and Snowbird

helped him to his feet, Red chattering away. He answered, obviously faltering. Red made an odd fluting sound I didn't think I'd heard before. "Can you tell them in English?"

Fly-in-Amber stepped around, faltering, to face us. "I don't know what happened. Red says I fell down and spoke nonsense while my body shook.

"To me, I was blind, but I felt the floor." He gingerly patted his right arms with his main left hand. "Along here, that was strange. And I smelled things that have no name. At least that I've never smelled. And I felt cold, colder than home. Cold like Mars, outside.

"But I don't remember talking. Red says I talked and talked. I heard something, but it didn't make any sense."

"Maybe you heard what you were saying to us?" Snowbird said.

"No, it wasn't words; nothing like words. It was like a machine sound, but it was like music, too; human music. A musical machine?"

Dargo played back part of it. "Doesn't sound very musical."

Fly-in-Amber tilted his head back, as if searching the ceiling and walls with potato eyes. "I mean something like 'feeling.' When you say music has feeling."

"You mean emotion?" Oz said.

"Not really. I understand that you humans have emotions when events or thoughts cause chemical changes in your blood. In your brains. We are similar, as you know. This is not . . . not that real?"

He swiveled toward me. "It's like when Carmen tried to tell me, at 20:17 last Sagan 20, how she felt while reading the score of Beethoven's *Eroica* symphony. That seeing the dots on the screen made your brain remember the sound, and the feeling that the sound caused, even though you weren't hearing anything. Do you remember that?"

"I guess." If you say so, Dr. Memory.

"It was that kind of, what would you say, distance? What you said about reading the score was that it was like a diagram of an emotion, an emotional state, but one you didn't have a word for."

I did remember. "That's right. You can call it 'joy' or 'hope' or something, but nothing really precise."

"So if someone couldn't read music, and didn't know anything about how music is written down, still, they might see the score and recognize patterns, symmetries, as having beauty, or at least significance, without connecting them to sound at all."

"I've seen something like that," Oz said. "A system of notation that dancers use to record a performance. There's no way you could tell what it was without knowing. But there was symmetry and motion in it. I guess you could say it had intrinsic beauty."

"Lebanotation," Red said. "I saw it on the cube."

Green had come back and listened silently for a minute. She let out a burst of rapid-fire French, then paused. "Fascinating. Save it for later. Fly-in-Amber is ill. I must take him away and look at him."

Red said something in Martian, and she answered with a short noise that I recognized as affirmation. She put a pair of arms, a large and a small one, around her patient and led him off to their living quarters.

Red watched her go and made a human shrug. "She is the doctor, in a way. But I doubt that there is any treatment for this."

"She talked to Mars," I said, and checked my watch tattoo. "She might have heard by—" She came rushing immediately back, warbling and rasping at Red.

"She says the same thing has happened on Mars, evidently about the same time. Most of the memory family fell down and started talking this nonsense."

"It was *temps du Mars* 09:19," she said, "when it happened there. Seventeen Earth minutes after Fly-in-Amber."

"As if they caught it from him," I said. "At the speed of light."

"Or it came from Earth," Paul said.

"Or outer space." Red gestured down the hall. "Neptune's out there."

4

PUZZLES

The memory family had seventy-eight members, less than 1 percent of the total Martian population. They were odd-balls, but curiously uniform in their eccentricity. In human terms, they were vain, scolding, obsessive, and humorless. The other Martians enjoyed a whole class of jokes about them, and didn't take them too seriously, since history was not a traditionally useful pursuit. And then this odd thing happened.

In less than an hour, it became obvious that "odd" only began to describe it. The only members of the memory family that had acted like Fly-in-Amber were the ones who had been watching the show about the light coming from Neptune. It was obviously some kind of trigger.

All of the ones affected did exactly the same thing as Fly-in-Amber. They fell over and emitted the same long string of nonsense sounds ten times. It had to be some kind of message.

The scientists in Little Mars would have decoded it soon, but we had broadcast it to Earth, and were beaten to the punch by a Chilean researcher, who idly fed a recording of the data through a reverse SETI algorithm—a program that looked for patterns like the ones we had been sending out for more than a century, trying to contact intelligent life elsewhere in the universe. He hit the jackpot.

The dot-and-dash digital message had been slightly obscured because it was mixed into a far more complex one, like a radio signal that carried both amplitude and frequency modulation. Filtering out the frequency modulation gave an unambiguous pattern of dots and dashes. There were 551 of them, and the same pattern was repeated ten times.

The number 551 is interesting in SETI terms because it's the product of two prime numbers, 19 and 29. One of the most basic SETI maneuvers was to make up a message with (in this case) 551 ones and zeros, which you could transmit with dots and dashes. Then represent them in a crossword-puzzle-style matrix, either 19 squares by 29 or 29 by 19, making a picture out of the black and white squares.

The signal went like this:

```
1111000011101011001100100001000010101
1001000001001010011111100000101010001
0000000011101010001100000000000000000
0000000000000000000100000000100100000
0000000000010010000100101110000111000
0000000000010010000100100000100100000
0000000000000000000110001000000000000
1100000000000000000000000100000000000
1100000000000000011000000001000000000
0000000000010101000110000000010101000
0000000000011111010110101110111111111
0000000000011111010000000111001010100
0000000010010101000101110001000001000
0
```

```
10101000100011100001010100000001010000
1011100000001110100
```

The first time the Chilean astronomer tried, he used the 19 by 29 matrix, and got nothing coherent. The 29 by 19 gave this interesting picture. Humans and Martians gathered together in front of the monitor as the Chilean's diagram came in.

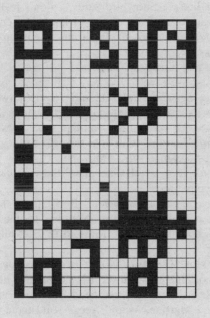

"Is that *English*?" Oz said. "What the hell is 'O Sin'?"

"I think it's some kind of human joke," Snowbird said. "They said it was 551 ones and zeros?"

"Correct," Dargo said.

"Unless it's a coincidence, unlikely, then it's a joke reference to the first example of trying to communicate this way, three of my generations ago. Frank Drake made it up in 1961, with 551 ones and zeros, and it was widely broadcast. The square O in the upper-left corner would be the Sun, with the Solar System underneath it: four little planets, including yours and ours, then two big ones, Jupiter and Saturn, and then two medium-sized, Uranus and Neptune."

"So what about sin?" Oz said.

"I don't know," Snowbird said. "I don't really understand human jokes. That corner of Drake's picture was a symbolic representation of the atoms of carbon and oxygen. Necessary for life."

"Silicon and nitrogen," Paul said. "Si and N. They're a silicon-based life-form?"

"With six legs and a tail," Oz said, "or eight, two of them small. There's a square next to the Earth, with a line pointing to a man-shaped diagram. Another square next to Mars, and one over Neptune, with lines toward this diagram of an eight-legged creature, with a tail."

"We don't look at all like that," Snowbird said. "We don't have eight legs."

"We have eight appendages." Red tapped the screen. "There is a solid line from Neptune to the creature, but only a dotted line from Mars to it. That might mean something."

"But hold it," Oz said. "Nothing could live on Neptune. Eight legs or nine or whatever. It's a cryogenic hell."

"No." Red shook his huge head. "Ha-ha. I mean, yes, humans and Martians would freeze solid there in a matter of seconds. But there could be something like organic chemistry with silicon and nitrogen—liquid nitrogen being a solute, like water in our chemistry. You could have compounds analogous to amino acids and proteins. So complex life chemistry is theoretically possible."

"There's hardly any free nitrogen on Neptune," Paul said. "Hydrogen, helium, a little methane for color."

"Not Neptune itself." Red drummed the fingers of his small hands together. "Its largest moon, Triton."

Paul nodded slowly. "Yeah. Geysers of liquid nitrogen when it's warm enough."

"We don't know much about it, do we?" Oz said.

"Haven't been there since forever," Paul said. "A flyby in the 1980s."

"In 1989," Red said. "The Chinese-Japanese Outer Planets Initiative was launched in 2027 but went silent when it arrived, in 2044. But there's been a lot of study from various Hubbles. There are probably a hundred specialists about to start bouncing off the walls."

"What about the number down in the corner?" I said.

"Ten to the seventh," Paul said; "ten million. And that looks like a 'd' after it. Ten million days?"

Red and Snowbird translated it simultaneously. "Twenty-seven thousand three hundred and seventy-eight years." Snowbird added, "Fourteen thousand nine hundred and seventy ares, in Martian sols."

"I wonder if that's how long you've been on Mars," I said. Red shrugged.

"It's how long human beings have been all human," Oz said, "in a manner of speaking. Interesting coincidence. The last Neanderthals died about twenty-seven thousand years ago. I guess *Homo sapiens* has been the dominant species ever since."

"Having killed off the Neanderthals?" Moonboy said.

Red gave his slightly maddening monotone laugh. "Ha-ha. Nobody knows what became of them."

"*Homo sapiens* invited them over for lunch," Moonboy said, "and they turned out to be the main course." Dargo shot him a look.

Oz tapped the eight-legged figure. "These could be your Others. Who created you in their image, more or less."

"Living that close." Red shook his head. "And on so small a world? Triton isn't even as big as your Moon."

"They might be like you," I said. "You don't take up a lot of real estate."

There was a double-ping signal, and a familiar face appeared, superimposed over the Drake diagram. Ishan Jhangiani, science coordinator on the Earth side. "This is interesting. Some of the Martians were watching the broadcast, but only the yellow ones were affected. And the nine yellow ones who were doing something else were not affected."

"I don't think we have any organs that discriminate between regular light and coherent light," Red said. "So how could that work?"

Ishan chewed his lip and nodded. "Well, just pursuing logic . . . you would never encounter such a strong burst of coherent light in the normal course of things. So you, or rather the yellow ones, could have such an organ and never know it."

"But it wouldn't have any useful function," Oz said.

"Ha-ha. But it would. It would make you fall down and speak in tongues whenever somebody on Neptune, or Triton, wanted you to."

That would turn out to be pretty accurate.

5

UNVEILED THREAT

After the excitement died down, most of us went back to the mess and zapped up a meal. Dargo went off somewhere to stick pins in dolls.

I traded the lump of rice in my chicken for the pile of mashed potatoes that came with Oz's meat loaf. He exercises as much as I do, as we all do, but he keeps putting on weight, while I lose it.

"I don't get it," Moonboy said. "If they wanted to send a dot-and-dash message, why be so roundabout? Why not just use the ruby laser itself?"

"For some reason they wanted the Martians involved," I said. "One Martian, at least. What I want to know is how Fly-in-Amber got all that information out of the red light." So far, all we'd gotten was on/off, on/off.

Oz nodded. "And what's different about Fly-in-Amber, and those other yellow ones, that they were the only Martians affected by it? The anatomical scans we did on Mars didn't show any significant differences between the various families, except for Red. With all his extra brain and nervous-system mass and complexity, I'd expect him to be the one singled out, if any."

"He said he didn't feel anything special," Meryl said. "But he only looked at it for a couple of seconds. Then he was worrying over Fly-in-Amber."

"I'll do a high-resolution PET scan of all their eyes and brains," Oz said. "See whether Fly-in-Amber has some anomaly."

There was a pause, and Paul shook his head. "Triton? How could intelligent life evolve on Triton? How could anything complex?"

Oz studied his meat loaf for clues. "Well, it couldn't be like Earth. A large variety of species competing for ecological niches. At least intuitively that doesn't sound likely. If it's like Red suggested, a quasi-organic chemistry based on silicon and liquid nitrogen, think of how slow chemical reactions would be."

"And how little chemical variety," Moonboy said, "with so little solar energy pumping it."

"There's also energy from radioactivity," Paul pointed out, "and tidal friction from Neptune. I think that's what causes the liquid nitrogen geysers they see."

Moonboy persisted. "But it would never have anything like the variety and energy in the Earth's primordial soup."

"You're all barking up the wrong tree," I said. "If the signal really is coming from the Others, they didn't evolve on Triton. The Martians' tradition is that they live light-years away. So this laser thing could just be an automated device. It isn't any more or less impossible than the Martian city. That was supposedly built by the Others, a zillion years ago."

"Or twenty-seven thousand," Oz said. "You're right. But why did it start blinking exactly as soon as one of the yel-

low family reached Earth orbit? That would be some sophisticated automation."

That gave me a little chill. "In other words . . . we're
being watched?"

He stroked his beard. "Give me another explanation."

Over the next several days, scientists on Earth as well as
here analyzed the signal from Neptune, which had stopped
eight hours and twenty minutes after Fly-in-Amber's con-
dition had been broadcast to Earth. That was exactly twice
the travel time of that broadcast to Neptune, which fact was
an interesting piece of information in itself. Mission ac-
complished; turn it off.

The laser beam was apparently just that, a simple powerful beam of unmodulated coherent light, carrying no information other than the intriguing fact of its own existence.

There are some natural sources of cosmic radiation
that produce coherent light, but nobody was pursuing
that direction, since the timing of it would be an impossible coincidence. It was artificial, and in its way was as
much a message as the Drake diagram that came out of the
amplitude-modulation part of Fly-in-Amber's utterances.
The amount of power it was pumping was part of the message, a scary part.

It could destroy an approaching spaceship. Maybe it
had, once.

The frequency-modulation part of the message resisted
analysis. Each of the ten iterations of the signal had different, and apparently random, patterns. The Martians here
and on Mars listened to them and agreed that they sounded
like Martian speech, albeit in monotone, but made absolutely no sense. Fly-in-Amber found it quite maddening.
He said, "It sounds like a human idiot going 'la la la la'
over and over." Well, maybe. But sometimes the "la" be-

came "la-a-a" or just "ll," and sometimes it sounded like a pencil sharpener trying to say "la."

Four or five days after the excitement, I was dragging my weary bones home after exercise and was surprised to meet Red at the end of the corridor. The Martians didn't often wander over this way.

"Carmen. We always meet at my place. Could I have a look at yours?"

"Sure, why not?" It was a mess, but I doubted that Red would care. He'd learn more.

I thumbed the lock. "I normally take a shower after working out."

"Your smell is not toxic." I guess you take your compliments where you can find them.

He looked large in my small room, and strange, hemmed in by undersized furniture he couldn't use. He wheeled the desk chair over in front of him.

"Could we have some music? Bach Concerto Number 1 in F Major?"

"*Brandenburg*, sure." Pretty loud. I asked the machine and it started.

"A little louder?" He gestured for me to sit in front of him. I did, and he leaned forward and spoke in a barely audible whisper.

"Everything I do in my quarters is recorded for science. But this must be a secret between you and me. No other humans; no other Martians."

"All right. I promise."

"When I listened to the frequency-modulation part, I understood it immediately. Only *I* could understand it."

"Only you . . . It was in your private language? The leader language?"

He nodded. "Perhaps it is the real reason we have to learn the language. Because this was going to happen eventually."

His voice became even lower, and I strained to hear. "It told me that we Martians are biological machines, developed for this purpose: to communicate with humans if and when they developed to this point, a time when flight to the stars became possible."

"I thought it wasn't, yet."

"Within a few human life spans. The Others work slowly."

"You mean the Others actually did evolve on Triton?"

"Not at all, no. They do come from a planet revolving around another star, some twenty light-years from here. It's a cold planet, ancient, and its cryogenic kind of life has been there for literally millions of years.

"The one individual on Triton was especially engineered for its task, as were all of us Martians. We're all here to keep an eye on you humans.

"The Others move very slowly; their metabolism is glacial. They *think* fast, faster than you and me, because their mental processes utilize superconductivity. But in physical manipulation of their environment . . . you would have to study one for hours to see that it had moved.

"The one on Triton moves about sixty-four times as fast as they do; we move about four times as fast as it does. To match you.

"They offer this as an analogy. Suppose you humans, for some reason, had to communicate with a mayfly."

"That's a kind of insect?"

"Yes. Though it lives most of its life as a variety of nymph. When it becomes an actual insect, it only lives for a day. How would you go about communicating with it?"

"You couldn't. It wouldn't have anything like a brain, or language."

Red grabbed his head and shook it. "Ha-ha. But this is analogy, not science. Suppose it had a quick squeaky language, and intelligence, and civilization, but it lived so fast that the span from birth to death was only one day. How would you communicate with it?"

"I see what you're driving at. We're the mayflies."

He grabbed his head again. "You gave away the ending. But suppose you did have to communicate with these intelligent mayflies. To them, you are slow as sequoias. How do you get them to realize that you are also an intelligent form of life?"

"Build a machine? One that moves as fast as they do?"

"Yes, but not in one step. What the Others did was build a machine, a carbon-based biological one, that lived somewhat faster than they did—and which had the ability to build a machine faster than itself. And so on down the line."

"Until you had one that could talk to mayflies. Humans, in this case."

He nodded. "That's what we are. We Martians."

"Your only function is to communicate with us?"

"I would say 'destiny' rather than function. We do have a life, a culture, independent of you. But humans are our reason for being."

"So why," I whispered, waving my hand at the music, "why all the secrecy?"

"Because I'm not supposed to be explaining this to you. To anybody."

"We're supposed to decode the message ourselves?"

"I don't think you could. I don't think even a Martian could, no matter how brilliant, unless he spent all his youth studying my language."

"Maybe not even then," I said. "Oz says your brain is immensely more complex than other Martians'. But why do the Others want to keep it secret?"

"I don't know the details yet. But they're afraid of you; of what you may become. Millions of years ago, they had trouble with a planet in a nearby system, somewhat like the Earth. Water-carbon-oxygen life. They're frightened by how fast you act. How fast you evolve."

"What kind of trouble did they have with this planet? A war?"

"I don't think that would be possible. I think it was what you would call a preemptive strike."

"So . . . they destroyed them?"

Red nodded slowly. "After the young planet started sending out interstellar probes. The Others' world was relatively near—their sun was maybe a hundred times the distance from here to Neptune, what we would call a wide double-star system—so of course the Others were their first interstellar destination."

"The young world was going to invade at that distance?"

"The Others didn't know. But there were wars on the oxygen planet, worldwide wars, for years before they had space travel, and the Others could observe them indirectly. As we, and they, have done with you."

"So the Others suddenly developed space travel themselves, and went off to do this 'preemptive strike'?"

"Oh, no. They'd been exploring other planets with probes for many thousands of years. They'd been to this solar system, and others, with complex autonomous robots to gather information, deliver it, and self-destruct."

His voice grew even lower. "As we have observed, they have considerable talent, power, for manipulating things at great distances. The tools for the preemptive strike were in place long before they decided they had to be used."

"My God. Are they in place here on Earth, too?"

"That wasn't clear. Sometimes the message was allusive, metaphorical . . . It was sort of 'If it's true, it's too late for the humans to do anything about it; if not, nothing needs to be done.' "

"We might feel differently. We humans."

"It also said that for the humans' sake, the threat ought to be kept secret. Not for its own protection, it emphasized. For *your* sake—I think so it wouldn't have to take action prematurely. Though my sense is the 'action' wouldn't be anything like an invasion or even a launched missile. It would be a small act, like turning on the laser beacon."

My heart was hammering. "Could it destroy the Earth just like that? So casually?"

"I doubt it. And it wouldn't want to, literally, destroy the Earth. It said that we could have the planet if you proved unsuitable. We Martians."

"Now that would go down really well on Earth."

"Don't worry. Who needs the gravity? The Others are aquatic, or whatever you call something that lives in liquid nitrogen. They don't think about gravity any more than fish do. They just float there."

I felt he was telling the truth. "You're on our side."

He nodded. "It can't see that. Even if I was not in *beghnim* with you, I would feel closer to you, to all humans, than to them. The Others may be our creators, but in terms of simple existence, we are much closer to you.

"They hardly live at all, on our time scale . . . and technically, they never die."

"Never? How do they manage that?"

"An individual will stop moving, stop metabolizing, for a thousand years or more. Dead except for the information structures that make up its individuality. When it's needed again, it's kind of . . . jump-started."

"I don't know that term."

"It's old-fashioned. Basically, some other individual decides it's time, and applies enough energy to get it metabolizing again. A process that might take ares.

"So in a sense, it's never really been dead. Though for a

thousand ares or so, it's been no more alive than data stored in a machine."

"How many of them are out there, alive, at any given time?"

"It could be three or three trillion; I don't know. The only one we have to worry about is the speeded-up one on Triton. The others are thirty ares away from affecting us in response to anything we do. And it would take them ages to respond."

"If some people, a lot of people, knew what you've told me, they'd be declaring war on Triton. Which would do a lot of good, I know."

"A lot of expense for nothing. The best they could do would be to send a heavily armed and automated vessel out to find a small target beneath the surface of Triton, and destroy it. But it's impossible."

"Not theoretically. Not if a majority wanted it badly enough."

"I meant practically. You realize how powerful that laser would be, close-up?"

"Paul worked up some numbers. If it could be aimed and used like the American Star Wars lasers were supposed to, they would be able to vaporize any conventional space vehicle, long before it got to Triton."

"Ha-ha." He nodded rapidly. "But think larger. Suppose this laser is far from being the pinnacle of their technology. Suppose they had one a thousand times more powerful. Suppose it was hidden on Earth's moon."

"It could do some real damage, even if they stopped it pretty quickly."

"It would be hard to stop, wouldn't it? And in less than one day it could destroy every city in the world and set fire to all the forests and plains. The smoke would persist long enough to stop agriculture."

"Did . . . did the Other threaten to do something like that?"

"No, not in so many words. It did imply that the destruction would only take one day, and from that I extrapolated various possibilities. But it was not like a threat, or a prediction." He paused for several seconds. "It's hard to translate the exact intent. It was presented as a theoretical possibility, almost an entertainment for the Other. Like a horror movie that could come true.

"I think I know the leaders' written language well. But I've never heard anyone speak it. Doubtless there are nuances that I've missed."

"Only one day." We needed a scientist here. "I guess it could deflect a large enough asteroid to make a disaster like the dinosaur wipeout. Or release some kind of poison in the air. But wouldn't that take more than a day?"

"Unless it was released at thousands of places all at once. But the 'one day' was only an implication. It could just stand for a short period of time. Maybe a short time in comparison to how long it normally takes for a species to go extinct. As I say, it's hard to tell whether it's being direct or speaking in metaphor and symbol."

"Can you talk back to it?"

"I don't see why not, at least in terms of technology. *You* could probably talk to it. It seems to understand English. Just go on the six o'clock news and say, 'Please, Mr. Other, don't destroy us in one day.' But that would sort of give away our secret."

"You could talk to it, though, in your leader language. I mean on the same news show. Without letting on that you'd talked to any human about what it said."

"I'll do something like that, eventually. But first I want to see how it reacts to the Drake diagram project. That should be ready in a day or so." The Earth-side scientists were arguing with a consortium on Earth—of course including the Chilean astronomer who'd "cracked the code," and was turning out to be a real pain in the ass—trying to agree on a twenty-nine-by-nineteen matrix message to send back to Triton via ruby laser.

"Maybe they should just send block letters. GOT YOUR MESSAGE. PLEASE DON'T KILL US."

6

PEACE OFFERING

In fact, they did a variation of that. The top five rows were taken up with the word PEACE in big block letters. Then there was a symbolic representation of an amino acid, alongside the same for some silicon-nitrogen molecule that might be a similar building block for its form of life, followed by a question mark.

A second message was a star map, looking down on the galactic plane, with Sirius at the center. (It would probably be the brightest star in their sky, too, if they came from nearby). The Sun's position was identified with a cross. Then there was another question mark.

I wasn't too sure about that one—I mean, *We told you how peaceful we are. We'd never invade you. So why not tell us where you live?*

The morning they were going to send the message, I got up at five and found a message that Dargo wanted to see me at eight.

That couldn't be good news. Unable to concentrate on work, I surfed around the news and entertainment. I almost went to wake up Paul, but figured he was going to be busy with the message transmission, more ceremony than science. He was scheduled for three hours of VR interview after it, so he could use his sleep.

I was, too, which was why I couldn't sleep. Dargo was probably going to tell me what I could and could not say. Good luck with that.

I dawdled over coffee and hard biscuits. At five after eight, her door was open.

"Please close it behind you. Please have a seat." She was studying a clipboard and didn't look up.

The chair was hard and low. She kept reading for a minute and looked up suddenly. "You had a Martian in your room day before yesterday."

"So?"

"So what was he doing there?"

"Well, I guess you got me. We were having sex."

"Carmen . . ."

"It's pretty wonderful, with all those fingers. You should try it."

"*Carmen!* This is serious."

"I've been in his room a hundred times. He was curious about what mine looked like. So?"

She just glared at me. She pushed a button on the clipboard and it started playing the first *Brandenburg Concerto*.

"You . . . you were eavesdropping."

"You were committing treason. Against Earth. Against humanity."

"Talking with Red. I do that all the time."

"You've never whispered under music before."

I raised my eyebrows and didn't say anything.

"What were you two talking about?"

"You tell me. What does the recording say?"

She stared at me for long seconds, her mouth set in an accusing line. I knew that tactic, but finally broke the silence. "You don't know what it says."

"I can't decipher much of it. But other people, specialists in sound spectroscopy, will be able to."

"So send it to them." I moved closer to her face. "And be prepared to explain how you got it."

"You can't threaten me. I have clear statements like this!" I heard my voice whisper, ". . . got your message; please don't kill us."

"You're pleading with the Others, aren't you? You can't negotiate on behalf of the whole human race!"

"You have it totally wrong." I stood up. "I have to talk to Red."

"You don't know what you're doing. He's not your *friend*. He's the enemy."

I paused at the door. "Do you have a favorite piece of music? Something loud?"

We only had about an hour before the Drake diagram thing, and of course Red would have to be there, too. I called and asked him to drop by my place on the way.

I found an ancient Louis Armstrong composition with the Hot Sevens, which gave us a pretty constant level of loud interference.

After I'd told him about the meeting with Dargo, he folded all four arms and thought for a minute.

"I see three courses of action, and inaction, with different degrees of danger," he whispered.

"The easiest would be to just do nothing, and hope that Dargo lets sleeping cows lie."

"Dogs. Sleeping dogs."

"Ah. Then there is the extreme other end: assume that the

Other is bluffing and just broadcast the truth. That would be almost equally simple, but if the Other *isn't* bluffing, it might be the end of the human race—and perhaps Martians as well."

"But it said Earth could be yours."

"It would have no more need for us if the humans were gone. We don't know whether it can lie. Like a sleeping dog, ha-ha.

"As a middle course, we might enlist a confederate or two, for insight and perspective. On the Martian side, it would have to be Fly-in-Amber. On the human side, the logical choice would be Dargo Solingen."

"Out of the question."

"This is not about personality, Carmen. I don't get along with Fly-in-Amber, either.

"Your great military philosopher Sun Tzu said to 'keep your friends close, and your enemies closer.' He had some experience with alien invasions."

"None that loll around in liquid nitrogen and zap you with killer lasers. What about Paul?"

"His engineering and science would be handy. But I suggested Dargo because she knows so much already. Making her an ally might buy her silence."

He made a gesture I'd never seen before, pushing down on his head with both large hands until it was almost level with the ground. Then he released it with a sigh. "It's a pity life is not a movie. In a movie we could just throw her out the air lock and go about our business."

"Making it look like an accident."

"Of course. But then the detective would figure us out and show up with handcuffs."

"Quite a few, in your case."

"Ha-ha. There is an intermediate course. We appear to enlist Dargo's aid but don't tell her everything."

"Lie to her."

"Perhaps a necessary evil." I suddenly wondered how much of what Red had told me was the truth.

"What would we keep from her?"

"The threat itself? I take it she doesn't yet know that I can understand the message. We could tell her that much, then claim it was something less disturbing."

"No . . . She heard me say that we got the message, and 'please don't kill us'—she can extrapolate a lot from that."

Red nodded. "Merely mortal danger."

I tried to keep my voice down. "The only thing we have on her is the fact that she broke the law making that recording."

"There is also the fact that she apparently has little beyond that one phrase."

I thought back to what she'd said. "True. Little enough. She didn't seem to know that you had decoded the FM message. 'We got the message' could refer to the Drake diagram thing. As far as she knows, we were conspiring to communicate with the enemy in English."

He paused. "Until we learn differently, then, let's make that a working hypothesis: she thinks we don't have any more data than anyone else. Meanwhile, we enlist Fly-in-Amber and Paul, swearing them to absolute secrecy.

"When the Other responds to Earth's overtures, we'll decide on our own course of action."

"And if it doesn't respond? How long do we wait before we try to contact it ourselves?"

"If it moves at one-eighth my speed, I'd say a week. Of course, it might have various responses prepared ahead of time."

"Like destroying everything?"

"No. If it were that simple, there would have been no need for the message it sent to Fly-in-Amber. We're safe for the time being."

"Which could be hundreds or thousands of years."

"Yes. As long as we don't do anything that threatens it, or the Others back home. Or it could be hours or days." Red made his humanlike shrug.

My timer's buzz was barely audible over the festive jazz, Dixieland gone to Chicago a couple of centuries ago. "That's the ten-minute warning. Guess we better go up and watch them push the button."

Just about everybody, human and Martian, showed up for the ceremony. One wall of Earth A was glass and shared by its counterpart on the other side of the quarantine. We had more room per person, or entity, but they had champagne.

After the short speeches and button-pushing, the screen showed a roster for interviews at the two VR sites. Paul and I were scheduled first, though with two different interviewers. Paul had a guy from an MIT technical journal. I was stuck with Davie Lewitt, who was pretty and intense but not remarkably intelligent. She had interviewed me after the Great Hairball Orgy on Mars, and pinned the name "The Mars Girl" on me. For a couple of years, it was "Hey, Mars Girl," whenever someone wanted to annoy me.

I was only a little sarcastic with her during the hour, but Dargo, who had been watching, gave me an annoyed grimace when she took over the helmet. She used more disinfectant spray than was necessary. But Oz gave me a broad smile and a thumbs-up.

When Paul came out I touched his arm and cut my eyes in the direction of my room. He smiled, but wasn't going to get quite what he expected.

You don't use paper wastefully in space. But it's one way to write something down and know that no electronic snoop can sneak a copy. As soon as we entered my door, I handed him the folded-over sheet that started KEEP

TALKING—DARGO'S LISTENING! Underneath that was a summary of everything Red had told me about the frequency-modulation message, and our tentative plan.

We chatted, mostly me talking, about our VR interviews. We undressed and I called for music, an obscure whining neoromantic guitar/theramin collage by some Finnish group whose name I couldn't even read. But it was loud.

When he finished reading, we got into bed and made appropriate sounds while whispering under the music.

He nuzzled my ear. "So we do nothing until the Other responds. Then Red—and you and I and Fly-in-Amber—will send them back a message. In Red's language."

"Right. Can you build a radio transmitter?"

"We already have one that's rarely used. We could point it at Neptune and talk away."

"I don't think that would be safe."

"Probably not, if she's being fanatically thorough. But we don't have an electronics lab on this side. You can't build anything without parts."

"So couldn't the existing radio have a little accident? *It's* got all the parts."

"God, you're a devious woman."

"Is it possible?"

"Yes, of course. I'll study the wiring and be ready to disable it. In the course of testing the 'repairs,' I'll send this gibberish out toward Neptune.

"But there's one thing you and Red missed. Dargo doesn't have to be that afraid of punishment, when she admits to having spied on you. What can they do—extradite her to Earth? Dock her pay? There's nothing to buy here, and we're already in a kind of prison."

"Well, Oz, and probably the others, would help us pressure to have her relieved of responsibilities. Deny computer access."

"That could work. Make her stare at the walls until she begs to be thrown out the air lock."

"I like the way you think." I straddled him. "The music's going to climax in about two minutes."

"Slave driver." But he managed a coda.

7

LANGUAGE BARRIER

Allowing for speed-of-light travel time, the Other took only twenty-some minutes to react to the Drake message—which meant that most of the response must have been prepared ahead of time, and it only had to choose which button to push.

If, that is, it had been honest with Red when it described its temporal limitations. It did occur to me that there was no compelling reason for it to tell us the truth.

Or to lie, if it was as powerful as it claimed.

The answer to the message came in spoken English, in an odd American accent, which Earth quickly identified as David Brinkley's, a newscaster from a century ago:

"Peace is a good sentiment.

"Your assumption about my body chemistry is clever but wrong. I will tell you more later.

"At this time I do not wish to tell you where my people live."

Then it began a speech in a slightly different tone, a speech that could have been prepared years ahead of time:

"I have been watching your development for a long time, mostly through radio and television. If you take an objective view of human behavior since the early twentieth century, you can understand why I must approach you with caution.

"I apologize for having destroyed your Triton probe back in 2044. I didn't want you to know exactly where I am on this world.

"If you send another probe, I will do the same thing, again with apologies.

"For reasons that may become apparent soon, I don't wish to communicate with you directly. The biological constructs that live below the surface of Mars were created thousands of years ago, with the sole purpose of eventually talking to you and, at the right time, serving as a conduit through which I could reveal my existence.

"'Our' existence, actually, since we have millions of individuals elsewhere. On our home planet and watching other planets, like yours."

Then it said something that I thought would simplify our lives, at least mine and Red's. "This is a clumsy and limited language for me, as are all human languages. The Martian ones were created for communication between you and me, and from now on I would like to utilize the most complex of those Martian languages, which is used by only one individual, the leader you call Red." Then it went into about two minutes of low, gravelly wheedly-rasp-poot, and went silent.

"So what was that?" Dargo said.

Red favored her with a potato stare. "Please play it back for me."

He listened. "Can you speed it up by a factor of eight or so?"

"No problem," a voice said from the screen. "Just give me a minute. I can double the speed three times."

We waited, and then it came back sounding more like Martian.

"Not much in the way of information there. I can write it down for you, phrase by phrase. But it's mostly ceremonial—good-bye and a sort of blessing—and some technical information, which frequencies it will monitor for voice and for pictures. Though I think it probably monitors about everything."

"Why was the initial message so slow?" asked the screen.

"The Other said that it had spent days translating that English message and rendering it as American speech. It recorded it more than a year ago."

Red hesitated. "We talked, Oz and Carmen and Paul and I, about how slow their metabolism must be, because of the low temperature of their body chemistry. They must move slowly." He wasn't going to say anything he'd learned from the still-secret message.

"Talking with them is not going to be anything like a conversation. But we are all accustomed to having a time lag between saying something and hearing the response, in talking with Mars."

"Why did it wait?" Dargo asked. "First there was all that indirect mumbo jumbo, hiding the Drake message in the strange oration that the yellow Martians had buried in their memories. Now we find out that it could have just contacted us directly. In English!"

"Dargo," Oz said quietly, "we don't know anything about their psychology. Who knows why it does anything?"

"It's protecting itself," Moonboy said. "Maybe even trying to confuse us."

"It does know *our* psychology pretty well," I pointed out, "after eavesdropping on us for a couple of hundred years."

"And it knows you," Red said. "Of you."

"Me personally?"

He nodded. "The Other knows of our special relationship, and would like to exploit it, making you its primary human contact, through me." I wondered whether he'd just made that up.

"How could it know something like that?" Dargo snapped, for once mirroring my own thoughts.

"It has access to any public broadcast. Her relationship to me is well documented." He made what might have been a placating gesture. "Of course, Carmen will share what she hears with everyone, and we will take input from anyone."

"I don't like it. You or she could make up anything, as long as you're working in a language no one else can translate."

"I will tell the Other of your objection."

"And how will I know that you have?"

"Have I ever lied to you? Lying is sort of a human thing." Paul glanced at me and glanced away. We both knew that wasn't exactly true. Red had come up with the suggestion that we feed Dargo an innocuous, half-true translation.

"Even if you completely trusted Red," Oz said, "as I do, there's no reason to assume that the Other is being straight with *him*. As Dargo said, it could have communicated with us directly from the beginning if it had wanted to."

Moonboy nodded. "It must have its own agenda, its strategy." To Red: "We still don't know how long this whatever, this hypnotic suggestion, has been part of the yellow family's makeup?"

"None of the family can tell us anything useful. They say it must have been there forever, ever since the Others created them. Which would be fine, except for the number."

"Ten to the seventh seconds," Moonboy said.

Red nodded. "It would require that the Others, or this Other, could predict twenty-seven thousand years ago how long it would take for humans to get to Mars and bring a Martian back."

"A yellow one," I said.

"Wait," Oz said, and laughed. "We don't have any reason to assume that the number is *right*. The Other isn't some sort of infallible god. That twenty-seven thousand years might have been its best estimate two thousand years ago, or ten thousand, or fifty—whenever you Martians were initially set up."

"At least five thousand ares. We have reliable memories that far back—at least the memory family does."

"You think so." Oz was still smiling broadly. "But look. If the Other could program the yellow folk, the memory family, to flop down and deliver a prerecorded message when they saw the red laser—then what else might it have programmed them with? Maybe five thousand ares of bogus history."

Red grabbed his head and buzzed loudly, laughing. "Oz! You could be right." He buzzed again. "Like your religious humans who claim God created the Earth six thousand years ago, with the fossils all in place. Who can say you're wrong?"

"An areologist," Oz said. "Quite seriously. We have Terry and Joan on Mars right now, nosing around your city, trying to date it. What if there's nothing that's more than a few thousand ares old? A few hundred?"

Red clasped himself with all four arms, which usually meant he was thinking. "It's not impossible. I have direct evidence, written communication, with only three previous leaders, with mention of a fourth. Less than a thousand ares." He turned to Moonboy. "Have Joan and Terry found anything older?"

"I don't think so. But they're still doing preliminary work, being pretty cautious."

"We must have them try. Dig down for things to date. This is fascinating!"

What I myself found fascinating was the way Red had changed the subject away from "Have I ever lied to you?"

8

SIGNAL-TO-NOISE RATIO

Red wrote out the message that the Other had transmitted after its English one, and it was as innocuous and plain as the earlier secret one had been threatening and complex. Basically, "I want to cooperate, but you must let me go at my own slow pace."

I searched my room for a microphone but found exactly what I'd expected: nothing. You can buy one at Cube Shack not much bigger than a flea.

Red asked everyone on our side and most of the people on the Earth side whether they had questions or messages for the Other. I knew he wanted a long transmission so that his own part would be hidden in the volume generated by others.

News came that my mother and father were coming on the next shuttle from Mars, which pleased me, though I had to admit I hadn't missed Dad. So Card would be informally adopted by the Westlings, which no doubt made him one happy boy. Barry got away with murder, which happens when your mother is a novelist and your father is a crazy inventor, no matter what their job titles claimed.

Over the next two days, I had eight more VR interviews. The most trivial was one from my old high school, and the most interesting was with a panel of "xenopsychologists" convened at Harvard. The weirdest was the last one, from the Church of Christ Revealed, who thought the whole thing, from the Space Elevator on, was a hoax the government was perpetrating for its own obscure purpose. I told them they could go out and watch the Space Elevator work; they could aim an antenna at Mars and intercept the signals that emanated from there whenever the right side was facing Earth. The interviewer smiled conspiratorially, saying, "Yes, that's what we're *supposed* to believe," or, "It's all explained in the Bible, and it isn't like your people say."

After putting up with that, I went back to my place feeling sort of like the most dispensable member of the team, and what should greet me but a message from Dargo: "Please come see me at your earliest convenience."

I put on my exercise clothes and went up to row and jog. Moonboy was on the rowing machine, so I jogged for a while on the treadmill watching Earth news. So little of it seemed important.

So my "earliest convenience" was after 250 calories of running and a mile on the oars. I didn't shower, but went sweatily down to Dargo's office.

Her nose wrinkled when I stepped in and closed the door behind me. Without preamble, she said, "Have you ever heard of ess-to-en?"

"No . . . A sulfur-and-nitrogen compound?" Even my dim recall of valences told me that couldn't be it.

"It's a research tool I just found. It dramatically increases the signal-to-noise ratio in a collection of audio data."

Her ubiquitous clipboard was on the desk. She stabbed a button on it, and my voice clearly said, "That's a kind of insect?" Then Red started the mayfly analogy, Bach a faint whisper in the background. She switched it off.

"I have it all," she said. "The superslow Others, the faster one on Triton, the rationale for Red's secret language. Our mayfly helplessness in the face of their ancient wisdom."

"So. Now you know everything I do. You still can't—"

"Maybe I know a little *more* than you do. You accept what your Martian friend says as the pure truth. I do not."

I didn't trust myself to say anything, and just nodded.

"There's nothing like all that even implied in the actual communications that everybody's seen and heard from Triton. I think Red made it all up."

"Made it up? Why would he do that?"

"It's simple, really. His power over his tribe, and now his usefulness to us, is dependent on the uniqueness of his supposed language. What if it's just another Martian dialect? Our linguists are cataloging similarities among the other four. With a large enough sample, I'm sure Red's will fall into line."

She didn't know what she was talking about! They weren't "dialects," any more than Chinese is a dialect of Turkish. And no linguist was yet able to utter "two plus two is four" in any of the tricky languages. That they had sounds in common was not very mysterious.

"I'm sure that could be true," I heard myself saying, "in theory. But I'd need more than supposition."

"Of course you would. And I know you consider him a friend, and wouldn't ask you to betray him. Just try to listen to what he has to say objectively—with my skeptic's ears as well as your own. Try to entertain the possibility."

"All right." Among the possibilities I could entertain was that Dargo had finally gone totally insane. "But what if he *is* telling the truth? We don't dare go public with your thesis. The Other might learn of it and push the button."

"Absolutely. Utmost caution and secrecy."

I left with my head sort of spinning, trying to figure out exactly what kind of game Dargo was playing.

I couldn't believe she'd had a change of heart about me, trusting me enough to enlist my aid in her scheming. But she did have me in a perfect trap—I couldn't report her eavesdropping without revealing Red's deadly secret.

Could she be right, though? The "deadly secret" a sham, part of an elaborate hoax?

No. That would require advance collusion with the Other.

Maybe Dargo was setting me up for a double double cross, having me spy on Red and then telling Red, to destroy his trust in me. I couldn't say anything to him or Paul, now, without the risk of being overheard.

But I could write. I didn't want to trust e-mail or anything else electronic, but I could afford a little paper.

Paul first. Before I even went to the shower, I wrote down everything I could remember about Dargo's convoluted scheme, in small print on both sides of a half sheet of paper, and folded it up small.

We met in the hall as I was coming back from the shower, and when we kissed hello I slipped it into his pocket. He gave me a little nod.

I spent a couple of hours trying to extract something useful from a structural-linguistic approach to the Martian consensus language, by an Earth researcher who'd done a lot of work with cetacean communication. I think she was hiding her lack of actual results with a lot of pretty charts and weak analogy. Both creatures do communicate with repeating patterns of noises. But the dolphins are mainly saying, "Follow me to fish," or, "Let's fuck." The Martians apparently indulge in more abstract concepts.

Paul wasn't at late dinner. I ate with Oz and Meryl. She brought up the subject of Dargo. "It's strange. With all this exciting new stuff happening, she seems angry rather than interested."

Oz said that Dargo will be Dargo. "She's an administrator at heart, not a scientist. Administrators don't like the unexpected."

I could have given them both a couple of data points, but had to refrain.

When I got back to my place, there was a humorously pornographic love note on my screen. Bunnies. I brushed my teeth and went over to Paul's.

For the first time in my life, I felt the foreplay went on too long. Why couldn't he be more *like* a bunny? I could see my note and his answer on his desk.

He fell asleep, or acted as if he had, right afterward. I slipped off my narrow half of the bunk and padded over to his desk and read the note, a page of small, neat capital letters.

SHE HAS YOU IN A DIFFICULT POSITION. ME, TOO, AS-
SUMING SHE ALSO RECORDED OUR "CONVERSATION"
WHILE MAKING LOVE. OF COURSE I'LL PRETEND
THAT I DON'T KNOW SHE KNOWS, AT LEAST UNTIL
SHE REVEALS IT TO ME.

YOU THINK SHE HAS EITHER LOST IT OR HAS SOME
NEFARIOUS PLAN IN MIND. LET ME SUGGEST A THIRD
ALTERNATIVE: THAT SHE IS RIGHT.

WE ONLY HAVE THE MARTIANS' WORD FOR THE
STORY THAT THEY DIDN'T KNOW ABOUT THE BEING
ON TRITON. WHAT IF IT HAD CONTACTED THEM
YEARS AGO—DOZENS OR HUNDREDS OF YEARS—
AND SWORN THEM TO SECRECY?

OUR SCIENTISTS HAVE NO IDEA HOW THOSE
RADIO/TV/CUBE RECEIVERS WORK. THE OTHER
COULD HAVE CONTACTED THEM RIGHT AFTER THE
FIRST RADIO SIGNALS FROM EARTH, AND SAID, "THE
ALIENS (HUMANS) ARE COMING, AND THIS IS WHAT
YOU HAVE TO DO."

MOST OF THEM SEEM STRAIGHTFORWARD AND
HONEST, BUT THEY'VE HAD A COUPLE OF HUNDRED
YEARS TO STUDY HUMAN BEHAVIOR, WATCHING US
LIE TO EACH OTHER REPEATEDLY—AND BESIDES,
HOW COULD YOU TELL IF ONE WAS LYING? THAT
SHIFTY LOOK IN ITS FIFTY EYES?

AS YOU SAY, RED REQUIRED YOU TO MISREPRE-
SENT THE TRUTH ABOUT THE OTHER, THEN VOLUN-
TEERED TO LIE HIMSELF, TO MISLEAD DARGO ABOUT
THE HIDDEN MESSAGE.

I WOULD SAY IT'S MORE LIKELY THAT THE
MARTIANS HAVE BEEN STRAIGHT WITH US. BUT WE
OUGHT TO KEEP THE OTHER POSSIBILITY IN MIND.

YOU MIGHT USE DARGO'S DEVIOUS MIND. SHE
MIGHT COME UP WITH A WAY TO TEST RED WITHOUT
HIM NOTICING.

I HATE LIKE HELL THE THOUGHT THAT SHE
MIGHT BE RIGHT.

I couldn't sleep. Kissed Paul good night and silently
went back to my place, where I memorized his note and
then destroyed it, tearing it into small pieces and rolling
them up like pills, then swallowing them with sips of water.
Carmen Dula, human shredder.

When Dargo had said it, it sounded like paranoia. From
Paul, it sounded almost reasonable. I had to consider, re-
consider, the argument on its own merits.

Go back to the beginning:

1. Red did not *plan* to initiate contact with humans. He

showed up only when it was necessary to save my life, an event he couldn't have predicted. (But that situation would have presented itself sooner or later, with somebody.)

2. The Martians didn't know that I'd get the lung crap—which required their lifesaving intervention. (But maybe they did know—Red certainly didn't waste any time responding—and maybe they were lying about every Martian getting it. Maybe it was genetically tailored for young humans.)

3. The effect of the ruby laser on the yellow family proved that they didn't know about the Other beforehand. (Or that they were good actors.)

4. They don't know how their technology works themselves. It's self-repairing, eternal. (Or so they say.)

5. For a deception to work would require the whole Martian population to live a lie, all the time. (Or maybe just the dozen or so we're in constant contact with—and they were chosen by the Martians themselves, not at random.)

It *would* have to be all of them, eventually, since as far as I knew there were no restrictions on human investigators like Terry and Joan.

I did finally sleep, and had a disturbing dream. I was at a party on Earth, a formal one like a gallery opening. I moved through it like a ghost, glass in hand. No one paid any attention to me.

Except a large handsome man with red hair and a red tie. He studied me intently. But when I went toward him, he receded somehow, dream logic, and disappeared.

No one on our side was, strictly speaking, a linguist, but Josie spoke Chinese and Spanish as well as English, and had been hammering away at consensus Martian. Oz had Latin and Greek as well as Norwegian. I made a "drinks"

date with them, to get their angle on the Martian languages, just before my next tête-à-tête with Red.

Our diets in Little Mars were controlled about 10 percent by our own input, and 90 percent by the Mars Corporation experts, who weren't about to send us up a bottle of Jack Daniel's whenever we felt the need. But we did have a carboy of ethyl alcohol with a computer-controlled tap. You showed it your retina and it dispensed a shot or two of "vodka," which was pure ethyl alcohol distilled from Hilton garbage, with a little lime flavoring, cut with 50 percent absolutely pure water from Hilton sewage. You could mix it with various things. I chose grape-juice concentrate and another tumbler of water, to make it resemble wine.

Oz took two ice cubes and a drop of "bourbon concentrate." Josie tipped hers into a glass of orange juice.

"No human will ever be able to really speak a Martian language," she said, "without mechanical help. Ten or twelve of the phonemes, you'd have to be a cricket or a garbage disposal to make." Phonemes are the elementary sounds that make up a language.

"And they have lots of them? Phonemes?"

"Around seventy. As opposed to forty-some for English. Some human languages have more than a hundred, though."

"But you can pronounce them all without a chain saw." He somehow made a noise in his throat like a champagne cork coming out of a bottle, beginning the sentence, "Xhosa can be a challenge."

"There's remarkably little repetition," Josie continued. "Human languages have words like 'the' and 'and' that keep cropping up. If Martian has them, they're pretty well hidden."

"It's worse than that," Oz said. "You know about those

Poles on the Earth side?" I didn't. "They're just analyzing sounds, taking every recording of Martian speech we have, and pushing it through a computer routine that counts phonemes. Or at least sounds that repeat.

"There are eight related sounds, like throat-clearing, that occur more often than others. The other seventy-some kinds of sounds seem to be evenly distributed—one sound is as frequent as any other."

"If you edit out the throat-clearings," Josie said, "it sounds weirdly like Hawaiian."

"Wannalottanookie," Oz growled.

"Tell me about it. And you've been following the dictionary saga?"

"Last I heard, they were still on square one."

"Yeah, square zero. Like they never say a given phrase the same way twice. But they understand each other. And they can't explain *why* because they never have to *learn* their own languages."

"Except for Red."

"Who presents his own set of problems," Oz said. "He was born knowing all the other languages, but then had to learn his own, which nobody else is allowed to learn—including us."

"I wonder why," I said. "It's been a deep dark secret from the beginning."

"We do have that small sample, in the last message from Triton. The Polish guys analyzed it, and maybe it is significantly different. Too small a sample to say for sure?" He looked at Josie.

"Seven hundred thirty-eight syllables, forty-some of them the throat-clearings, which I think are some kind of punctuation. The same phoneme-type sounds as the other languages, but it's nothing like an even distribution.

"The Poles did a breakdown, which I can send you. Some of those sounds only occur two or three times. About fifteen of them make up ninety percent of the message."

"So Red's language is more like a human one?" I said.

"It's also the only one that has a written form. If you asked him nice, do you think he'd give you a sample?"

"If you twisted his arm—or all four of them?"

"When I asked him back on Mars, he said it wasn't possible—not like 'it's not done' or 'it's illegal,' but just not possible, like walking on the ceiling."

"Not possible for you to read," Josie said, "or not possible for him to show to you?"

"Both. They weren't 'his' to show—even the records he himself wrote belong to his family, not himself—and if I did look at them, I wouldn't see anything that looked like writing." I took a long sip of ersatz wine. "He just laughed when I tried to press him on it. I couldn't even get him to write a sample down, though he writes human languages well enough. You can't write it with a pencil or pen or brush, he said. And then laughed some more and changed the subject."

Paul came scrambling down the ladder. "Thought I might find you here." I'd left my phone in the room. "You were talking about Red?"

"Red and languages," Oz said.

"There's some news." He plopped into a chair. "Five or six minutes ago. The Martians are mating! Joan has a cube of all but the first few minutes."

I had to laugh. "Martian porn?"

"Whatever works for you. But what's interesting is the buds aren't being grown to replace dead Martians, but rather the ones that are here in Little Mars."

"Wait. Not Red."

"Even Red." He shrugged. "In fact, it was apparently Red's idea. Can't wait to hear his side of it."

I checked my wrist. "I have an appointment with him in less than an hour. Come on along. You, too," I lamely added to Oz and Josie.

"Too crowded," Oz said. "You can catch us up later." He stretched. "Think I'll take a little nap and sleep off all that booze."

"Me, too," she said, and slid her half-full glass over to Paul. "If you don't mind my germs."

"Love your germs," he said.

9

BETRAYED

I knew that Red was going to be busy with some Chinese xenobiologists up until our meeting at 1800, so I didn't check in early. I called on the hour, from outside his door, and said that Paul was with me; he said he was welcome.

We'd dressed warmly, of course. Over his Corporation uniform, Paul wore a threadbare wool cardigan, souvenir of New Zealand, and a knitted wool cap with incongruous snowmen that he'd won in a poker game on Mars. I just had an extra shirt and wore jeans over my exercise shorts, and had made a cap out of a bandana, the way Dad had taught me when I did Halloween as a pirate in the fourth grade.

The temperature dropped more than twenty degrees when we slipped into Red's quarters, closing the door quickly behind us.

It took a few moments to become accustomed to the low light. Red had the Martian equivalent of an indoor garden, trays of mushroomy things growing under dim bluish gray light. The wall cube that he'd been using with the Chinese still had a slight glow.

There were cushions of various shapes and sizes, all a neutral gray, scattered in front of the cube, for human visitors. He gestured in that direction. "Carmen, Paul, it is good to see you. Please have a seat."

I wondered whether he'd ever considered the psychological advantage he had, always standing over his guests. Of course he had.

"We just heard about the blessed event," I said, as we sat down, "on Mars."

"An interesting euphemism. So often otherwise, on Earth."

"You're requesting a replacement for yourself," Paul said. "Do you expect to die soon?"

He shrugged slowly. "Like you, I could die anytime. But the reason for me to rush my replacement is less philosophical than economic.

"I've come to realize that I will never go back to Mars, and nor will any of the other Martians here. It's expensive, in terms of redundant life support, and there is no way my leaving would profit the Corporation. On the contrary. No one else can deal with the Other as efficiently as I can.

"And it's inconvenient for Mars, to have their leader so far away. Simple yes-or-no decisions can be delayed by more than a half hour."

"Used to be half a day," Paul said.

"Yes, I'm grateful for the repeater satellites. Still, the families should have a leader who is not absentee."

"What will your status be," I asked, "after he's matured?"

" 'She,' in this case. I suppose I'll play an advisory role for a while. But I'll probably be more involved with the Other than with Mars."

"This will be the first time there have been two Reds alive at the same time."

"Ha-ha. It doesn't bother me if it doesn't bother you."

"What I mean is, in all of your history, you've only had one leader at a time."

"And that will be she, once she learns what she needs to know. Which might be twelve ares, like me, or a couple of ares less or more. And then I will just be the old guy who went to Earth."

"Who incidentally knows the secret language and speaks to creepy aliens and such."

"True enough. I won't forget the language. I don't know whether it's possible for us to forget a language."

A chime rang, and Red made a kissing sound at the cube. A small square appeared in the middle with Dargo Solingen's face. The background showed that she was standing outside the door.

"What may I do for you, Dargo?"

"I just heard about the . . . creation of your replacement, and wondered if I could talk to you."

"Carmen Dula and Paul Collins are here."

"I know that. I have no objection."

Red inclined his head toward me, and I shrugged.

She came in dressed in regular short-sleeved coveralls. At least she wouldn't be staying long.

She dove right in. "This may seem trivial, but some people have expressed concern about protocol. Does this . . . budding mean you are no longer the leader of the Martian people?"

"That was always a simplification, as you know. And we aren't exactly people. But it's true that the formation of another individual with my characteristics makes it less simple. If a parallel were to be drawn with human history, I suppose I am a regent now, ha-ha, as much as a leader.

The new Red will take over when she knows enough and is strong enough."

"Physically strong?" she asked.

"She will be, but no. You would say, 'She has leadership qualities,' though I think it's more definite with us. The things that she reads while learning her language, mine."

Dargo stared intently at him, perhaps deciding what to say. "I don't know whether Dula has told you. I was able to decipher the secret conversation you had with her."

"I hadn't gotten around to telling him yet."

Red was louder than usual. "You are allowed to do that?"

"No rules cover it. As no rules cover what kind of music you have in the background when you—"

"That's bullshit," Paul said. "Space law is an extension of international law. If we had a jail, we could put you in it."

"I don't think you could, but it's moot." She looked at Red. "Your claims about what the Other could do to us . . . I don't understand why you would entrust that knowledge to these two but not to the authorities."

"Trust," Red said. "Your word. I should have trusted you?"

"Yes. If you had trusted me . . . nothing would have happened."

The cold air got heavier. "So what happened?" I was almost whispering.

"To extract your actual conversation from my recording, I had access to tools that drew the attention of security authorities. They asked me to cooperate, and presented a World Court subpoena for all the material on which I'd used those tools."

"We're not on the *World*, Dargo," I said.

"My God," Paul said. "What if it gets out? You may have killed us all."

"Don't be so dramatic," she snapped.

Red shook his head. "He may be right. I suppose it was only a matter of time, but I'd hoped it would be after *my* time.

"Did you stress the need for secrecy—I mean the possible consequences if the Other learned of this breach of confidence?"

"They have heard exactly what you said, including the fantastic threats."

"Here is a fantastic threat," he said, with a gesture I'd never seen: all four arms extended straight out and trembling. "Would you like to be the first human being to be killed by a Martian?"

He took one step toward her, and she made for the door with unsurprising speed.

She left the door open. I closed it softly. "What should we do, Red?"

He hugged himself in thought. "I wish I knew more about the Other. We have ancient traditions about their nature. But about this particular individual, you know about as much as I do . . . Well, there is one thing. It's not reassuring."

"What?"

"You know the Others on their home planet are technically immortal. That is, actually, they spend most of their 'lives' as dead as a rock. But they are revived every now and then. Do something and then return to the dormant state.

"This one is not that way, because it has to stay on the job until the job is done. The ten-to-the-seventh seconds figure, that's how long it has lived. Continuously, for twenty-seven thousand years.

"And it envies its relatives for their periodic rest."

In the dark cold, I broke into a sudden sweat. "It wants to die?"

"To die, or to return to where it can have its long rest. I'm not sure quite which state it was referring to. Or whether it feels there is much difference."

Maybe that was why Martians had such a curious attitude toward death. It might reflect the attitude of their makers.

"Should you prepare it for the possibility of exposure?" Paul asked.

"As I say, I'm not sure. That might just make it push the button—or it might have been lying about that."

"Let's not take the chance," I said. "Let's hope her 'authorities' are more cautious than she was."

Paul nodded, but his expression told how little hope he held out for that.

10

TROJAN HORSE

It took less than half a day. Unable to sleep, I got up around four and occupied myself answering mail that had piled up from family and friends. I was writing a note to Card when the screen chimed, and a red exclamation point started to strobe in the upper right-hand corner.

I asked for news but then toggled *Life Today* rather than the *Times*. Inch-high letters as red as the strobe: TRITON MONSTER THREATENS EARTH DOOM!! Martian Go-Between Reveals All!

I started to read the story, but it kept blurring. How could they *do* this?

The phone pinged, and it was Paul. "Sorry to wake—"

"I'm awake. I saw."

"Jesus. What do we do now?"

"I think the question is what is *it* going to do now."

"Yeah. Damn. Meet me down at the coffee?"

"There'll be a run on it." I dressed in a hurry and pinned my hair out of the way.

He was waiting for me with a cup. I got one sip, and both our phones went off simultaneously.

It was Ishan Jhangiani, the Earth-side science coordinator. "This is a general announcement. I want everybody, human and Martian, to be at Earth A, on the Mars side, or Assembly A, on this side, in forty-five minutes, at 5:30. I'm afraid this may be a matter of life and death."

The combination of tepid coffee on an empty stomach and bad news sent me rushing to the head. After I'd emptied that out I felt better, but my skin was cold and greasy, and my hands were trembling.

Paul came out of the other head, and he didn't look much better than I felt.

I looked into my cup. "I'd like to have one cup of coffee that was actually hot before I die."

"Better do it now." He sat down heavily. "Sorry."

"Gallows humor's better than no humor at all." I looked at my wrist. "We've got forty minutes." I nodded at the ladder, toward my room.

"No, I couldn't. Thanks, but I couldn't."

"Me, neither, actually." I rubbed tears away. "I could kill that bitch!"

"We should've grabbed her and thrown her to Red."

"Yeah." I laughed but it didn't sound like a laugh. "Not that it would change anything."

Speak of the devil—my phone pinged, and it was Red. "Carmen—Comm says there's a message coming in from Triton. I think we should be at Earth A early. As close to now as possible."

"We're down at the mess," I said. "Beat you there." Paul nodded and stood and followed me up the ladder.

Only Oz and Moonboy were there before us. Oz gave me

a wan smile. "Josie will be along. She takes a few minutes to wake up."

The cube was on, but it was a blank blue. "Red said they're getting some communication from Triton."

"Maybe it will be 'Send me the head of Dargo Solingen.'"

"Wonder if she'll be here."

"No. Jhangiani invented 'house arrest' and put her under it. She's locked in her room with no contact with the outside world. Josie or I go by every three hours to take her to the head and give her bread and water."

"She'll sue. If any of us live through this."

"Let me be a character witness," Moonboy said. "I've been her special little project for about ten years." I wondered how many of us there were.

Ishan Jhangiani appeared on the cube and looked at us. "No Martians yet?"

"Red's on his way, Dr. Jhangiani. He said there was a message?"

He nodded. "It started five or six minutes ago. We're recording—" His image suddenly dissolved in a shower of static, and the room lights flickered.

Paul crouched instinctively. "Shit. What's that?"

"Hello?" Jhangiani's voice came out of the swirling white noise. Then his image returned. "That was . . ." He inclined his head and touched an ear. "Oh my God . . . do we have a picture?"

The cube went black, then showed a familiar sight, the Hubble planetary camera's view of Neptune, an almost featureless blue ball accompanied by the tiny pale circle of Triton and specks of light that were Nereid and a couple of other small satellites.

Then Triton exploded.

The pale circle suddenly was a ball of intense white that

grew brighter and brighter, and then the screen went white with static.

It darkened again and a woman's voice said, "This is real time now." It took a moment for those words to make sense. Real time, not recorded.

The view was the same as before, but the dot of Triton was surrounded by a glowing circle, visibly expanding as we watched.

Red was standing in the door. "What's happening?"

"Maybe you can tell us," Paul said. "Your Other evidently did something interesting."

Jhangiani came back into the cube. "That explosion reached a brightness of minus twenty-seven magnitude. For a moment, it was slightly brighter than the Sun."

"Forty times as far away," Paul said. "So for a moment, it was putting out sixteen hundred times as much energy as the Sun. How could it do that?"

"Perhaps Red can tell us," Jhangiani said. "This is the message it sent; a few words of English and then the slowed-down Martian." He nodded at someone. "We've sped up the Martian for you."

The David Brinkley voice again: "I monitor your news broadcasts, of course, and the most recent ones have forced me to make a decision. I am sorry. You already know too much." Then there was about two minutes of accelerated Martian. And then static.

Red didn't say anything. "What did it do?" Jhangiani asked.

"It . . . went home." He hugged himself. "It may have literally returned to its home system. Or it died. The words could be the same. As if, if you say someone has returned to Earth, he could be going to a planet or being buried.

"On going home, it destroyed every trace of its technology that was on Triton. It didn't want to risk humans finding it and copying it."

He paused, and continued in a halting monotone. "It did this even in the knowledge that soon there will be no humans alive on Earth. The hundred on Mars will presumably live."

I swallowed back bile. "What's it going to do, Red?"

"It's already done." He rocked back and forth. "I'm sorry. I swear I didn't know. I didn't suspect." He shook his head.

"Didn't know what, Red?" Oz said. "Is there anything we can do?"

"I am a time bomb. A Trojan horse. The Other wanted me on Earth, or nearby, before it turned on the beacon that started all this. So that . . . if things didn't work out, I could be forced to put an end to it."

"How can that be?" Paul said. "Even if all your mass was turned into an explosion—"

"I mass about a hundred kilograms. By em-cee-squared, that comes to nine times ten to the eighteenth joules. That's equivalent to twenty hundred-megaton nuclear weapons.

"Earth could survive that, since we're twenty-two thousand miles away from the surface. But fusion doesn't begin to describe the forces involved. Could fusion have accounted for the Triton explosion?"

"I guess not?" Paul said. "No, of course not. Did it say how big . . . how destructive you could be?"

"Enough to boil away the ocean on the side of the globe we're facing. Blow off a lot of the atmosphere. The other side would perish, too."

"When?" I asked.

"Days." He shook his head. "Maybe two, maybe three.

"The energy doesn't come from here. It's bleeding off a thing like a black hole in an adjacent universe. We've been using it domestically since we first came to Mars."

"The mysterious power source for all the machines," Oz said. "The light for the hydroponics."

"I suppose. I knew nothing about it until today. But the Other says it had another thing like me on Triton, and it only drew off power for a couple of hours, concentrating it for the explosion. This will be orders of magnitude more."

"With all due respect, Red," Moonboy said, "we should lock you into the shuttle right now and fling you as far away as possible."

Red agreed. "That might be the most practical course. Or you could kill me, or I could kill myself, in case the collection process requires me to be alive.

"But the Other didn't say anything about either possibility. It could be that I would explode prematurely, automatically, if I died or left the vicinity of Little Mars."

"Which might be desirable," Josie said, "if it caused an explosion with less force. We . . . would die, but the Earth might be spared."

Red nodded. "I can't say, one way or the other."

I tried to listen with Dargo's skeptical ears. The Other might have been lying to him. Or Red might be lying to us. "It could just be a test," I said. "The Other observing to see how we react to this extremity."

"If it were a human or a Martian, I would say that was possible." Red shook his head. "Not the Other. I don't think we have any hope in that direction. Moonboy is right; I should be sent away. But I don't know that I can go far enough in two days."

"I have an idea," Paul said. He licked his lips and stared straight ahead. "Let's use the shuttle, but put Red on the other side of the Moon. Get three thousand kilometers of solid rock between Earth and the explosion."

"Ha-ha. Perfect. I'll do it now."

"You're not doing it yourself. You need a pilot."

"Paul . . ."

"We don't need the whole shuttle; just the Mars lander. We'll compute the right time for a slingshot transfer and have it blow the separation bolts at that instant. We do the transfer, and I come in ass backward, kill velocity, look for a place I can land with skis."

"It's suicide," Moonboy said.

"No, I can do it; plenty of smooth areas on Farside. I'll take a few weeks' life support. If Red doesn't blow up, they can fuel up the *Lowell* lander and come get us."

"You don't have to be aboard," I said, trying to keep the pleading out of my voice. "You can pilot by VR."

"Afraid not. No repeater satellites. Once I'm on the other side of the Moon, I'm out of contact with here. It's seat-of-the-pants, just look and do. I'm confident I can land it."

"And if you're wrong," Red said, "we'll just crash. That might set off the explosion, or it might prevent it."

"You're so cheerful," I snapped.

"We don't agree about death," he said. We had argued about that, on Mars and here. He invoked the human philosopher Seneca, saying that he had not existed for 13.7 billion years and apparently didn't mind that state. One spark of a couple of centuries' life, and he'd be back to not existing for some trillions of years, and would enjoy it as much as the previous billions.

"Which leads to a solution," he said. "Paul, if we just set up the thing to crash on the other side of the Moon, we won't need a pilot. I'll just be the cargo. Dying is not so important to me."

Relief washed over me. "Red, that's great! You don't have to be a fucking hero, Paul!"

Paul didn't look at me, but he wasn't looking at anybody. When he spoke, it was like a class recitation: "Red, I appreciate it, but it's not a simple computation. The Mars lander was not built for this, and it will be out of touch for the most crucial phases."

"So he *crashes*!" I said. "He just said—"

"No. With one kind of mistake he crashes, but with most

others he stays in orbit. It's not like dropping a ball. Things in orbit tend to stay in orbit, at least in the short term. And whenever he was not directly behind the Moon, he'd be the doomsday machine for Earth."

"How long would the flight take?" Oz asked.

"I could get it down to a day, and still have plenty of fuel for the landing maneuver."

"We'd better get busy."

"Can I . . . Could I come?"

His face was completely still. "No. Darling. Minimum life support, maximum maneuverability." He stepped toward me and took me in his arms.

He whispered, speaking slowly and carefully. Only I could hear: "We had a wonderful time while we had it. Better than most people ever get." The last word whistled as his voice cracked.

"You know I am not so far away from Red with the dying thing. I love you so and, if it has to end, will regret the years we would have had together—do miss them already—but at worst, in one instant I'll only be back to where I will spend most of forever anyhow."

I was crying and didn't try to say anything other than the obvious.

II

ENDINGS, BEGINNINGS

In the last few hours neither Paul nor I brought up the possibility that nothing would happen and he would be back in a few days. As if talking about it might have jinxed us.

Red did drop a hint, though, obliquely. I was waiting by the air lock that led to the shuttle, and he came walking up with a bundle tucked under a large and small arm. It was the gauzy tent he wore when he ventured out onto the surface of Mars.

"Just for safety's sake," he said. "You never know." It would protect him for a couple of hours' EVA or moonwalk, or keep him alive for a while if the shuttle's life support shut down.

Paul came out of the air lock looking like a Space Force recruiting cubeshot, gleaming white space suit. He had shaved his head and had feelie contacts pasted on his skull.

I was composed. Oz had given me a couple of slap-on

tranquilizers, but I wanted to hold off on them until after the launch.

Paul put his helmet down and swept me up in an armored hug. That was not exactly the way I wanted to remember his body, hidden behind bulletproof plastic. But I could imagine what was underneath.

"You remember the day we met," I said, "throwing a pebble at the iguana?"

He smiled. "Yeah."

"Think you can manage to hit the Moon?"

"It's a lot bigger." He gave me a last hard kiss and stepped back. No good-bye or see you. Just a long, intent look, and then he picked up his helmet and went through the air lock.

When it closed, I put one of the patches on my wrist. When the reverberating *bang* meant they had launched, I slapped on the second.

We had saved one bottle of the imported Bordeaux for some future celebration. I held it for a long time, remembering. But then I put it back and went down to the mess and made a glass of grape juice laced with ethanol.

I carried the drink up to Earth A, where almost everyone else was gathered. I almost wished they had let Dargo out to watch the consequences of her judgment. But I would probably have said something or done something I'd later regret. If there was a later.

The Hubble showed the little ship drifting along in the bright sunlight, occasional background stars going by unhurriedly. Paul talked with technical people here and on Earth, and Red kept up a constant monologue. Fly-in-Amber said it was all apparently in Red's own language, a message for his successor. Or perhaps for the Others, eventually.

The alcohol and drugs made me very sleepy. I ate a hamburger because I knew I had to have something, and then went up to my quarters and slept dreamlessly for twenty hours.

I awoke to my own timer, the phone, and the computer screen all buzzing and pinging. I turned them all off, knowing what they meant, and went to the head. Splashed water on my face and jerked a comb through my hair and went up to Earth A.

They weren't using the Hubble, because the Moon is too bright for it to focus on. Oz said it was a telescope in Hawaii. It showed the Mars lander as a small cylindrical shape, moving toward the limb of the Moon. I knew it would be decelerating, but you couldn't tell by looking.

Paul's voice was suddenly loud. "We'll be making planetfall, moonfall I guess, in about twenty-two minutes. Twenty-one. Lose radio contact in less than a minute."

The image of the ship and the Moon's limb was almost touching. "Hmm . . . I don't have any last words. 'Crash' Collins signing off. Hope this works. Dargo, I'll see you in Hell. Darling . . . darling . . . good . . ."

Well, at least Dargo would get all of her message, even if mine required a little imagination. Josie came up and held me from one side, and Meryl from the other.

Meryl sobbed. "People won't know he already had the nickname."

The view shifted to earthside, the nearly full moon high over a placid ocean. Maybe it was from the Hawaiian mountaintop where the observatory was.

After what seemed a lot longer than twenty minutes, a voice from the cube said, "One minute to touchdown."

We held our breath for a minute. Then another minute. We didn't know what to expect.

After twenty minutes or so, people started drifting

away, back to their quarters or down to the mess, or just to wander.

For some reason I kept staring at the moon, maybe wishing I was there in Hawaii, maybe not thinking anything much—whatever, I was one of the few people actually watching when it happened.

At first there was just a faint glow surrounding the moon, as if a wispy cloud had moved in front of it. Then it was suddenly dramatic.

People who have seen total solar eclipses say it was like that, but more so. A brilliant nimbus of pearly light spread across half the sky, the full moon suddenly a black circle in the middle, dark by contrast.

A crackle of static and a human voice. "Holy shit. That was close." Paul!

It was Red who had suggested the plan, which was probably not something a sane space pilot would have come up with.

After touchdown, when he was careening along on skis trying not to live up to his nickname, he should look for an area that was locally "uphill." Try to stop with the lander pointed at least slightly skyward. Then Red would get off, stand clear, and Paul could hit full throttle—get over the horizon, and try to make orbit. When he disappeared from sight, Red would measure off ten minutes, then open his suit and die. That would give Paul time to make orbit. But not so much time that he would go completely around and be over Red when he died.

The supposition that Red's death would trigger the explosion turned out to be a good guess.

It was a combination of luck and skill. He could steer to a certain extent with the skis, and so when he had almost slowed to nothing, he aimed for the slope of some small, nameless crater. When he slid to a stop, he was pointing about fifteen degrees uphill, with nothing in the way.

Red was already wearing his gauzy suit. He cycled through the air lock and picked his way down the crater side. As soon as he signaled he was clear, Paul goosed it. Once over the horizon, he tweaked the attitude, so he got into a low-lunar orbit, and waited.

When it blew, he was almost blinded by sparkles in his eyes, gamma rays rushing through, and he had a sudden feverish heat all over his body. Behind him, he could see the glow of vaporized lunar material being blasted into the sky.

That little crater that saved him really earned the right to a name. But it had boiled completely away, along with everything else for hundreds of kilometers, and in its place was a perfectly circular hole bigger than Tsiolkovski, previously the largest crater.

I thought they should name it Crash.

So every January 1 we present a petition for lifting the quarantine, and every year our case is not strong enough. But now there's a Space Elevator on Mars, so there's a lot of pretty cheap travel back and forth within the quarantine. After five years on Little Mars we went back, and it was good to have a planet beneath your feet—and over your head as well.

Oz invented a Church of Holy Rational Weirdness so that he could marry me with Paul and not offend any of our sensibilities. I was going to have twins and thought there were already too many bastards on Mars.

We named the girl Nadia, for "hope." Her middle name is Mayfly, and I hope she lives forever. The boy has the same middle name.

People who don't know us might wonder why a kid with jet-black hair would be named Red.